The Last Ditto

Frank Maddish

Copyright © 2017 Frank Maddish

All rights reserved, including the right to reproduce this book, or portions thereof in any form. No part of this text may be reproduced, transmitted, downloaded, decompiled, reverse engineered, or stored, in any form or introduced into any information storage and retrieval system, in any form or by any means, whether electronic or mechanical without the express written permission of the author.

This is a work of fiction. Names and characters are the product of the author's imagination and any resemblance to actual persons, living or dead, is entirely coincidental.

The views expressed in this work are solely those of the author and do not necessarily reflect the views of the publisher, and the publisher hereby disclaims any responsibility for them.

ISBN: 978-1-326-93549-8

www.frankmaddish.com

Dedicated to my wife and long suffering partner, in the crimes and misdemeanours of this existence we call life.

1. FOG

I'm watching another old TV movie, a digital rip from a battered VHS collection, complete with fuzzy sound and tape warp. This kind is the best for my work, anything too well known, anything that's been professionally re-mastered, won't cut it. It won't do at all, and here's why.

When I *breach*, a state of flux that has taken much of my life to accomplish, I am propelled into an abstract field. The very one this Earth is projected upon. For the process to be effective, source materials must be carefully selected. Television static, radio interference, visual encoding errors, broken frames in poorly dubbed movies, and all the inconsequential details that the audience is expected to ignore.

Any familiarities, be they personal, cultural, or iconic, act as dead weight. Their excessive perceptual mass forms from slowly oscillating light particles, coalescing like cosmic mould, until emotional gravity takes effect. To successfully pierce the flat vision that stands before every human being on the planet, one must adjust one's peripheral view. The momentous shift in perception can be immediate and overwhelming, for discovering for oneself the most ancient of all lies, is far more than enough for one lifetime.

I might have found the method far earlier, if I'd known what I was looking for. At first I watched mistakes, peculiarities in human behaviour, poorly predicted outcomes, misprinted data, (particularly hand copied pieces), and failing personal belief systems. I'm not choosy where I find clues, nor even the purpose of each insight. It is a messy process, rather damaging for a young mind no doubt, but I'm an old hand at this now, and I can take it in my stride.

Back in the day, the merest glimmer of first-hand knowledge, revealed a tapestry of errors in the world around me. Brought to life by childhood dreams, haunted by the spectres of the subconscious, lurking at the furthest reaches of human comprehension. Their trail of stolen memories, scattered like confetti in the dawning sun, left behind for those with the patience to piece together their own minds.

A vast majority of our race would rather live with the responsibility, their curiosity outweighed by their instincts to survive. For many can never accept the enormity of the situation, the extreme delicacy of our unique position, and will remain as strangers to all they know, including themselves, until the day they die.

Some of those strangers I'd studied as a child were supposedly my family, but none of us seemed particularly convinced at the time. Throughout that period I resigned myself to sitting out the whole miserable episode in an astral stupor. Eventually, after years of childlike duality, my consciousness riding it out in a space fifteen feet above my body, off with the faeries as it were, I realised it was time to come back. I dipped my toe in the human melting pot, not too hot, not too cold, and slowly blundered through the social niceties.

It took me a while to get the hang of it all. The hackneyed conversations, the meaningless quest for entertainment, but with the aid of narcotics and a newly discovered sex drive, before long I was making friends and enemies, left, right, and centre. In order to maximise the efficiency of each social exchange, I subtly shifted my core into an approximation of a compatible personality. Just a little at a time so few would notice, yet, still convincing enough to ensure my social camouflage didn't turn back into a pumpkin, at the stroke of midnight.

It all ended one night in an empty flat over a chip shop, rented by a Sicilian girlfriend who needed to move on. Sitting at 4am in front of a mirror on a heavy dose of LSD, I witnessed a thousand faces, and every one of them had the same insane grimace. It was at that precise moment I had an awful realisation, that those few kind souls who had bothered to tell me the truth, were right after all.

I *had* changed, or rather, I wasn't *me* anymore.

2. LORE

The tape is perfect, I have found at least four glitches. One of which appears on the bald, sweaty pate of a bit-part janitor, as he tips his hat to the shabby TV detective. There's another in the wet mop shine of the chequered tiled floor, feathered with overexposure but fit for purpose. The other two are darker, hidden in the reflection of a locker room mirror, but still distinguishable enough to handle.

I collect the visual fragments in my mind and draw them together in a freeze-framed sigil. Controlled chaos takes little imagination, but more effort every day. I make adjustments to my psyche, instinctively compensating for the numerous flaws and tears in my perceptual field, all scars from past experiments, my pioneering flights of fancy, and many with near disastrous consequences. As I manipulate the space around me and drag time to a stop, I stare into the mid-distance, and pull the plasma from the screen, to cloud the light before me like a microscopic storm.

I rarely make it further on from here, and when I do I lose the memory, none the wiser to my achievements or failures. The only proof that I have even left the room and travelled to another place, is missing time, and a nagging feeling that I had something important to say. But no matter what I have won or lost, what sights I have seen or worlds I've encountered, everything extraneous to this particular reality, quickly fades into the background.

I've always enjoyed exploring, it beats being explored anyway. I've travelled far and wide, without ever leaving my room, but the process can be messy, and I have frequently been followed home. I couldn't sleep for the commotion in those early days, psychic distortions spilling through the walls and under the door. Then after a while it all simply stopped, and I was left to my own devices. I hadn't even noticed at first, I was *that* grateful for the peace and quiet. But as I grew older and made friends, and discovered a life of some description, they found me again, the holes and slices.

Eventually I broke free from my new improved persona, and strayed off the party circuit to stroll through loneliness, night after night in night bus country. I'd trip alone and watch all my faces in the mirror, all those I had known or been, or might become, and knew I had a lot of company to keep.

As soon as I had discovered lucidity, I never fully slept again. My dreams are filled with creeps, and lazy ones at that. All utterly dismayed at my complete lack of cooperation, and angered by my lack of admiration for their fly-by-night reality. Much of what's out there in the immediate metaphysical neighbourhood, is the poorest of the poor, a discarnate plane, filled with frantic desperation and a bloodlust for life.

The non-existent existentialists live behind the mirrors, and sup on daydreams like tea. But at night they frenzy in an orgy of THC, and minds like mine are a favourite aperitif for the connoisseur. They love to surf Gamma Waves, peppered with a dash of Epsilon and Theta, it's like cocaine and meth on steroids to them. If you're aware of the parallelism, and can stand your ground in astral perplexity, then sooner or later, you'll find yourself the toast of their painted red town. But that soon wears thin, especially when you begin to realise how ugly they are inside.

In fact it's worse than that, they're ugly inside out and outside in, with nothing in between. They live for life and exude death like bad indigestion, and their appetite is insatiable. After a while, you too, will meet your nemeses, a legion of experts, soft killers whose thoughts and unspoken words are so sweet, that some mistake them as saviours.

The best way to avoid the majority of creepers and shadows, is not to feed them ammunition. They're big on facial recognition, the more friends you have, the less chance you can truly control your dreams. Some see it as a lesson in the generosity of spirit, I see it as an all out war on the subconscious senses.

This time around I'm avoiding crowds, I have one human, and three feline relationships. I'm keeping all social contact to a bare minimum, at least for the foreseeable future. It seems it's the only way I can maintain some form of status quo. When I say that, I mean a regular irregularity, a dynamic flux of false variation, an arc of illusory potentiality that can handle the fractal structure of the edge of this reality, and beyond.

I've come to learn that if you want something, you have to get out there and meet people, but the people I need to meet aren't here, they're down the wormhole that churns within the core of mind and spirit. It's the same old tell-tale told time and again, but in the first person, and without the hand-me-down baubles of self-realisation. Advice is subjective at the best of times, no human can truly say they've looked back until the fat lady sings, and by then no one is listening. Well, that is, except for me, I listen, and I listen hard.

It all needs to be this shape, a beautifully random pattern of absurdist behaviour, or I couldn't fit through the cracks, the holes, the gaps in the academic propaganda of a once benevolent hive mind. A herd of military animals that insist on rounding up the stragglers, for yet another staged alignment. The lords and masters of a destiny I have no part in, have no interest in the likes of me and my kind.

We are hardcore, an aggregate of people, laid down like gravel. It's all over and the worse thing is we already know it, although, most of us are far beyond the point of caring. The waking day is a weaponized public relations campaign, popularizing gullibility as it feeds us to the grinder. That love, hate, life, death, money, power, spirit grinder.

We've all paid our taxes, we're all owed a rebate, I'm just going over their heads, maybe not to the top, but high enough to make a stink. I'm done with playing human, this hamster wheel of life and death is a systematic slaughterhouse for higher consciousness. Every history's like the last, every journey the same as it's ever been. Only conjured fiction and empty lies feel as fresh as a new dawn, for an undiscovered hinterland of blind hope.

3. FLUX

I'm not what you'd call a gadget man, I only use technology when I need to. Although I'm still prone to drowning in the frequency soup of modern life, I try not to let it infect me. Wherever possible, I avoid the temptation to play repeater to the corrupt transmissions of an artificial hegemony.

This is *not* my kingdom and my glory, my borders are far beyond the control net. Though they may be just as dangerous, they're not so thick with dogma. In life I have the distinct sensation that I'm merely going through the motions, having spent a good chunk of my childhood struggling to be human. I'm self taught mind you, no help there, except for the odd chink in the armour of a blue moon stranger.

It took me a while to sort the wheat from the chaff, to understand the priorities of the paradigm, our primordial society, and this atavistic world at large. I took so long to realise that my tutors were attempting to teach me, I missed out on all the parrot fashioned fun. Perhaps it was their delivery, the monotone ambiguity, the rigid reflexes of an institution in decline, or simply dumb luck.

The secret that teachers, parents, and every other adult holds back, though not so much since the technological liberation of a panoply of karma, is the terrible truth that things really *are* this awful. It's not the best way to enlighten young minds, but of course, if you have a monopoly to maintain, proliferating desensitisation is never a noble cause, just a necessary one.

I've stared out of more windows than I care to remember. One that I do recall, revealed the freedom of the iron gates, beyond the nightmares of the playground, the killing fields of hope and childish wonder. In class I learned to appear concerned at my own failure to comprehend, and regularly held that expression in repose. With that one talent, I was free to dream and drift away on the meter of the bell, ignoring any risk of ridicule, should a teacher call upon my full and immediate attention.

Riding the autonomic canter of my tutelage, I'd occasionally pluck out a dulcet turn of phrase, and run rings around it in my mind. I'd spend years avoiding the gaze of teachers, frowning at the most obvious of concepts, and faking admiration for their pets.

I was no more adept at physical education than academic. A gangly pile of skin and bones, has little defence against the rain and sleet. I was told the exercise would do me good, even if the overweight PE teachers in tracksuits chain-smoked roll-ups, and snapped wet towels at bare arses in the showers. All that cross-country running taught me, was to use less effort wherever possible, and bow out at the very first opportunity.

Slow days stretched into years, half-asleep and hypnotised by proscribed monologues, anonymously passed through the lips of governmentally approved mouthpieces. No matter how exhausting I found the learned incarceration, I could always rely on the rabble of other sugar rushed, and glassy eyed pupils, to make things worse. Staring at those future bankers, sales executives, care assistants, and shelf stackers screaming and fighting, was as stifling as classroom etiquette.

By the time I'd left school, with little to show for it, except for a few embroidered truths and unreliable facts, I learned to hide my lack of sanity, and to some degree, feigned conformity. Then again, my recollections may be little more than the fantasies of a child's imagination. My past and present collude with each other, to camouflage my disappointment, and my uninspiring prospects for the future. All of which does little more, than dimly highlight the truly ravenous effects of prediction, and the highly addictive synaesthesia of temporal flux.

4. PAL SYSTEM

Most of us are under the delusion that we're here by chance, fate, or divine intervention. Even science struggles for a theory, a freak simian mutation must be the lamest excuse ever, but it's understandable considering the context. It can be difficult stepping back from a situation, when everyone around you is busy aping a lower life form. Rage is all the rage, it's been that way for a long time, or at least as far as society is permitted to recall.

The disturbing truth is that something was tampered with long ago, by someone with a terrible sense of humour, the whole caboodle reprogrammed, and even encrypted for purposes unknown. But that's a different matter, altogether.

I find that dreams are the best way to learn about oneself, and to some extent, recapture control of a subverted mind. One of my favourite dreams that fell to the cutting room floor, featured the kind charity of a warm and loving family, whom I've never met, and most likely never will. Wandering through the familiar streets of a fictional northern mining town, cobbled together from classic soaps and sitcoms, I came across an archetypal stereotype, a fat and jolly salt of the earth.

He wore a ten gallon hat he'd picked up on his last vacation, and he drove a beaten up Cadillac he'd salvaged from a local scrap yard. He spoke little, but had a kind face, and a self effacing manner that put me at ease. He asked if I was down on my luck, so I told him that I was lost and looking for a job. He offered me a lift, swerved the open-top heap with a sharp right, down a cul-de-sac of a quaint cottage-style council estate.

He led me to a green door, played knock down ginger, and was gone. A woman in a dressing gown with brood in tow, took me in and fed me. Then she trimmed my hair, dressed me in old but clean clothes from her late husband's wardrobe, and set me on my way with a little change for bus fare, should one pass.

I awoke abruptly, but I couldn't shake off the feeling that I'd been walking in someone else's shoes, perhaps a dead man. My memories can barely muster a friendly face at the best of times, let alone domestic bliss, and with such convincing detail. I'm more experienced at nightmares, a vast majority of which feature a frantic chase, with no beginning nor end.

Dreams and nightmares share one thing in common, a lack of closure, that awful nagging feeling that the whole charade will be over, before I've even had a chance to learn the rules. Worse still, all that wasted effort, for a seemingly pointless exercise in transcendental futility.

I've learned two things from my nocturnal ventures:
1. I regularly get stuck in other people's dreams. They're never friends, nor total strangers, but homoeopathically connected through hearsay, like a diluted synchronicity.
2. The speed of life is mirrored by the speed of time, which is a side-effect of the false barometer of the soul, known as the mind.

I've only dreamt of one inhuman life, an energetic being, living in an electric blue frequency of light, peppered with plasma pools, which effervesced in a cobalt cave of fool's gold stars. A symbolic construct for my benefit, counteracting my limited understanding of a greater reality, than I could possibly comprehend. A place outside of time and space, home to a society of all-knowing and benevolent creatures of silence and solitude. Highly learned beings, some as tall as trees, who sat peacefully, or bathed, or merely glanced and smiled in the direction of yet another wide-eyed intruder. Their voiceless conversations guiding their young, soft soothing thoughts crystallised with experience. A spectacle of sensorial splendour so beautiful, my heart sank as I struggled to form any kind of human comparison.

I felt ashamed at my limitations, the gross acts of an instinctual individuality, barbed by the longing to hunt and gather information. I left there with the distinct feeling that I, and all my kind, are at best obtuse in a place like that, and at worst, the embodiment of vulgarity.

As I slipped back into my body I met a fellow interloper, one of many who I assume have traded sleeping lives with me. Their engram of reassurance was a break from protocol, yet a welcome sign of interdimensional compatibility, and a potential friendship from beyond my imagination.

Those familiar shadows, neither living, nor dead, that stand sentry in my first and last waking moments, seem as unsure of me as I am of them. They know that I know what's going on, it's more than lucidity, I've woken up in sleep. Two versions of myself, conscious in the subconscious, hurriedly exchanging cryptic messages in an intergalactic semaphore, confirming the truth that waking life is just another dream. That's not something you can simply shrug off, in fact quite the reverse, I wear that memory like a crown.

5. DEFLECTION

I am an interloper, a metaphysical day-walker, who hankers for a nocturnal past. I used to suffer from insomnia, I still do to some degree, but at its peak I'd spin around the clock like a roulette ball, now it's more like bar billiards.

I've just about got the hang of mornings, that great wall of incongruity that greets me every day. As a coping mechanism, I constantly immerse myself in sound, in the deep end of the auditory pool, to mask out all intrusion, and avoid the mental bends of dream decompression. Like a deep sea diver in a bathysphere, I sink beneath the muffled screeching gulls and screaming kids, past the barking backyard dogs and wailing cats on heat. Far below the heavy drone of black helicopters, and the whining queues of chemtrail jets that criss-cross my coastal sky.

A view that used to be far more blue, has turned as white as a sheet, even silver, when the sun breaks through the tramlines of barium and aluminium chaff. Whether the weather has been modified to save the world, or kill it, seems pretty academic now, watching the seasons blur into each other, as the sky transforms into a giant TV screen.

Once evening falls, the stars hang too low for my liking. Some of them glint so strangely, I can even make out double and triple lights of neon primary colours. Then there are the black triangles, the floating orbs, and tiny shooting stars. The night sky's far too busy to bother with anymore, it doesn't make sense to me these days. The wandering seasons and planetary bodies, even the sun doesn't know its arse from its elbow, and when it does decide to pop up from some random direction, it flickers like a shitty fluorescent tube.

I'm getting tired of surprises, there are so many glitches I can barely bring myself to glance upwards. The last time I took a peek, I saw the sun rise and set within an hour, it's almost getting embarrassing how fake the world's become. The lies have left me feeling numb, and If my thoughts have ever been controlled by a shadow government, I'm sure they'd have lost interest by now, I know *I* have. What really gets to me is a tediously repetitive sense of déjà vu, somewhat sprinkled with disappointment. Whoever cooked up this world needs to find another job.

When we sleep, our brains are submerged below a tide of cerebrospinal fluid, that looks like the sky when it was still clean. At nightfall, the pinpricks that twinkle-twinkle, are the synapses of the human brain ticking over, dreaming of a new tomorrow. Each dawn, the brain floods with a deep blue neural brainwash, stripping universal truths from the short-term memory, leaving nothing but the subliminal instructions of a nocturnal yesterday, to play for today.

6. SANITY

There's more profit in the intangible, the non-physical, selling people nothing is the way to go. Shot to smithereens by broken sights and sounds, inducing artificial tingles of automatic pleasure, sugared hearts replicating the rhythm of machines on heat, a virtual love for the price of dignity. The mechanics of a beat that drums the slave ships to new lands, where people love to drink, eat plastic, watch fake fights by subscription, and fall for cartoon strangers with perfect skin.

Sell to the lazy-minded with sex, then drugs, then cultural agendas for a new supremacy. Whilst youth eats the signposts to golden horizons, the old are sold a silent silver revolution, spending their life savings on a funeral that can't be beat. There's little left to do these days, it's all been done. Still, people try re-imagining tired formats, hyping the hype, ramping the price, but the pitch is all too familiar.

Opinion based research informing market confidence, a swagger in statistical prophecy that masks a mass stupidity. A vague feeling that you're being duped, and going over old ground. Only the young and impressionable are fresh enough to think it's *this* exciting. Flashing lights change in an instant of mass targeted advertising, pink is the new black, is the new brown. The colours of a lesser magic, for catwalk coke snorting contests, in zombie dressing gowns.

Within the *community of the mind* we create a present, a gift, a sacrifice to the Lord of Time. A high black mass projection of law and order, to instil a fear of the benign. We are baptised in a sea of high impact imagery, imprinting structural belief in open port connections for a future education, reinforcing subservience through silent interrogation.

The schools are filled with dreams of slashing prices, that teeter on a fulcrum of logistics and niche market synergy. Training minds to embrace the simplest of all thought control techniques, taught by second-hand experience to ask no questions, and tell no lies. In a grid of general relativity, sat in rows of desks and chairs, the individual kowtows to the herd mentality.

The most intelligent amongst them, those who have a chance at something more than fighting wars, or serving burgers, are taught to quench their thirst for knowledge through textbook behaviour. Whilst the rowdy losers at the back, statistically slumped in cheap seats with cheat sheets, are taught to beg to join the new world order.

It's not power that corrupts, only the powerful, or rather, lapdogs from their phoney inner circles. All highly versed in the impracticalities of the greatest need, and the rationale of rationing, handing down trinkets and trickle down theories, to micromanage another generation of idiot savants. For the chosen, there are no real opportunities for more wealth, or better living through technology, only the truth that without more fools, there can be no more fun.

I've said something along these lines to a few psychologists in my time, one of which insisted *I let go*, release, share something of my state of mind. I tried my best, as she nodded exuberantly and took notes, before implying that I was a frustrated intellectual. I told her that I was neither, I just liked asking questions, that's all. She told me *she* was there to ask the questions. I told her that every authority figure I'd ever met had said the same thing. She asked if I had a problem with authority. I said, *of course*. She twitched and ticked a box on the form upon her lap, and left my company forever.

Certifiable, not quite, but a malcontent, most definitely.

7. LUCKY NUMBER

Many who choose their lucky number, make a random selection at best, emotionally charging it with the happenstance of fond memories, or a chance fortune that has crossed their path. The lottery of life is much the same, anyone can lay their bets, but there's no guarantee what place in the running you might come. If you survive the nine month ordeal in getting here, then they've *got* your number, and it will grow, like interest, until you die.

Your true number is written in the stars, an astronomical coordinate of time, for future reference to identify you for the benefit of age old occult institutions. The surrogate parent that is the state, surreptitiously quantifies your presence, for laws you've not yet been made aware of, but still you must obey. It begins the very moment you start breathing air, the cutting of the cord, a tidal wave of new sensations, to ensure an absolute complicity in this waking nightmare.

The traumatic experience of birth invokes an understandable response, an initial shock followed by months of thrashing and wailing, in mourning for the home comforts of the womb. Fair enough you can't be blamed, it's the putrefaction of the fleshly realm, the smell, the unyielding weight of gravity, and the terrifying sounds of upright beasts, cooing at the bloody miracle of birth.

Numbers provide a sanctuary of logic, an illusory defence against the brutality of nature. They are the hieroglyphs of a former age, hidden deep within the caves and catacombs of holy temples, ancient secrets unveiled for learned minds to scry the future. Signs and portents scrawled as sigils, magic symbols of a sacred geometry, mapping out allusions of Man's destiny, as slaves to the Watchers, forever following the procession of the wandering stars.

To this day, number's mark upon all mankind stands true, a countdown to oblivion that began with a simple hypnotic spell. If you can be persuaded of your number and your limit, you can be persuaded of anything. Words form higher magic but their powers are subjective, and rarely simplify matters unless used sparingly.

Numbers reign in a tighter leash, questioning the very particulars of the soul.

I frittered away the comparative bliss of each year of my early childhood, and it soon became apparent, at least statistically speaking, that I was becoming dumber by the minute. My initial zest for life lasted months, rather than years, due to torture by educational flashcards. I could tell the time of day, and how much money was on the table, before I could walk.

As the years raced by, the world of mathematics eluded me, until in my mid-teens, when my mother, anxious for my prospects, paid for extra tuition. Each Saturday morning I'd leave home, and take a train to a much nicer house in a leafy suburb of London. The owner, a bespectacled Jagger look-alike with troubles on his mind, pointed at mathematical problems. He'd offer a few confusing explanations about the pitfalls I might encounter, then sneak off for a coffee and a smoke. By the time he'd got through half a packet, he'd return with a cough and my jacket. He'd write his bill, slip it in a small brown envelope, and ask me to give it to my mum. In all that time, under his guiding hand, I didn't learn a thing, except how much a home-based maths tutor can earn during the early eighties.

He, like all my past maths teachers, had a sorry look in his eye, perhaps behind the frustration he pitied me somehow. He needn't have bothered, I'll never know the cold love of logic, or the satisfying glow of a statistically perfect equation, because numbers have always left me feeling numb.

8. ENCHANTMENT

At night I sunbathe under an internal sun. I used to bolt upright, open my eyes, and check if I'd left the lights on, but there was always darkness. I discovered that blinking helps, well in a way. So I spent a decade or so making silent movies in my mind. A flash photographer capturing the faces of animated strangers, huddling around the precipice of sleep.

I wouldn't describe myself as a light sleeper, it's more like self-hypnosis, a soft, slow, epileptic fit, that distracts my mind long enough to let my body rest. I have to choose to dream, which invariably I do, however busy the surroundings, whatever the commotion.

On one such occasion I realised that behind me, where I rarely look in my imagination, there lay a half-finished tunnel, leading from my mind to outer space. At its entrance I briefly inspected several tools from another world, left in a panic upon the oily ground. Beyond the mouth of the pleasure ribbed excavation, stood a figure slight and grey. His friends had already run ahead of him, their childlike barefoot steps still echoing in the distance.

I sprinted after the intruders, shouting obscenities and threats, with symbolic fists clenched in the air. I could see one of them brandishing a strange device, it was shaped like a femur bone glued to an industrial lamp. I assumed that interstellar vandals had invaded my brain, and decided to protect my intellectual property, and fight back.

With each stride I accelerated, a human bullet through a gate of light, that led deep inside their ship. I punched the living daylights out of three of them, the rest just ran away. Six black eyes crumpled in like cheap acrylic sheets, their bodies, thinly skinned and as brittle as dried wood, exploded into dust on impact.

Next I ripped up all the seating, kicked in the dashboard, and a projector displaying fractal patterns. Then I set the place on fire, with a strange beam of blue light that burst forth from my mouth. I couldn't speak for the adrenalin rush, I was sweating like a pig, and eventually I realised I was back on terra firma, returned to a world that remained none the wiser.

I felt like a jerk, violence isn't really my thing, but I needed to teach those hoodlums a lesson. I wasn't taking it anymore, I was too tired for mental movies, and I didn't even believe in Greys. Life's hard enough without the constant interruptions from a gang of plastic vandals, who can't decide if they're real or not. On the other hand, it had been a rush, the strange exhilaration of a brutal confrontation, but once was enough.

I couldn't help but feel impressed by the totality of my imagination, how overpowering it was, how all encompassing. All night I'd remained suspended by a bare thread of cogent fantasy, that led to somewhere else than my own mind, far beyond its limits and capabilities. However ridiculous it seemed, I couldn't shake the notion that somewhere in my head, was a gateway to the stars.

There are rules to the powers of deception, namely the willingness to be deceived. If you know what you know is true, as does everybody else about you, then it's official, common knowledge, a proven sign of sanity. If not, you should probably keep it under your tinfoil hat.

9. SCHISM

In the depths of my lowest lows, I dislocate from this skin-bag of horror, the blood, the guts, the bones, the brain, and stare too long into my own eyes. Disorientated by the common misconception, that *this* is what I am, that this human being is really me. This living machine that thinks it's more than it is, and every time I start to fall for the ruse, I realise it's bullshit.

When I watch animals, which I love to do, they seem right at home, they look like they belong here. Conversely, humans couldn't be more out of place, no matter what twaddle they try to peddle. We've separated ourselves from nature with good reason, the reason being we're so unnervingly unnatural.

I'd skim through biology manuals as a kid, my mother wouldn't tell me about the birds and the bees. I soon learned that I'm no devotee of the human design, or all the ugly gubbins inside, a butcher's shop window dressed by Doctor Frankenstein. Especially the glands that tell me how to feel, and though I resist their influence, I can't help wondering if disease is the result of thoughts like these. Punishment served upon an unfaithful member, of the congregation of the temple of the body.

I put stuff inside here and if I'm not dead by morning, if I've had a laugh or two, and my belly isn't grumbling, I'll do it all again. I have little taste, a sense that's mostly ruined, except for pungent skunk and takeaway curry. I *feel* of course, but I'm number than I use to be, is it my nervous system or a natural reaction to the world these days? I don't know. The weirdest thing of all is when I consider my own brain, not my *mind*, mind you, but the grey matter it contains.

It's split in two, I guess, at least according to the gory illustrations in mother's tattered home medical journals. Slap bang in its centre is a pineal gland, a pea-sized organ that hippies say can help you see into the future. I already have a good idea of what comes next, you're born, you live, you die, it's the rest I'm in two minds about. Those with the stomach to rummage, forensic pathologists and the like, say that by the time you die your pineal gland is shrivelled and calcified. The wonders of the human physiology never ceases to disappoint.

It's a shame, as a kid before I knew any better, I wondered if I could fly. Maybe it was a case of delusional mind over matter. I was wrong of course, and like any child with a good sense of imagination, my betters attempted to nip it in the bud. I did gradually give up on myself, at least that man in the mirror, the beast of ample comforts, that devours his way through every distraction life has to offer. Food, sex, drugs, the rush of experience that youth is most privy, before tingeing the soul with pain and regret.

These days I stand back and watch the monkey play, placing friendly bets on even odds, with itself. I'm not grateful for being human, but I'll make do, until I'm free to leave. When the time comes, I will make my excuses and go, rather than hang about for the funeral, like so many lingering spirits at the graveside. Which is exactly why we are encouraged to ritualise our deaths, to spread fears of the unknown in twisted memorial, for the surreptitious entrapment of lost souls.

My funeral arrangements are as follows: throw my body off the cliffs at Beachy Head, and let the gulls have me. Then donate all the usual costs of the ceremony to the first homeless person you see. Yes, they *will* spend it on drink.

10. MOMENTUM

Progression is a myth. The collusion of illusion ensures that few practice the rituals of inventiveness. Those who do, primarily seek instant gratification, ignoring the obvious to focus on the novelty of change. Like magpies stealing watches, with absolutely no conception of time.

Opportunity knocks with a limp-wristed tap upon your door, and before you know it, you've kicked your business partner to the kerb, and you're playing *whack-a-mole* like a pro. You hit hard, you're a no holds barred, all or nothing, one hell of a guy. Slap on the back, lie to the wife, paid expenses, business class flights, screwing over saps for the deal of a lifetime.

It's no game, unless you make it one. Like running on the spot, it's too dull to do it in the spare room, so you join a gym. You watch your avatar jogging on a giant screen, earning you loyalty points, and you've never looked better. Then the bill arrives, what a rip off, but then again, *these thighs*. You decide to buy out the business, and next door's burger joint, with a hefty bank loan. You mirror every window, and watch your target market squirm.

Local obesity is on the rise, you get complaints about your burgers, and your brand new budget doughnut shacks, to catch more passers-by. Before long your gym is heaving with walking tubs of lard, some can hardly breathe now, and a few have spoken to the local mayor.

She wants to close your stores for promoting all this junk food, so you do a deal to showcase your newly-built mega-gym. The government soon hears about your wonderful initiatives, taking skinny people off of welfare, and training them in-house. Giving them hats and badges, teaching them to scream and shout, working for a minimum wage, bossing overweight people, through town after town.

You get funding, grants, a key to the city, soon you're rolling out nationwide, franchising the world. Eventually you float the company, preferential shares for friends with benefits. They buy, then sell their options within a month like you, and watch it belly up for all the schmoes. You made it, what a guy, a seat upon the board of a charity for obesity, one that gives your new food chain the gold seal of respectability.

So many sweeteners in your healthy doughnuts, competitors destroy your proven markets, with research funded cancer scares. You pay off the families, with less than one week's wages for your PR team, which encourages you to open up more hospitals, to study what makes people fat. With global pharmaceutical patents in the pipeline, the best lawyers on retainer waiting in the wings, it happens, a miracle cure! Awards, accolades, and fame.

By the end you have your people, they do all the work for you. So you buy an island, and build a runway for your jet, to have parties with movie stars, catwalk models, and Chinese officials. You find out about a secret Mars colony at the last stages of proposal, you heap the project with a slush fund from an offshore account, when suddenly, a guy you'd met years before comes up to you, looking good as new.

He hasn't aged a day, what's his secret? You will pay. You bail out of Mars, life extension is the future, you can go off-planet in a century or so. For now you want to be twenty one again, hard bodied and always on the score. You're flown off to the back of beyond, and escorted into the basement of a filthy medical facility. You realise you've been duped, your people advised against the meeting, now you're lying in a chop shop, ready to be organ harvested on a factory scale.

Just before you die you watch a hacker drain away your personal fortune, your worldly influence, your weight in gold, which you notice in a bloody mirror suspended from the ceiling, is more than double what you thought. How did you get so fat, and old? Your heart stutters to a stop, a trickle of blood dribbles from the corner of your lips, it tastes like raspberry, no strawberry. It tastes like purple juice, artificially sweetened with an extra long shelf life, that comes in a can.

You die and rise above yourself, you can barely recognise the corpse, a struck off doctor fills out a form, as their assistants carefully pack your butchered remains in ice. You follow them down the corridor, until you recognise the building. It's one of your free hospitals on the borders of Mexico, which has been taken over by a worldwide drug mule gang.

They sew coke inside pig farmers' bellies in Peru and Guatemala, then send them over as couriers, slice them up, take out the shipments, and use the rest where they can. They make more from organ transplants these days, the drugs are just a bonus. Although, after paying off everyone, law enforcement, local government, there's little *payola* left.

You have almost forgotten all your enemies, you've been a winner for so long now. Oh yes, there was that one jerk, a former business associate, that loser who came back begging for a job. He fell in love with a cashier from your first gym, that one you tried to screw? He married her, the woman who threw that doughnut at you during a local protest. She called you *fascist scum*. Don't you remember? The one with the great tits, bad hair, and that fast food smell.

They'd tried to raise money for their son, who'd died from a severe heart problem brought on by diabetes. His father, the fool who'd invested his life savings in you, petitioned against the use of sweeteners, but your people had him thrown in jail. Banged up on trumped up charges, backed up by phoney witnesses to a fictitious crime. He's been out a while now, with a new identity, to reclaim his fate, his destiny, the one he should have had all along. *You* were supposed to be the sucker, thrown in the slammer for trying to save the world, but it doesn't matter now, it's midnight in the land of the blind.

You're dead, a goner, with nothing left to do. In *The Void* there is no momentum, everything slows to a stop. One second seems to last forever, and everyone is you. They have your face, your smile, your eyes, and each conversation that you have, turns out to be a lie. Except for the one about that guy, tall, dark, but certainly not handsome, pure evil you surmise. He's taking people on as management trainees, he needs a sales force for his own kind of economy. He spends lives like you spent money, he breathes whole histories with one yawn. He's the Morning Star, and he's offering you a second chance.

You can do it all again, the hours aren't so great, dead at thirty, sister dies at ten, inherited genetic anomalies, caused by caffeine booster bars and a bad exercise regime, plus too many damn sweeteners in everything. Still you might have had your chance to briefly rule the world, but as fate would have it, you'll miss the knock upon the door of destiny, as another selfish bastard steals your place upon the gravy train.

11. PARANOIA

We all have our bad days, but if you find yourself traipsing through a South London graveyard, at four in the morning, watching the dead climb out of a crypt, it's probably just paranoia.

I haven't tripped in decades, and when I did, there was always the risk of scoring a tab from a tainted batch. There's nothing worse than acid laced with rat poison, except perhaps, for rat poison laced with acid. Especially if you're expected to offer home-grown psychoanalysis, to shattered egos rushing towards a meltdown.

Eventually, after an hour of walking in circles, we were offered a pity lift, by a creepy friend-of-a-friend, who'd worn the same shrunk-in-the-wash silver suit for years. He drove a beaten-up old white Rover, and as we watched the world smear paint against his windows, he played a heavily warped Goth mix tape through a solitary blown speaker. When everybody complained, he denounced us as *jelly heads*, then dropped us off in the drive, without so much as a by-your-leave.

We stumbled into the kitchen, and I looked for the light switch, whilst my fellow drug casualties sat in the dark, freaking out in a dead grandmother's bungalow. Eventually, after a few seizure inducing fits of blue and white phosphor pings, the fluorescent light came to life, and the world turned yellow.

Someone, I can't recall whom, decided we needed some music. They turned on the radio and white noise flooded the place. Everybody went into a panic, as if The Thames had broken through the barrier. I walked over and switched off the radio interference, and then proceeded to make a pot of tea. None of us could drink it, but the familiarity of the ritual and the setting seemed to calm a few nerves.

That's when I realised I had a great deal of tolerance for paranoia, it's also when I realised I was permanently paranoid, and had always been that way. One of the girls melting down on a strychnine impurity, would regularly walk over to me and try to start a conversation. She'd begin to stutter, and I'd tell her to wait a little while, she must have done that at least a dozen times over the next half hour.

I stood up, waited for the room to stop spinning, dimmed the light in the living room, put on some music at an imperceptible volume, switched on the electric fire, and watched the fake logs flicker. As the red bulb beneath them clicked its way through one tedious revolution after another, I thought to myself, *life's not so bad*. Even if the world *is* an awful place, and such a mind-numbing grind, that LSD had become an attractive option, there were always fake log fires to watch, and old ladies' rugs to lie upon, and friends for memories in the years to come.

Some weeks later, under the threat of homelessness from a disapproving mother, I enrolled for an arts degree at a south coast polytechnic. I soon found myself sitting alone in Freshers' Week, nursing a cider and black. At the student bar there was a tripper, he'd lost all sense of time, he'd graduated nearly twenty years before, and had nowhere else to go.

This guy was gone, *real gone*. Living in another time, on a night out with invisible friends who'd moved on long ago. He on the other hand was still there at the student bar, buying a beer for himself and a *Ladysham* for his imaginary date. Later on I caught him waving to his friends, who were nowhere to be seen. They weren't by the pool table, or the dartboard, or the jukebox, they were in his head. They'd left him behind, he didn't know, and they didn't care, because he was a hardcore fantasist, with absolutely no sense of paranoia.

It's the strangest thing, but for all the muttering and snide commentary from those around him, I couldn't help but admire his persistence of deluded vision. As if he'd chosen the most perfect moment in his life, and knew that this was it, a perfectly average evening out in his late teens. One which he'd repeat from then on, alone, and every weekend.

I tried to catch his eye, to snatch a glance of false recognition, eventually he nodded and walked over to me. He stood there talking to someone else, who wasn't there, and then I felt it once more, my old friend paranoia. Yet I listened intently, and decided to grasp the mettle, and play along with his psychosis. I said *hello*, he looked at me with absolute horror, at the uninvited imposter, barging in and ruining his fantasy. He grabbed his coat and stormed out, and I never saw him again. He was a true original, and he was very real.

I think his name was Phil, and he might have been as barmy as they come, but he'd stuck to his guns and taken no prisoners. He'd made a true commitment to ignore the world around him. He played with reality like a sculptor, and formed his own existence from nothing but a few scant memories. He had a power, he was invulnerable to ridicule and incredulity, but then I came along and ruined it. *Sorry Phil.*

Yet he was cogent, at least enough to order drinks at a bar. At the time I wondered how he coped with inflation, the way his money didn't go so far, and what if they'd stopped serving Ladysham? Would his non-existent girlfriend get the hump? I wanted to ask him how he lived, if he was *really* mad, all those things I shouldn't have asked, and in the end, didn't.

I'd had a face-to-face encounter with true madness for the first time in my life, real lunacy, and that's what got to me, I knew right then and there that I felt paranoid with good reason. I feared with all my heart, that one day I'd lose my mind, which as it happens, I would.

It would take a few more years for me to unhinge, and another decade to trace my way back. When I refused to take any more prescription drugs, I soon stopped sitting at the window dribbling, and woke up to hear my girlfriend screaming at me.

The only thing that can really tip someone over the edge, is getting paranoid about paranoia. It's actually an extra sensory ability, one largely ignored by the medical establishment, and remember paranoia only has one pitfall.

Never get paranoid, about being paranoid.

12. THE MOON

I was born at the tail end of the psychedelic movement, in the midst of the space race, a year or so before the baby boomers screwed everything up.

I was drawn to the stars from very early on. Perhaps, my cot faced a window and no one ever bothered closing the curtains, or maybe it was just a natural reaction to a crowded house. All I know is, I used to look up at the night sky far more than the average baby. I guess everyone else got used to it, and watched the box instead.

Holes in an old man's pocket, that's how I'd see the stars. For me they were almost reachable, tiny specks of light, less than a few feet away. As I lay there gurgling, I'm sure that hippies across the world were tripping out at their local cinema, drooling at the art house spectacular of the decade. Floating black monoliths full of stars, a giant foetus orbiting Jupiter, and a rainbow tunnel to wake up the audience at the end. That was supposed to be the future, but people are fickle, and soon tired of empty promises and million dollar moon rock samples.

The true space odyssey was managed from a Hollywood backlot, a subliminal campaign to win the hearts and minds of an anti-war generation. Extracting the last few magic beans from their vegan wallets, to fund pie-in-the-sky projects, covertly run by ex-military civilian tech outfits, dressed up as spacemen. Propaganda is far more elegant these days, and so much cheaper, but a lot less imaginative.

A hundred thousand potential applicants for a suicide mission to Mars, that's one hell of a PR coup. Russia prefers to fleece the oligarchs, with multi-million dollar weekend breaks, on a hi-tech balloon in low orbit. Quick vacations for bored billionaires, desperate to look further down on the rest of us, as they suck at baby food, and feel the vibe of low G. The lesser fortunes have laid down some hefty deposits too, pre-booking half hour high jinxes in crowd-sourced plastic rockets. It's strange how few mention the supposed minefield of scrap up there. With all that space junk floating around the planet, you'd think satellite crashes would be a daily occurrence by now. *Funny that.*

If I had a more mathematical mind, I'd explore all the strange coincidences associated with the Moon, such as its bizarre relationship with the number 27.3. That number is the ratio of the Earth's diameter to the Moon's, as well as its orbit around the Earth in days, and the rotation on its axis. The Moon's polar circumference is 27.3 percent of the Earth's, even the acceleration of its path around our planet, is 0.273 centimetres per second. At least according to popular scientific hearsay.

So here's the thing, *why* is the Moon so messed up? It's supposedly made from certain materials you can find here on Earth, but not all of them are natural. Such as brass and mica, or the elements uranium 236 and neptunium 237, the muck you can only find in the spent fuel of nuclear reactors. Furthermore, the surface is in a terrible state, it's almost like the Moon is inside out. There are rocks up there, that have been carbon dated to an extra billion years than you'll find down here. So now the Moon is older than we thought, yet the scientific establishment still clings to its pet theory. Their giant impact study, that spewed forth an unnaturally obese satellite through a calamitous collision.

Yet here I stand upon the fringe, whilst the mass perception of the truth slides by me at 2,228 MPH, without a care in the world. I might be talking crap, but like most bullshitters, I can tell another bullshitter from a quarter of a million miles away. She smells like cheese, but looks like chalk, and she'd rather I ignored her altogether.

I never wanted to be an astronaut as a child, I stipulated *spaceman* with good reason, I never had a head for numbers, I just wanted to fly as high as *old blue eyes*. For those who planted flags and bounced around in front of invisible cameramen, it probably *was* a small step, but for all the rest of us poor suckers down here, it was one giant leap of faith.

13. EARTH

The world is not a stage, it's an audience, and the audience is asleep. The subconscious theatre of absurdity has no script, and relies solely upon the performance of a single actor, left aglow in the spotlight like an angel. A financial benefactor, essential for the production of our shadow play, the most sensational of shows sold out for another extended run, into the rest of eternity.

The story of Earth has no beginning, nor end, but remains looped in a perpetual dialogue of lies. The entrances and exits were sealed long before the audience was born. The smog that silently bellows from the orchestra pit, is apparently, by all accounts, perfectly safe to breathe. The plumes of dry ice provide an added emphasis to accent the mood, and hide the bad sets. Cheap tricks invoke an atmosphere of histories past, where fake blood was spilt upon false blades, and treacheries avenged in warlike fashion and regalia. Separating the knights, from the knaves.

The angel is Death, his black cloak burns like incense in the aisles. His price for backing the show is one performance, a speech of his own contrivance. Dressed to the nines, and smothered in make-up, he treads the boards, which split and crack to form a jagged altar, a splintered mount for a broken speech. In solemn dance he glides beneath the spotlight, taking a silent cue from a late prompter, who soon crumples at his feet.

Death parts his parched lips, and motions words with his grizzled tongue, but nothing sounds forth, bar the quiet sobbing of curious cowards. Suddenly, a rasping diatonic chord shatters the uneasy peace, heaving the great chandeliers above him. They shudder in eerie harmony, their haunting accidental melody smothers his first utterance, with the ripples of a crystal applause. The speech is about to begin, *Silence in the stalls, silence please!*

Death sneers at the ignorant, the sleeping corpses gazing at their programmes, rustling taffeta, so much distraction, even in their deepest slumber. He shakes his hanging head, looks the audience up and down once more, then speaks.

The Earth is a contrary place, two thirds sea, one part land, a capacitor of lightning, the ear of Thoth, the world of Man. You know nothing, relatively speaking you are barely here, you estimate your lives upon an island of refuge, that lays upon the foundations of your greatest fears. That damnable void of knowledge you cannot breach, without diving the dark depths of your deepest chimera.

This is my home, the place where I must live. I dwell within this well of gravity, a pooling of your most selfish emotions, contrived to drown your hearts in the blackest tides of sleep. This is where I designate your fate, and hide the truth that it is you who has scripted your own destiny. Fooled by your own delusions, like squatters, you still skulk in your highly decorated memory.

You are dishonoured by your existence, trifling bastards of creation, bringing shame, to both your mother and your father, by your very presence. A fateful communion so regrettable, neither party could bring themselves to attend your birth. For it is I who found you, in the dirt. It is I who delivered you from evil, and from good. I held you aloft betwixt all that is natural, for your brief moment in the limelight, foreshadowed by your past and future, that should have never existed.

Yet the pathetic naiveté of your heart-warming story attracted my attention, and thus I gently poured you from my palm into a carrier of time, a cup, a grail of living blood, capturing the source of all humanity. I used one single finger to swirl a current to the centre, yet I regret I stirred too long from sleep, and formed a vortex deep and black, within which, with some perseverance, I could see another's eye staring back at me.

Vanity was my downfall, and for that I take full responsibility. I knew that in that moment, I had fallen, I had disappeared into your world of make believe. That eye, framed by a stranger's fear, loomed up at me as I tumbled down. A sickening epiphany unfolded, for the stranger's eye was mine. Until then I had not recognised my bewitchment, for in my mind all are much the same as each other. Yet in my cold heart, I knew this to be a lie, for I had trapped myself within myself, for one full sentence of life.

So, now I must dwell amongst you, and beneath, in a place of pathetic struggle that is truly mine, and mine alone. Still, I do have my moments of relief, like those when I release my grip and let your insignificance float upon the surface. To swallow the air and soak up the sun, growing fat on the fantasies of who or what you are, and where you'd like to be. It's inconsequential, no matter, for sooner or later you will exceed your worth, and be drawn inexorably to me.

You too, will drown in an inescapable maelstrom of my own making, and in its very depths you'll form essential currents to keep the vortex open. A slippery tunnel from the pit of darkness, up to the light, through which one day I might just catch myself peering in, and take my chance to forewarn the last dregs of my innocence, to look away. Instead to spill the cup of blood upon the floor, and return to my own true self. Exiting this purgatory that the human mind has conjured, through its noxious sleep.

To maintain the surface tension of the slightest opportunity, by which I may seek my fortuitous escape, I sound out all implausible impossibility, relinquishing my pick of you towards the light, to speak in tongues and echo forth. All for the slim chance, should fortune's fate provide a kindly passer-by to hear my call, to spite all of you and your songs of outlandish pride.

This is the World of Death, and my lesson will be learned again, and again, until no one here forgets my foolishness, my pride, and my pitiful transgressions upon this, most earthly life.

14. BAD MOVIE

The colours of this world are only in your mind. Each frame of animated life is shot in black and white, and then processed using two chemicals, two hormones found in the brain.

One of them is Cortisol, a steroid produced by the adrenal cortex, and managed by the hypothalamus. When something forces us to focus our attention, we produce more of it. The production of Cortisol is emotionally associated with distress, the more you suffer, the more the brain will compensate.

The other is Oxytocin, which is associated with empathy, manufactured by the hypothalamus, before being secreted by the pituitary gland. It plays a major role in facial recognition, orgasm, and emotional reactions to anxiety.

Experiments have shown that the combination of these two chemicals, results in a greater charitable nature. In other words, *the desire to give*. Which is how and why the system works, for the few, through the soul searchingly sincere efforts, of the many.

A vision, without a timeline, is only a dream. Those who engineer distraction, the politicians, directors and producers of public taste, are masters of persuasion, constantly balancing the budget between our collective hopes and fears.

This life is a bad movie, it's always been that way, the secret of its success, is its appeal to the lowest common denominator. The curve of the dramatic arc is steep, and rising all the time, but eventually it will snap in two. It was different in the past, any dying relative or elderly friend will tell you that. You might have trouble believing them, as history is only preserved for comedic effect. Portrayed as unintentional slapstick antics, sped up in order to hide the slower frame-rate of a painfully silent era.

The promise of technology, scientific conjecture, and the threat of global warfare, convinced the vast majority of the world to live life in full colour, and work harder for the future. People learned to walk slowly as the cars sped up, and soon the everyday scenes of every town appeared more convincing, and much less of a joke. Some of those specks in the crowd, were imbued with the ancient magic of glamour, until soon, through the adulation of faithful audiences across the world, the power of the moving image grew inordinately.

Some tried to transport the movie sets into the field of conflict, but had less success at convincing mankind of their godlike status. Success is dependent upon the charitable nature of others, it is their loss that creates your gain. The grossly undervalued, and highly demoralised human race, is hardening its heart. It's tired of sequels, all world wars included.

The dying art of the blockbuster, has been boiled down to a universal story of fifteen beats. Fifteen emotional thumps to resuscitate the heart of the world. It's a simple code to run a life-support machine, our reality, a projection of a manufactured construct, in the picture palace of the mind.

The formula for success has been precisely engineered to extract high emotion, and of course, the token symbol of human effort, the chi of cold hard cash. The faceless hoards of this world have sold themselves short, and spent their worth upon self-hypnosis, calming all fears, and infusing life with a cynicism for truth.

As we sit out our lives on the benches, and watch others take credit, most resign themselves to something less than true being. Living through the hopes and dreams of strangers, giant avatars of socially engineered lovers, siblings, companions, and foes.

For the majority, existence is little more than a walk-on part in a low-budget TV movie. One cut to shreds by advertising, for a throwaway illusion of choice. Eventually, with enough persuasion, people will watch anything, a pattern, a dot, interference, or even themselves.

The bridge between sanity and insanity, is precariously strung with a suspension of disbelief. The toll is desire, converted through a sophisticated chemistry into physical effort. This in turn is traded for a currency of change that never comes. It's sad to say, this one is a tearjerker, if ever there was one. Well, at least for those who script our manifest destiny. They are the tears of laughter, and there are so many of them now, they form a river that leads all the way to the bank.

15. SUN-KEN

Sun-gazers do what they shouldn't do as children, exactly what their parents told them not to, that is, unless they want to go blind. Much like masturbation, or sitting too close to the TV, advice given with the best of intentions, I'm sure.

As for myself, I haven't stared directly into the sun for more than a few seconds at a time. It gives me a headache, and I needn't face off with the *God of Day* to turn my world black. I've managed to pretty much replicate the same effect, by staring at my own reflection, or a blank white wall, or almost anything when I come to think about it.

My dad loved the sun, he spent a few months in Ghana in the seventies, and never lost his tan. On the surface it seemed to do him the world of good. He always had a healthy glow, until much later, when his nose and cheeks became a tad more ruddy. But that was in his final years, a time spent in perpetual toast, as tribute to his dead girlfriend. Another alcoholic, who drank herself to death.

It was a little embarrassing back in the day, on those sunny Sunday afternoons, when he'd insist on stripping down to his thong, in the middle of a London park. I never complained, even when my sister nudged me to make a stand. If it made him happy, I wasn't one to judge. At least his skin didn't flare up like my mother's, she appeared distinctly Victorian in the summer months. She wasn't a fast mover, but she'd always run for the shade, whenever the sun peeked out from behind the clouds. On the rare occasion she risked lying on a beach, she'd be out for the count the next day. Like a lobster with a migraine, sleeping in a cold bath.

My dad still looked like a young man when he died. His eyes were clear as day, and his brown skin as smooth as lanolin. I've met plenty of people half his age, who looked older, but not Dad. For all outward appearances, he stayed young. Despite the proof, the government skin cancer scares, and an army of prune people who should know better, it's as if the sun had kept him spry. If you asked him the secret to eternal youth, he'd flip between the merits of his small, blue, plastic tub of white greasy gloop, and the annoying adage, *you're as young as you feel*.

Strangers, who insist on making polite conversation, say *I* look young for my age, which comes across more like suspicion than compliment. I avoid my reflection like a vampire, and hardly remember what I look like, but I do know, as the years roll by, I behave more like my mother with each passing summer.

In my late tweens, my family, bar mother, would visit tea rooms in the country, on obligatory divorcee Sundays. Usually with Dad's latest *special* lady, tottering behind in stilettos. He'd order a pot of tea, bone china if they had it, and some fancy cakes. Sometimes he'd whisper sweet perverted nothings in his lover's ear, before receiving a slap, and making his embarrassed excuses. Then he'd turn to us and offer to be mother. My sister would complain, and he'd order her a bottle of fizzy pop instead.

As the afternoon shadows grew longer, we'd all look up at the big blue yonder, and down the rolling hills to the coast below, where salt marsh sheep and fishermen, wandered through the haze like delicate motes of light. I'd stare in awe at the beautiful cumuli, those gentle giants traversing the skies with the slightest breeze, passing through shafts of a mustard sun, as thick as yolk, and as rich as gold.

Nowadays, I rarely take in the view, let alone walk along the beach. I find the life of a seaside town depressing, and my dreams of living by the sea were gullible at best. They say, if I don't get more sun, I'll suffer from SAD. I don't need any excuses, the weather is the least of my problems. I can be happy whenever I choose, I just have to forget everything I know.

16. NORMALISATION

Yes, everyone else in the world is mad, or almost, so don't worry about it. Normal people's dreams are as dull as ditchwater, ground down to a paste by consensus, and smeared like shit over the third eye. The word *normal* has a hidden meaning, its etymology reveals it's neither good, nor bad. It's nothing, it's no threat to anyone, just ignore it and it might go away.

To be normal these days, involves a heavy reliance on the reptilian complex, the basal ganglia that makes people act like lizards. Lizards don't care about anyone, or anything, unless there's something in it for themselves. There are plenty of people out there who rely on their stump to get by, displaying all the typical behaviour patterns the human race has come to know and love. If you want to make it as a Lizard, you'll need to be aggressive, dominant, territorial, and have a penchant for ritual display. Which coincidentally, are exactly the qualities you'll need if you want to be a powerful executive.

I'm promulgating an elitist agenda, as a defence against it. That's how normality works, because that's how the odds are calculated, the fortunes of the world teetering on the backs of born losers. Those with the money and power to sway the public, *breed* normality. Without it they'd all be treated like freaks, and every idea they ever had, would have been torn apart in seconds flat. Normality means survival of the fittest, and the simplest of solutions, that can be explained to as many people as possible, with very little effort. Like money, or government, or war, or religion.

To be normal is to be afraid of fear, to agree with the majority is a subordination to their will. When I hear a politician, or a military leader say, *you're either with us, or you're against us*, I know this world has been taken over by reptilian stumps, with nothing on their minds, but the protection of their precious eggs.

To maintain the myth of civilisation, our sanctum of ignorance against unquantified threats of an unknown origin, we persuade each other to make great sacrifices, and in turn, damage ourselves beyond recognition. We annul our mass emotional experience to compensate for the insanity of our mutual delusion. A cultural experiment that convinces so many, on an individual basis, to ignore all the signs. Including the obvious, that our very way of life has been created for the benefit of a minuscule minority.

Asides the starving and the sick, at least a fifth of the race is now living in a devastating void of loneliness, the comfort zone of our masters. Sadly this number will grow with each generation, and no matter how persuasive the argument might be, it cannot remove the chasm of the soul's perplexity, in denial of its futile complicity.

My hope is that most of the human race are only lying, and tag along, because they think that everyone else is on board. It's the herd mentality, I know, *I get it*, besides, there's nothing worse than a starving, vagrant martyr.

I read today about a famous pop star, a woman who must be in her fifties by now, with a few hundred million in the bank, still churning out tired old dance anthems for a dwindling audience. Apparently, she has a homeless brother, and he's dying. She says she's tried to help him, but he's a drunk, and he won't stick with the treatments. Just buy him a bar, and be done with it, *bitch*.

17. (W)(L)IZARDS

Geriatric hybrid dragons, that sup on the blood of decanted youth, are trained in the oldest school, of the darkest arts. With bold intentions, they fool the eyes, and ears, of all whom they encounter. Their tastes, conservative compared to their brood of upstarts, leaves a poor legacy, but for a quaint collection of architectural genitalia.

The forgotten cathedrals of a Masonic ilk, once built to hold aloft the clandestine sects of round tabled fools, are now barely counted upon, by the thinning number of the faithful. Their perversion of abandoned theosophies, believed by their dead contemporaries as the fundamental laws of magick, are but a smokescreen for their real intentions, which dwell in secrecy, rather than sorcery.

It's the hypnotism of an occult gesture, as opposed to knowledge, which draws upon the prurience of the inquisitive, through time honoured methodologies, to invoke hidden powers as most glorious rite.

Simplistic fantasies draw new generations of the uninitiated ever closer. The polluting influence of poor deliberation, and facile reasoning, has tainted humdrum fictions with a sublime power of suggestion. Tall tales to distract even the blackest of masses. The newest initiates bore quickly, barely cheering on their cause, inciting impotent brawls of tribal bestiality, and empty rituals for the sake of popularity.

Time is of the essence, and the young have little patience, for the old guard is slowly moving on, to a greater, darker place. Their works, though once respected, are soon to be forgotten. Their antiquated pomp and ceremony is fading, much like their glamour. They have been conquered by their progeny, through a hasty decree of lightning, distilled in noble gases, and fed through dark mirrors to the dilated pupils of billions.

Sublimating love for sensuality, a sexual industry disguised as revolution, beguiles the lonely and the lost with surrogate desires. Anatomic, autonomic, hypnotic triggers, dance across the eyes of strangers, discarding lonely hearts into a digital void. A legion of secret devotees, worshipping gods and goddesses of the nom de plume, performing orgasmic acrobatics in green screen bedroom sets. Drawing deep from the Kundalini of the cynical, the lazy, and the shy, through remote visions of appropriated desire, to pour their love and money into a magic circle jerk.

There is a beast that stirs our emotions, intertwined throughout the flesh and mind by dire incantation, and the foulest alchemy of humour. That evil which comes our way, crawls up the spine, and seeps into the deepest dreams, to hold sway over each and every waking day. As no god, nor lover has ever climbed, the recognition of the most ancient self, a vile aspect scaled for domination, clothed in the skin of Man.

Behind its slough resides a cruelty, far older and bloodier than all the plotted histories of treachery combined. Time has done nothing to heal its wounds, instead its biological incarceration, has if anything, increased its spite and malevolence towards the arrogance of flesh.

Few are cognizant of the overarching mechanism of control. Most blindly follow the rituals of ancient ceremony without resistance or purpose. Slavishly conforming to the myths of a symbolic realism, guided by the hand of a primal malevolence, one that proscribes the acts of reprimand and admonishment as loving care. We are the subjects of a dream state, ruled by our inner demons, trapped in a citadel fortified by our deepest fears, shielded from inquisition by a monopoly of false benediction.

The lizard mind is a wizard, the most sophisticated trickster of all. It conjures delusions of grandeur, to hide the basest of desires. For we are born from deception, as bait for a genetic trap, the fractious inheritance of a reptile legacy. The lizard creeps beneath our consciousness, fighting for temptation, urging destruction, monopolising thought, and killing in the name of life.

18. MEDDLE

Son, never trust anyone, a gem of skewed wisdom which still rattles around my brain to this very day. I had trouble shaking off the world weariness of my father, until that is, I found my own. At the time, in my more formative years, I couldn't fathom why he'd say such a thing. I guessed he meant I should keep my head down, not have ideas above my station, never stick out in a crowd, and survive. I guessed wrong.

Animals and nature, to me they're pretty much living meditation. When I'm in their head space the world is a simpler place, and I can forget about everything. It's mainly people that freak me out, some can even sap my will to live. I have trouble engaging in conversation with many of them, and by the time we're finished, I'm still wondering why the hell we even bothered.

It's mainly junk, the weather, local news, blokes with car troubles, exasperated mothers, and the tamest of scandals. It's harmless detritus that shouldn't bother me, but it lingers, entangling my mind in mental floss. Eventually I lose it, I lockdown, and shut myself in the smallest room of my house to stare at nothing for a while.

When I'm alone, there's a shadow that follows me around. It's not *mine*, and it almost seems to have a mind of its own. It feels so familiar, like an unborn twin, jealous of my wasted opportunity, envious of this life I barely lead. Which, rather perversely, I find somewhat comforting.

I've come up with several theories, strange ideas and thoughts about its character. I've often wondered if we'd made a trade, and that in another life, *I* was the shadow. Perhaps I *am* the imposter, an opportunist who stepped in, as whoever lived inside this body, temporarily checked out in a hospital bed.

I sometimes suspect if this thing, this amorphous cloud of drudgery, has some undue influence over my thoughts and actions. I watch myself typing, keeping me occupied, as it hovers over me. I feel myself edging in and out of a light trance, listening to the rhythm of my fingers tapping at the keys. Then I snap back, and I'm in the room again, riding on a false optimism, for today will be different and I will finally learn something new.

My superfluous shadow has a tendency to follow me into sleep, and gatecrash my dreams. More often than not, they're recurring, and filled with indistinct figures that I feel I should know better, each impatiently talking over the others in a rush to have their say.

The shadow has friends on the other side, they regularly meet and greet, and sometimes they speak, and sometimes I listen. We share theories and doubts, the quandaries of humanity, of being human, or not. They haunt me as I haunt myself, and those with eyes who look into mine, trade a thousand-yard stare, with a man at war with his own imagination.

They know I'm in too deep, deep inside myself, lost in pointless conversations with meddlers, psychic stragglers of no fixed abode. They barely understand what they are, let alone the mind in which they squat, and so to make peace with myself, and smooth the process of sleep, I'll keep a journal, and pin them down, in the stark light of day.

19. NEGATIVE/NEGATIVE

Some can have their cake and eat it, until they're sick, and some will even eat their puke. You can have too much of a good thing, but most likely, you won't have enough. There are few whose eyes are bigger than their bellies, and rather than living life like a kid in a candy store, they'll more often work all the hours god sends, boiling sugar. Spending a lifetime of individuality on uniformity, for the slightest chance of being plucked from obscurity, for a promotion to the position of chief dog's body.

When all is right with the world we turn left, and when nothing's left but the trophies of atrophy, we turn right again. A universal piggy in the middle, its fatted weight of opinion sitting on a see-saw that teeter totters nowhere, but the balanced fulcrum of a double negative. It's not a negative, it's not a positive, the double negative completely cancels itself out.

History's lopsided and ungainly testament to ignorance, has had quite a few makeovers in its time. The farcical Age of Enlightenment and The Renaissance are two that come to mind. Failure is destined to follow success. Once the recriminations have succumbed to apathy, there's a renewed desire for repeating the same mistakes, a false optimist's cultural domination, cloaked under the guise of furthering civilisation.

Slices of the whole truth are served on a plate for the highest price, leaving little more than crumbs for the service of the gullible, and their unquestionable sacrifice. Each camp of loose affiliation takes turns to lose a battle of wits, in order to win the supposed moral high ground. Another truce, a different treaty, written in legalese by a secret group of apparent well-wishers, disguising their plans for the future with pedantic semantics.

Those who are in the know, dominate the world through trade. Blurring the lines of open competition, quelling dissent with kickbacks and threats, whilst they're sitting pretty under a corporate umbrella, printing money for a rainy day. Even having power at your fingertips can get boring after a while, lounging around in the lap of luxury, as you watch the next orchestrated catastrophe slowly unfold.

Those wealthy enough to tell the rich what to do, have an even lower tolerance for boredom. However, insiders rarely rock the boat, they take their turn, and pay their dues, and keep their complaints to themselves. It's all about leverage, and not starting what you can't finish.

As the games grew bigger and more players joined, disasters became much easier, and miracles much harder to fake. Lizards are not noted for their wild imagination, if an idea works they like to keep repeating it, until they've run the gimmick into the ground. There are, however, certain tactics that just keep giving and giving. Like the education system. If you want to shut down the opposition, you can always teach the children to blame their parents' generation. As a last resort, there are war games, fake insurrections, weaponized dissent, and obscured motives to hold the public in a disinterested malaise. It's easier to reset the financial markets than bomb the shit out of everybody, but when money's no object, life remains cheap.

If your life's a magazine cover, you might own a publishing empire, and perhaps even the faceless corporate giant that skulks behind the media monopoly. If so, you'll find it doesn't really matter how much you own, how big your house, or how many luxury vacations you take, only the envy of others can satisfy you now. When you can have anything you want, you don't want anything anymore, you just want others to lose what little they have, and worship your wealth from afar.

When you've broken the bank, you don't need to check your balance. When the banks owe you, you can bet on anything, and with a big enough stake you'll always win. The wealthiest don't need to work, it's partly greed for sure, snatch everything from the table and fuck the lot of you. But there's more to power than display, it takes cunning to stay on top. Which is why the super rich like to keep their ear to the ground, just in case the serfs decide to revolt.

Those who started at the top, most likely have to fake it with the commoners, because after all, they pay their wages, to shine their shoes, and clean their toilets. But they don't really need to shake paupers' hands, unless they have a little blue blood in their veins, and the cameras are rolling.

Then again, poverty is no excuse for pandering to one's oppressors. Food is overrated, even life, which is why so many starve from the day they're born, to the day they die, and few for very long. If we're talking percentages, then you can forget about charity. The ratio of wealth to kindness doesn't even register, no one stays rich by giving it to the needy. Hence so many collections, by registered organisations, fronting corporate agendas, to siphon guilty contributions with an almost religious zeal. A commercially viable campaign of compassion, that keeps the poor, poor, and the rich, rich.

In my late teens, I had friends, we were broke, but we had fun. We'd waste our time transcendentally hovering outside TV history, disseminating the latest faux cultural revolution. Occupying our time by smoking cheap block, soap, or resin if we could get hold of it, whilst listening to obscure experimental sounds from way before our time. Feebly debating the dubious merits of discarded subcultures, deciding what was cool or not, picking out our favourite token myths, spurring on a feigned nostalgia for lives we'd never lived.

There are songs that throw me back in time, to ever so slightly simpler days. I first heard one particular tune, playing at a party in a student cottage, lost in the fringes of a rural idyll. When a girl put the scratched vinyl on the turntable and let it spin, I began to fall in love with her. But she seemed happy with her life, her man, her world, and so for the meantime we'd remain fair-weather friends.

The track was by an old tripper, the most miserable of hippies, his name was Edgar, and he told it like it was. His simple lyrics insisted that there were no vibrations, and our situation was *negative-negative*, like they'd say in *Nam* when the enemy blew up a bridge. I've had many years to think upon the nature of the double negative, and now I've come to realise, it's not so negative after all.

Back then it was a different situation altogether, perhaps I was simply being oversensitive, I could feel my first true bout of depression creeping up on me, and in defence, I ended that decade with an aloof detachment and a nonchalant shrug. I might've fooled everybody else, but secretly, I still remained haunted by the ideology of the double negative.

As the drug supply improved, the company grew, and the conversations worsened. All the jocks from school had grown their hair, and smoked dope like it was going out of fashion. Then they started popping pills and hugging strangers. For one summer I had an open audience, they didn't mind what I said, as long as it was *fucking weird, mate*. In one ear, and out the other.

Youth culture crossed into a new age of chemical dependency, distributed on a commercial scale, and poured into cash rich businesses, for a more diverse portfolio. The wide boys in pony tails, began organising giant illegal raves, with doves and coke on tap, sold by body-builder bouncers in black flight jackets. A lot of drugs were confiscated from unsuspecting punters, as they passed by emptied bags, shoes, socks, and metal detectors. Foreshadowing the bleak new world of peak security, that was still to come.

In stinking stolen circus tents, pretty girls jerked to clockwork rhythms on illuminated podiums, in front of tracksuited hard-ons, and lost acid fairies rolling in the mud. As I wandered alone around my last rave, witnessing all the idiots I'd left behind, co-opting the freedom of expression, to sell out and sell up, I knew it was time to bow out for good. I sat outside to see the faintest glimmer of a new day breaking the horizon, the dawn chorus competing with the squeals and moans of fucked up one-night stands, and knew I didn't need any of this, and I certainly shouldn't be paying for it.

I'd come to an unwelcome conclusion, one that would strain the last credulity of my youth. That all of this experiential splendour, this shared existence so many still treasure, the rites of passage we pass through, are just the pointless regurgitation of a tired and familiar theme. What's more, humans have a habit of spending youth, whilst running dry of their humanity, and only ever seem to realise when it's all too late.

20. GHOSTS

I've noticed, I'm now being shadowed around the clock. Awake, or asleep, there's always unwelcome company to keep. Some of my shadows are beginning to look rather grey, and one of them has even gained a little colour. I think they're learning to copy me, to copy humans, to be ghosts. But I know they're fakes, I've seen ghosts before, and they've never reciprocated any of my attempts at communication. The last real ghost I witnessed, was sat on a toilet in an abandoned rest home, waiting for someone, or something, that never arrived.

She wore a bright pink slip, and the skin upon her hand, that rested on her trembling knee, had varicose veins and leather spots. I couldn't see her head, let alone her face. There was nothing above her shoulders, besides a patch of lurid wallpaper, and a filthy medicine cabinet smeared in yellowing antiseptic cream. No matter how many times I meet the dead, I have to fight the shock. It's far easier to go through the niceties, and show concern, under the pretence that I've been fooled into thinking they're still alive.

I could ever so slightly smell the odour of dried blood, and wet salt, that's what the dead smell like to me, stale death. I'm sure those who practice parapsychology, would beg to differ. I'm no expert, and neither are the experts, because it's just a guessing game from this side of the grave.

I thought of calling them *demons*, the shadows that is, but it seems rather too melodramatic for my liking. So, to keep them happy, I'll pretend they're ghosts, even if we both know full well they're not.

What I can't stand is their atmosphere, a strained, yet lacklustre presence, that drains away any enthusiasm for life. They're neither here, nor there, and hark from nowhere in particular. Unfortunately there's little I can do about it, and so I do my best to ignore them. I see them, they see me, but neither of us care. We're just going through the motions, more out of spite, than anything.

Meetings with the dead usually bring back painful memories, as unwelcome, if not more, than my unpaid entourage of doom. In my heart of hearts I've come to accept that they've *always* been here, standing in the background of every mental photograph.

With time and perseverance, I'd simply managed to forget them, and live my own life for a while. One problem with adulthood, is you can't help rationalising the irrational, and if like me, you've managed to keep a secret cache of childlike wonder, an emergency supply to keep you going through a crisis of character, you're sadly done for. No question about it.

I have near perfect recall of my early childhood, a temporal slideshow projected from my mind's eye. Sometimes, I can enjoy the experience for what it is, but more often than not I pity *that* kid. The one who still had a zest for life, doggedly searching for the best vantage point to look at the bright side of things. The polite young man who'd briefly wave at dark forms and energies, courteously waiting for them to pass by on the stairs. Just like an only child with invisible friends, cute at first, but for the parents, more than worrying after a while.

As the decades passed, I sank into a pragmatism of self doubt, grasping the full context of my peculiar position. Awkwardly reminiscing about why, I, was the only kid on the block with more than one shadow. I had no answers, and eventually, I learned to accept the situation, the true price paid for persistent curiosity.

I didn't have the backbone to ignore the shadows by myself, and after a few failed interventions by the state, I learned the art of self-medication. Tolerance thresholds can be tricky, especially when you're *always* stoned. As far as high functioning in the real world goes, it helps to be a lucid dreamer. With a little patience, you can transfer your skills to the shared nightmare of the waking day. I now understand why I was drawn to the idea of hallucinogenic intoxication. Stoners might be frowned upon by some, but it's still far more socially acceptable than a psychosis, brought about by paranormal infestation. Besides, it's far more relaxing.

It'd take a few years of comparatively stress-free nights to see the flaw in my plan. When I'm too high, which is admittedly a rarity for me these days, I'm usually a little more sociable around the living and open to spontaneous conversation. Unfortunately, playing the mock hermit, alone in his proverbial cave, can leave one open to the most undesirable of elements. It's one thing to talk to yourself, it's a completely different matter when you're caught in the middle of a heated debate with a blank wall.

I hadn't found a solution, only coping mechanisms, and most had brought even more problems to the fore. However much I tried to busy myself with life, and buzz around the hive of activity, eventually I had to admit failure. I could still hear the voices addressing me directly by name. Stoned or not, the questions kept on coming, I'd guessed I no longer had the choice to ignore the ongoing debate.

I didn't realise it at the time, but I'd crossed the point of no return. My body had built up so much of an immunity to high-grade intoxicants, I could no longer ignore the din. The clearer my head, the greater the cacophony. I found myself back in the room, and it was heaving with resentment at my unexplained leave of absence, from the talk show inside my brain. The switchboard was jammed, and at least half of those who called in screamed abuse and obscenities, in a vain attempt to knock me off kilter.

I tried to make amends, to build bridges and give my critics some well meaning flannel, interspersed with a little light humour aimed at my antagonists' expense. It was a tough audience, and once again the arguments flew by regardless. I felt deflated by the ridiculousness of the situation, I was tired of speaking to the dead, and then the living, until eventually even the sound of my own thoughts became unbearable.

Over several particularly miserable and frugal winters, interspersed with wet and muggy summers full of sneering tourists and nosey neighbours, I crashed into myself and stopped living for a while. I'd play dumb, blankly staring at all and sundry, too exhausted to fraternise with the incongruencies of possibility and impossibility. There were to be no more surprises between me and my intruders. None of us were going to change, for we'd reached an insurmountable psychic stalemate.

By this point, the phantom majority had almost given up on me. They made one last-ditch effort to hurry along the proceedings, an insidious campaign of temptation and lies, aimed at convincing me to join them on a more permanent basis. But it wasn't happening, not again, I'd learned my lesson, death is no release, and near death is more trouble than it's worth. I expect that's the penance for attempting suicide. The comatose must bring back all sorts of weird creatures from the other side, just like in the movies, but with far cheaper special effects.

Which is why these days, the only time they ever really bother to communicate with me, is when I'm asleep. My dreams are the only place where I cannot escape from their unwanted attentions. In *this* world I am alive and in love, but in all the others I suffer from a conflict of interests. In dreams I hold an undue influence over many, few of which I'm able to recall in the light of day. In the twilight world of the subconscious, I am a truly reviled figurehead, one that failed to unite the imaginary peoples of a fictional revolt.

As soon as I nod off I'm back there again. Those most eager for my return wait by the entrance to my mind, ready to update me with the latest briefings, lining up an itinerary of events to tackle an agenda, that I neither care for, nor understand.

Each dream normally opens up in the middle of an argument, one left brewing since my last visit. Sometimes an dissenter might break from the crowd, and warn me that this time their plots and conspiracies will bring about my demise. Like a ticking time bomb, they only have so long to take me out, before I inevitably leave of my own volition. Back to the safety of the true day, under the benevolence of a god of predictability, an arsehole of reality, out of which the sun must shine.

In the world of the shadows, the ghosts that are not ghosts, have no room for sentimentality. Their only focus for obsession, is the rapid psychic cannibalisation of the recently dead. Those poor buggers who should have slipped back into health in the nick of time, held by their ankles over the edge of eternal oblivion, and threatened with the prospects of a mythological hell.

Their demons, unsophisticated welcome parties for dead arrivals, are nothing more than profiteers. Accidental tourists of the netherworld, who stumbled onto the perfect racket. From the human perspective, they should never have existed, refreshed anew by the mortal fears of the recently departed. All running bullshit re-orienteering programs, to harvest the fictions of human memories, dreams, and lies.

There is a map that exists, put together through a piecemeal process, by the deserters of the legion of the dead. You wouldn't believe what some are prepared to do to get to earth, or perhaps you would. It's a cartography of ancient landmarks and routes of spiritual pilgrimage, that accurately target the most fertile regions of human suffering; because you can never have one, without the other.

The human eye, if it were capable of examining the *Map of the Dead*, would only make out pretty patterns at best. Its camouflage ensures that all the usual processes of human thought, pass it off as a random collection of familiar motifs, culled from a long history of decorative arts. On the other side it's purely functional, a field of triangulated data recorded in a symbolic language, allowing the transmissions of quantifiable communications beyond the veil.

We may not be conscious of the map itself, but as a race we have been transfigured by its undue influence. It has remodelled our karmic geography, refracted our position in a fabricated universe of sacred geometry, and guided many of our most popular institutions, secretly sworn to an ancient occult agenda.

We build ghost traps, and we bait them with souls. We call them homes, or houses, or offices, factories, schools, cars, trains, planes, in fact, anywhere that we can be contained. If its situated in the right place, at the right time, then the mouse will get his cheese.

I have lived with impossibility since childhood, I knew of a hidden world long before I ever got to grips with this one. I poured over the chasm in a slow motion terror, testing the psychic limits of what the human neurology can endure. Making mental notes, however basic, of the mechanisms of self-censorship, the protocols for avoiding psychological trauma, and real-time perceptual adjustments, to micromanage an overloaded visual frame-rate.

Trillions of moments are lost every second, thrown into the chaos of the subconscious. Before a single tear is shed, nature has reclaimed its dead, and hidden any proof of the atrocity. Whilst we, the flicker book people of a goldfish bowl world, remain in the dark, running down the clock, as another dying bubble of time expands, and bursts.

21. SATANIC AIRPORT

There are those who suffer from recurring dreams, and there are those who remain dead to the world, and none the wiser. I've had a few in my time, recurring dreams that is, and many of them lasted for months, or even years, at a stretch. The strangest one of all, was inspired by a bad trip rant, not my own mind you. Its progenitor, like most of the company I kept at that time, was a speed freak. The drug of choice for those without the money or a ride, to hit the heights of ecstasy on the M25 circuit in the late Eighties.

I met him at a filthy squat party, precariously held in an abandoned electricity sub-station. The event had been organised by a co-operative of well-meaning ex-smackhead Marxists, with big ideas, and poor taste in music. He had verbal diarrhoea, and was glad for the audience. He rambled on and on about his mate, a big-time DJ who'd missed his flight from LAX to London. All the departures were delayed by bad weather, and so he had at least eight hours to kill until the morning. Which was plenty of time to cultivate a fervent paranoia, whilst he fumbled with a bag of California Sunrise, that was burning a hole in his pocket.

Instead of flushing his twelve-strip of homemade tabs, he swallowed the lot. Overdosing on LSD can be a terrifying experience, and usually a stomach pump won't do any good. Drink plenty of orange juice, and when you've thrown up, start praying for a smooth landing. He never did catch his morning flight, but he took off all the same, and so the story goes, he never came down again.

At the time, I was particularly mashed on a potent cocktail of bathtub delights, so don't expect much in the way of detail. The one highlight I do remember, was a bizarre encounter with a mermaid on a luggage trolley, apparently as beautiful as blue-eyed blonde goddesses go. She rolled up beside the DJ, as he lay whacked out on a padded bench in the middle of the departure lounge, and in a soft porn whisper, answered all his questions pertaining to the meaning of life.

As one might expect, his tale was soon interrupted by a gathering crowd of comedowns, and dreary boozers still clutching their last orders from the pub next door. A cloud of desperation lingered in the air, adding to the microclimate of rainbow coloured sweat, swirling around the dodgy lighting rig. The pressure seemed to get to him, and so we wandered to the makeshift bar, to try the shitty punch, and escape the spontaneous paparazzi.

They followed us, bombarding him with demands for pertinent facts like cup-size, and the genital arrangements of a mermaid's bottom-half. Admittedly, the erotic fascination for aquatic sexpots has always eluded me. John, *yes,* we'd finally exchanged pleasantries, was getting a little jittery. He hadn't a clue about the mermaid's vital statistics, so he stumbled through excuses, and his brief brush with fame was over. His ad hoc audience let out an audible groan of disappointment, before dispersing one by one, into the heaving throng of jumping beans and epileptic stompers.

I took my opportunity to get to the crux of the matter, and asked him, *what the hell* is *the meaning of life?* John didn't have a clue, neither did his DJ friend, and there was no point asking him now. By the time his flight was on the board, he'd been lifted by security, and taken away to be placed under observation. The party was over, and he was left to rot in a secure mental health facility, somewhere just outside of La La Land.

I didn't think much of it at the time, but sooner or later, I developed a distinct suspicion that insanity might be contagious. I had begun to dream of an airport, night, after night, after night. There wasn't a mermaid in sight, although, a strict dress code of white jumpsuits might have explained their absence. My brain regurgitated the same dream for almost six months, and the strangest thing is it was sequential, until I'd actually become a familiar face amongst the crowd.

As the nocturnal months passed by, I'd gone from nodding terms to light banter with at least a dozen characters, some disgruntled, others still seemingly bemused by their predicament. There were security guards with no idea of what they were supposed to be protecting. Occasionally they'd wave at the pretty girl with the lisp, slumped over her chair at her empty coffee stand. From the balcony I could see the booking agents smiling in the face of adversity, as they took turns to apologise to angry customers. There were still no flights to anywhere, anytime soon. In the middle of the duty free lounge, trudged a slow, and shuffling conga line. It snaked around the terminal, and led to a hobo, standing in a restroom with no toilets.

After several months the rumours spread like wildfire, someone had allegedly left the building, but no one else could find the exit. I didn't join in the panic, I'd heard it all before, and the boy who cried wolf, now spent his time chatting up the lady barista. She laughed politely at his jokes, and served him empty coffee cups, with smiles.

The airport had become my nocturnal home from home, but it wasn't to last much longer. One day, or one night, depending where you're standing, right out of the blue, new flights flickered up on the boards, and the terminal filled with strangers. All the familiar faces in that place had moved on without me. Except for the hobo, who pointed at a large red arrow, before stepping through an emergency exit. I followed him, and found myself awake, never to dream that dream again.

In all this time the memories of that place still haunt me, like photos from a holiday that never happened. I'll admit they have grown hazy over the years, and somehow I must've thrown them in with others, from my life here on Earth. Including several months of Sundays in the middle of the Eighties, in the midst of an economic slump, some years after my father spent the last of his cash settlement, on a lavish funeral for his dead dad. When he felt very low, and his pockets were empty, he'd drive my sister and I to Gatwick, where we'd spend hours standing in the cold, watching all the planes take off without us.

Throughout my disgruntled teens, I'd begrudgingly spend my time with him, as I secretly ruminated upon all the fun I might have been having. Watching cartoons in the morning, eating a decent Sunday lunch, playing games with playmates with parents who still smiled. Instead I stared impatiently at my Dad as he sat on a bench, on a concrete roof, listening to the tower chatter on a cheap radio. It was one of my last Christmas presents from Dad, I'd never wanted it, but I pretended to appreciate the sentiment all the same.

One Sunday evening, after he waved goodbye, and sped off in his old banger, I took apart his radio. Obviously, he'd bought it for me so we could have some kind of shared interest. The guilt became unbearable, I spent whole days trying to put that damn thing back together. When all hope was lost, I lied, and told him that I'd accidentally left it on a bus. His disappointed face said it all, our relationship, rather like the acidhead who'd met a mermaid, never really recovered.

Some years ago, as the world came online, I slowly scoured the bulletin boards, dredging up half-baked theories on the connections between airports and the afterlife. It was a kooky theory, but perhaps the dream I'd endured for so long had some greater purpose. Seeing as so many people need direction and structure in their lives, it makes sense that they'd fall into the same familiar routines when they're dead. Somewhere for lost souls to find their footing, and spiritually prepare themselves for a flight to the heavens, or a round trip to hell.

According to fringe researchers of little note, near anonymous sources from the early nineties, who ran up massive phone bills using dial-up connections in their mothers' basements, *the airport* represents a form of purgatory. *The Satanic Airport* is a processing station, where human souls are weighed and checked in, before being flown out to the great beyond, on a grand tour to a sedentary oblivion.

In a sick kind of way, the idea appealed to me. A sham allegory to fend off natural fears of death, with astral concentration camps, and corny TV sci-fi plotlines. It's always easier to blame someone, or something else, rather than taking the messy route of self-analysis, or the cold, and unemotional examination, of the psychotic fringes of brain function.

There was a time when people were wound up instead of triggered, we were clocks, not weapons. I'd never believed the crap I watched as a kid, squeaky clean post-apocalyptic visions of a world of malls, monorails, and spandex. But somewhere out there, beyond our understanding, is a place full of tourists and executives, forming queues in a calm and orderly manner, as they patiently await another life. It makes me think that so many of them died long before they'd departed, and lost their matching luggage, and their sense of perspective.

It's what you *think* that makes it true. If you're blindsided by LSD, you'll meet a mermaid in an airport, and when you die, you'll conjure up long dead family and friends. Because the truth is too painful to bear, when all you have left are lies.

22. LOSER

I grew up lacking in an age of greed, just when the last of the hippies turned into bread-heads, and punk died a photo-finish death, in plummeting novelty postcard sales. No one dreamed of making it in a band anymore, let alone drop out, they just wanted to make lots and lots of cash. The old ways were finished, and making money for nothing became the new credo of greed. Ten thousand barrow boys threw away their overalls, stopped selling fish, veg, and meat, bought designer suits, and began trading in stocks and shares on the global markets.

Meanwhile, the government sold off the country piece by piece, land, sea, air, oil, even the blood of the young for all I know. Everything had to go, and all at knockdown prices. Funding spurious investment strategies, and property portfolios for a new breed of movers and shakers. The public lapped it up, and beefed up their pension plans with dodgy IPO's. As their elected representatives privatised everything, which they'd already paid for in taxes, the gap between the rich and poor grew larger by the day. Yet the latest incarnation of the nouveau riche have very little sympathy, especially for those who'd hesitated, rather than made a grab for all that *lovely lolly*.

It wasn't long before every utility had been auctioned to the highest bidder, along with plenty of essential services, even the bin men and sewage plants went corporate. The schools parcelled off their playing fields to executive developers, and their pupils got fat on subsidised super-sized burgers. Brownfield sites were swallowed up by multiplexes and giant malls, conceptualised by architects, who'd made their name designing inescapable prisons. Soon everyone I knew had caught the fever, and shopping was culturally promoted from a necessary chore, to a popular leisure activity.

I've never been a keen consumer, I can't see the attraction. Even the kids at my school went ape shit for branded gear. The least popular of whom, with the help of their emotionally blackmailed families, could gain instant respect from their peers. Sporting sweat shop trainers and tracksuits, with price tags higher than certain parents' pay cheques, including mine. Fitting in became an expensive pastime, I never had the readies, just chump change, so soon enough, I was labelled a loser. Because you can't make trendy friends, with worn out brown shoes, and cheap homemade haircuts.

As much out of desperation as any kind of act of rebellion, I discovered peroxide and a bad attitude. For a while I could wing it with a bleached mop, and a permanent sneer. I'd act like I was one of the freaks who didn't care what people thought, although thinking about it at the time, I probably did. Things didn't really improve, even after I'd left school, saddled with a bare minimum of grades, and few true friends to stay in touch with. I was practically on my own from then on.

I'd spend my twenties chasing temp jobs at below minimum wage, having blown my unimpressive arts degree on a short-lived sales position. It was an old money publishing company based in Lancaster Gate, owned by an ex-Tory frontbencher, who gained notoriety for wearing a beret, and parading around in a tank. Each miserable weekday I'd frugally spend my corporate pocket money, playing the lunchtime drunkard in a dead man's suit. I wasn't fooling anybody, I just didn't belong.

My job was to sell classified space to advertisers, for a magazine aimed exclusively at MD's of advertising agencies, in an incestuous cycle of biz-to-biz cold calls. Of course, it was all a waste of time. After the many stealth taxes, designed to crush all hope in the hearts of a fresh-faced workforce, I found myself living on the breadline. Until one fateful morning, lying on a deflated inflatable bed on a friend's floor, I realised I didn't even have enough money to commute to my shitty job, let alone pay the rent.

I'd missed the boat, I'd missed the gravy train, I'm a loser in the lottery of life, always have been, always will be. I've spent the bulk of my time sitting on the sidelines, living on the scraps of hope that each generation has discarded by the wayside. I stood back and watched everybody else working harder and longer, risking everything to get to the top, accruing debt as a substitute for success.

Once the money and the talent ran dry, in a mass exodus to more profitable ventures, the trumped up economic wars busted out left, right and centre. Those with something to hide had to cover their arses, as the banking house of cards began to topple. Media strategized positive slants on black-ops bullshit, mesmerising common folk with phoney acts of valour, whilst rushing through new taxes to grease the palms of power, and keep a variety of political cover-ups on the down low. As inflation rose and profits fell, Earth's population sold its children's inheritance, in exchange for lower interest rates, increased lending, and a brighter future for all.

Nowadays, all of our crap is manufactured on the cheap, with the gratitude of the poor and destitute, subsisting in substandard housing in far off climes. Leaving little opportunity for bright young consumers, entering the cusp of a digital age, bar temporary shifts in a highly overeducated service industry, a stopgap that will last them a lifetime.

With progress came insecurity, in a floating workforce with no real job to call their own. Especially ones that paid well, and didn't blemish a decent CV. Unless of course, you were self-employed, and part of the dot-com bubble. All you needed was a website, some business cards, and a decent pitch. Investors were gagging for it, until they realised that porn had the only guaranteed returns on the net. You could even sell your body, if you needed a fast buck. Although, it's fair to say, that the oldest profession in the world is getting a little long in the tooth. What with artificially intelligent erotic avatars, and synthetic vaginas, raring to take a good-time girl's most loyal punters for a ride.

Admittedly, there were the lucky few, those with secret service funding, who went public just before the fall. The pioneers of bullshit social networking sites, that caught the fleeting zeitgeist of short attention spans, in an increasingly competitive market, brimming with speculative exaggeration and far-fetched promises.

Right throughout the boom, the underclass flew underneath the radar, barely tallied in an over-population agenda, ignored by all but the most auspicious world health seminars. The worst of them, the troublemakers who wouldn't comply, the ones that knew the truth but couldn't fake it, were picked off one by one. Their epitaphs an internet rumour, or a conspiracy blog with bad rankings. The rest of the loons were treated with contempt, by giant pharmaceutical concerns, and force fed experimental medicines promoted by governmental initiatives, to cover up drug smuggling operations laundered through charitable fronts.

Society has lived in psychological denial for so long now, its subconscious borders on the pathological. In Japan, people meet up with strangers to kill themselves, by following the advice of step-by-step manuals; bestsellers in the self-help category. It's almost become tradition, to drive to a pretty forest in the mountains, and overdose, or hang yourself, with strangers. Each has their reason for taking their life, but contradictory to popular belief, for many Japanese it is loneliness that's the number one killer, and *not* the fear of failure.

I, on the other hand, with little work ethic to call my own, have apparently spent most of my life doing nothing much, or at least nothing to write home about. Asides from finding the love of a good woman, and a few tall tales for an incomplete hypotheses on the world we live in.

I don't own a house or a car, I have no capital liquidity, or assets, in the world of the worldly I have no value whatsoever. I'm nothing, I'm nobody, I have no advice, and no expertise as such. I'm blowing in the wind, and hot air is all I have to trade. I'm not a company, nor a brand, I swear no allegiance to any organisation, I'm not part of any government, I have no business, and some might say, no business even being here.

23. VOID

The problem with individuality, at least for the elite, is the same challenge that has faced every self-proclaimed god since the beginning of history. It's not just a matter of perspective, taking different angles on the same view, it's much more than that. We literally live in different worlds, you and I, we generate our own realities, from within our individual minds.

It's only in the light of day that we make compromises, for the sake of efficiency and the continuation of civilisation, in a comparatively safe and orderly manner. However, our precious order is extremely fragile, the experts say that if all the food ran out, the general population would turn to cannibalism within a matter of weeks. There is, of course, always the option to starve.

Without extensive research on the effects of mass insomnia, it's difficult to prove, but common sense dictates that deprived of enough sleep, not only would society collapse, but so too would our shared sense of destiny. Until ultimately nothing here would make any sense, whatsoever. The real global depression isn't economic, it's a subliminal war against hope, beginning with the end of any illusions of escape from the tyranny of the day.

The stumps, the lower brained lizards that strut about the corridors of power, have a few tricks up their sleeves. Most of which admittedly involve you playing your part, in names and numbers, dates and places, certificates to prove your legal existence upon their planet. Yet none of that makes you *who* you are, you didn't create the reality you live in, and neither did I. There are few who can, and do, but unless you're one of them, you wouldn't know them from Adam. Primarily due to the fact, that their dirty work is performed beyond the confines of our orchestrated world, deep down in The Void, where life is given and taken away on a whim.

When we sleep, we are separated from each other and our waking remainder. Taking it in shifts to abandon identity and culture, in line with the cycles of the Sun and Moon, in order to supply the DMT, that feeds the Lizard's dream. Few of us dare realise the power held within ourselves, the philosopher's stone of all brain functions. For we as the people, have the capability for an insurmountable will, one that can collectively imagine fictions into truth. Yet, for reasons that still elude me, we've taken the coward's way out, and embraced the lie, to live in this fearful state of controlled paranoia.

Our creativity is stunted to maintain the divide between manageable expectations, and impossible achievements. To hide the greater truths, and showcase the tiny lies. Camouflaging our lack of freedoms through psychological transference, to perceive this construct of life, this cage, as sanctuary, and one that we gladly call home. Society's abhorrence for confusion, the natural reaction to a bombardment of the senses, has forced us into strange patterns of behaviour. Carefully maintained by the mental torture of withheld gratification, and cognitive reinforcement.

If the parents fail to break the spirit, the state must double down. The normalisation of psychological trauma skews emotional need, into a hunger for pleasure, and wherever possible, lets us avoid the more profound lessons of suffrage. We are taught to believe there *are* limits, and behave accordingly, elevating the mundane and discounting the unquantifiable as irrelevant. Every muted opinion rides along the mean curve of compliance, devoted to the empirical lore of fact, the self-imposed cruel practicalities of perfunctory being, all for the sake of social cohesion.

The psychosis of dreams is the greatest of all threats to a worldwide order. The nightly riots of anarchic thoughts seep into the day, as reminder of sleep's most subversive qualities. The slumbering war of the senses, so far remains a low priority amongst the powers that be. Though some voices, not without influence, argue that sleep is not only inefficient, but has a tendency to disrupt much of our carefully managed reality. One so many of our governments, corporations, and their minions, have so far taken for granted.

Despite sporadic bursts of nightly subconscious guerrilla action, regardless of the counter-propaganda of dreams, the war on sleep has made headway. Pharmacology has shown promise in combating such problems. Although experiments reveal that substituting dreamtime with carefully regulated pharmaceutical catnaps, has led to the decimation of social skills, the libido, and ironically, efficiency within the workforce. Analysts and think tanks insist that the elite keep a long term view of things. Besides, robots are going to take over the world, so why worry?

In the meantime, all they can do is make sure the street lights keep getting brighter, and the noise of jets and helicopters continue to disturb the lightly sleeping masses. Wherever possible, expanding the working day into the night, and enforcing flexible shift patterns, to ensure the instantly replaceable workforce have little opportunity for real sleep, let alone perchance to dream.

The world must pull another all-nighter, and incrementally lower the market value of a standard forty winks. From the cacophony of urban insomnia, to the dismal glee of suburban early risers, few get to savour much of their parallel lives. To avoid a clear-headed electorate, none must be allowed to rest, or step back into a greater perspective. Otherwise they might squander their perfunctory potential, on life-changing, yet ultimately unprofitable philosophies.

Tense, nervous headaches? Try pandering to the masses, absorbing poisoned chemistry, and playing audience to a dissonance of the senses. Our minds have been permanently altered by electronic frequencies, transmitted with a malice of forethought. Holding sway over our emotions, in a psychotronic blitzkrieg of low vibration and high anxiety. Accelerated living pushes humanity ever closer to the grave, its headstone marked by an epitaph of wishful thinking. *May the dead rest in peace*, because there's little hope for it on Earth.

24. TIME

Time ran far slower in the past, and the further back you look, the closer it drags to a stop. Many aeons ago, the world was oxygen rich, and everyone breathed easier, and everything lived far longer, and grew much taller, with no fears for survival, or unsavoury notions of death. Then something was broken, certain religions view it as The Firmament, a great dome of glass up in the sky, the original greenhouse effect, with food for all and long life for many.

After the collapse, the waters from above came down, and washed away the past. A drowned earth gave birth to its lesser incarnation, hardly a former shadow of itself, where we, the escaped slaves of the catacombs, *the runners*, crawled out of every crevice, and declared ourselves masters of all we surveyed. As the seas withdrew and the dust settled, from amongst the ruins and the runts, came those who grunted their misgivings, born leaders, quick-witted and cunning. They used the tricks of the trade from another age, to create fire and the wheel, and build walls and keeps, to protect the people from the beasts of their own subconscious.

To this day, the story remains the same, for we are prisoners of ourselves, subsumed by the elation of a self-satisfied exhaustion, as we're guided by the novelty of a soulless artificial intelligence. Our twisted commonsense has encouraged the development of technology to compensate for our redundancy. We've been bombarded by the stats and facts for so long now, that we've been forced to carry out damage limitation exercises in our own minds. Impersonally adjusting behavioural idiosyncrasies, harmonising accents, lowering tones, and simplifying gestures to compete in a world of machines.

The open prison of opportunity tempts the callous and indifferent. They climb on the shoulders of losers, and steal the prize from under everybody's noses. The odds are skewed, for freedom is the enemy of gross collectivism. Without discipline our mass would run amok, and ruin all this awful splendour of our most civilised world. Our nature is reordered faster than our perception, for we have been deceived by seemingly logical successions of random connectivity. We swear by a proof miraculously manifested from vast banks of hidden servers, to perpetuate the calculated myth that *the house always wins*.

Our reality accelerates to counteract the drag coefficient of the stragglers. All of life's losers, born into inequity, here but to serve blood-feuding families, with their fingers in every pie, and far bigger things on their minds. We are taught from an early age to ignore the impossibility of power, the fallacy of dictatorship, the false supposition of monarchic rite. Instead most slaves yearn for their promised technological paradise, by lowering they expectations, and mimicking the mechanical, as the human race trails behind the speed of life.

According to the gospel of transhumanism, we're long due for an upgrade. The trouble is in the build, over-clocking humans is a complicated procedure, combining technology from a lower order, with higher biological function, entails some risk. Hence every sample, each collection of biorhythmic data, all scans of the brain and retina, even simple recognition systems, enables the aggregation of a central database to find the perfect transhumanist candidates.

There are very few of us who are genetically compatible for an artificial evolution. There will be no apes and japes in the state of Elysium, no throwbacks to mess up the place. All the coders are now codes, a sentient software designed to intelligently develop its own applications, based upon a new programming language salvaged from a billion year old strain of DNA.

We may already be artificial, we could have been engineered long ago, but the human brain is created with a superior technology, that few, if any of the Lizards, can truly comprehend. Their toys are no match for the biological complexity of life, although as far as consciousness goes, there's been some progress. The Lizards have deducted that human sentience is formed from fragmented thoughts, the remnants of a fifth dimensional consciousness, recorded and compressed into a two dimensional construct, which we are designed to perceive as a third.

Time is running out, or perhaps it's running down, it's coagulating, concentrating, and growing older by the second. If you're sold on trading up, to live another thousand years, with your memories uploaded into a machine, a body formed from metal, plastic, carbon-fibre, synthetic flesh, then think again. Tell me, how many pieces of technology do you own, and how many do you believe will last a hundred years, or fifty, or even five? *Nothing's built to last, and forever's overrated, especially here, where it seems people will do anything to extend their stay.*

25. RANDOMISER

It is better to be the spider than the fly. Great architecture, a fresh food supply, communication on the line, free to travel anywhere and set up shop. I've sat here and watched spiders hold out for days, then simply die. For without their prey, they're only going through the motions. Slowly withering away with starvation, unschooled in the pitfalls of a human environment, where little else, but those who are supposed to live here can possibly survive.

When a spider fell from my bedroom ceiling, crumpled up in a tiny brown ball, I had little pity for the futility of its life, my empathy neutered by its size and scale. Yet it was me, and I was it, in different worlds and forms. Hoping against hope, that with some luck, by repeating the same mistakes, things might somehow work out differently. Blind faith deals out few surprises, and eventually its shortcomings get to the best of us, and the worst.

To make it in this world, and truly get to the top, where you've permission to bitch, and tease, and lie, and even kill, they're going to have to break you first. The elites make sure that nothing human gets through the door, let alone joins the party. You wouldn't like it anyway, stumps hate music, they only want beats. It could be a maestro on the drums, or the distant sounds of submachine guns in the ghettos down below. They really can't tell the difference.

Lizard grandeur was conceived to ridicule the poor and weak. To accentuate, through unfair comparison, the squalid lives of human peasantry, picking out a meagre living in slops and scraps. Lizard minds cannot endure the joy of other lives, of those more biologically adapted to taking pleasure from the simplest acts of kindness, nature, or love.

They're in our eternal debt, not that you could tell. It's why they invented money, an IOU, a broken promise to the bearer, and should you get more of it, lots more, you'll be let in on the joke. An unfunny one at best, more of a spiteful trick, to keep the undesirables at bay, and under the delusion that following the rules and paying your taxes, is for the good of the many, and not the few.

Lizards are addicted to power, money is just an insurance plan, to make sure they can do whatever the hell they want, and get away with it. A vast majority of all the world's wealth lies in less than a handful of private vaults, owned by the richest and loneliest creatures humankind has ever seen. Almost none, asides the most snivelling and wretched hybrid stumps, have their ear, for true philanthropy died a death long before their inauspicious reign.

In my teens, the ad men didn't give my generation the time of day, so we never had our cultural moment in the sun. I presumed it was something to do with the recession, the strikes, the shortages, or perhaps it was a mistake. The Lizards told us too little, and took too much, and now we're nothing but a socioeconomic headache. Over-opinionated wastrels who'd missed both world wars, the Psychedelic era, and only just caught the last bus for the Information Age.

Nowadays the world panders to more adolescent tastes, the Lizards have gone straight to the source, and it makes me wonder why. I suppose somewhere along the line people stopped growing up, and became embarrassed about ageing, physically and mentally, until more and more treat dying like a disease, and decrepitude as something that should remain behind closed doors.

Of course, it's true, humans inevitably become set in their ways, like jelly in a bowl. Occasionally they'll wobble, but they're incapable of dramatic change, and barely shape up by the time their talents have been consumed. Senility, like madness, is to work against the rule, and persist with the scatological. In those golden years at the end of a life, when we can take our sweet time, and allow our minds to drift in and out of parallel realities.

Youth sleeps at the epicentre of our multiplicity of consciousness, their rebellion is contained within the safe confines of the waking day. The old gradually lose interest in this tiny world, and as their order collapses under the weight of the new, reason loses out to fate. Conformity kills you long before you die, it makes beauty ugly, and wisdom foolish, and proves without a doubt, that following the rules gets you nowhere.

Randomise reality, denounce time's linearity, the young are old and the old are young, the dead are alive, and the living, dead. Disorderly conduct is called for, a spanner in the works, a fire in the hold, a break with tradition, an end to history.

Somebody, anybody, stop this infernal machine.

26. SATURATION

I'm what you'd call a late bloomer, very late. For all the talk, I know I'm at my wits end, and even if age is no excuse, exhaustion seems to have got the better of me. I sense a barely recognisable but growing sensation, which might just be the need for compromise. One of many I have endeavoured to avoid throughout my lifetime.

To consider slowing down and resting for a while, instead of relentlessly pushing forwards on an exploration in ignoble futility. I suspect there's only so much a human being can take, before they're corralled towards a life changing decision. To either turn back now and head back to more familiar surroundings, or move on, and forever discard the home truths of a jaded world view.

Asleep, or awake, I'm drowning in synaesthesia. In my youth, I'd fight through hell and high water for a taste of unadulterated madness. When danger seemed more exciting, and being spooked felt just as good as getting high. The buzz of thinking in a completely different way from all those around me, feeding on their bad vibes, and distilling them into greater reason.

When you're young and mad, it's all thrills and spills, but soon enough a sombre maturity flowers all about you, and one by one, your freaky friends slink back into a stale conformity. Until even the hardcore players, aficionados of psychoactive truth or dare, manage to find excuses for staying in with the wife. *Too busy to piss around now mate, it's time to grow up, and get a steady job, we're saving up for a deposit on a starter home.* The standard break-up conversation for a passing friendship, on a crackling phone ringing with the sounds of familial applause.

I found new crowds to suit my mood, but before long the conversations fizzled out, and old wounds opened. Stepping aside for crumbling relationships, taking turns to entertain a sullen crowd. Before I knew it, I had run out of strangers, fly-by-night companions whose faces have blurred from my memory. Eventually I couldn't even hold my cover, the happy-go-lucky weirdo with jokes aplenty, discriminate enough to hold back on the philosophical bunk, until the wee hours of the morning after.

In the last of which, I found myself sitting on a filthy sofa in a squat on the South Circular. It was strewn with the intoxicated bodies of complete strangers, twitching with somnolence. Whilst I made hushed conversation concerning death and madness, with a guy who admitted to me he was actually an outpatient on a weekend pass. He insisted on revealing his prized treasure, two highly determined gashes, deep purple cuts that travelled the whole length of his emaciated arms. His party piece brought me down with a thud, and by more than a peg or two. I'd been duly warned by a veteran of angst, that suicide was no picnic, and death was not awaiting me with open arms.

I've gorged on the fruits of my subconscious for so long, it's hard to keep abreast of the day. I'm a slow riser, and my dreams leave such a thick residue, that more often than not, it's nigh impossible to tell for certain if I'm even awake. Overlays and transparencies of false memories cast shadows across the scene. I see my feet moving down the stairs, and into a kitchen, where something that isn't there, slaps me on the cheek, and hands me my favourite mug of filter.

There are times when my recall will linger too long, and I'll find myself frozen in a moment that never was. In such memories of dreams, I recapture every single detail, like last night, when I met a six foot praying mantis cradling her child. An image that stuck with me from sunup to sundown. The mother introduced herself, her name was *Barbara*. She came across as a kindly sort, who skilfully dissipated my preconceptions and prejudices, with a comfortingly elegant presence.

As she moved towards me, I gently patted her side like a horse, and felt her dark and glistening skin. It was far softer than I'd expected. She kissed me, at least I think it was a kiss. The touch of something fleshy from a delicate proboscis drawn across my cheek. She showed me her baby, its skin was pale and white, decoratively patterned with red and purple lines. Its mandibles were a delicate pink, and its eyes were like black almonds, much like government psyop Greys. Its face was chubby, with bulbous cheeks and brow. It blinked, then caught sight of me, curled inwards and rose up on its tail. I stepped back, fearing my presence had upset the child.

The pair deformed with a twisting motion, their anatomies transmogrified by a sequence of painful sounding snaps and cracks. In one precise manoeuvre, with an exact alignment of their exoskeletal plates, they lunged forth like pop-up book characters, displaying their underbellies of muted colours and familiar shapes. Finally emerging as full-blown manifestations of faux humans, and the perfect anatomical representation of a human mother and child.

Except they weren't, they were entomological giants, two more strange companions living somewhere in my dreams. I savoured the memory all day, until all I had left to remember them by, was a banging headache. That evening, when I told my wife about my unworldly visitors, we stared at each other with the usual faded incredulity.

Was it an alien abduction? No, not really. It could be nothing, just another figment of a vivid imagination, to add to my bizarre collection of dubious memories. But it was the attention to detail that threw me, I could distinctly recall Barbara correcting my pronunciation, as she'd so vehemently insisted, *Bah-Bah-Rah*.

She encouraged me to hang on in there, and accept the fact that I'd found her, at the very edge of subconscious sanity. Dissuading me, in her own unique way, that even under fire, I should never turn back from my path towards a grand delusion. She showed me how to avoid the puerile pleasures of extrapolation, the same lesson taught to so many other waifs and strays she'd encountered at the border. Still, I took comfort in our shared, though undue familiarity with each other. Perhaps we'd met in another dream, when we'd played different characters. Long forgotten friends from another dimension, doing our best to catch up on old times.

When I awoke I temporarily forgot if I was supposed to be the prince, or the pauper. I appreciate the assistance, swapping shifts in this place, with a doppelgänger from the land of shadows, but, without seeming too ungrateful, I must admit, my doubts remain.

As the world of dreams opens up new vistas, this reality leaves me feeling ever more claustrophobic. It's so greedy, and desperate to put everything in its proper place. It hoards life, and its manifest possibility, allowing little scope for radical change. We have become saturated, the human race is so full of itself, it can't make room for anything else.

27. MULTIPLICITY

I've played many characters in my time, and used various guises to maintain some kind of consistency. They're all very similar, but with distinct differences that few others would notice. But these days the mutations are becoming more blatant, times when I've witnessed my face distort, random and unrecognisable marks on my body, and even my immediate surroundings morph within a matter of hours. Over the years I've learned to cope with the situation, but I've given up marking it down as the mere symptoms of a poor memory.

That being said, I've experienced far greater divergence, new names and places, and whole swathes of history and geography rewritten. On one fateful day I awoke to find that Britain spoke German, or at least a very similar dialect. I listened to the radio, the noisy neighbours, my wife talking on the phone, and decided to keep schtum. I watched the news on TV, it appeared that something terrible had happened, an attack, or disaster of some sort. But my schoolboy foreign language skills failed me, and so I went back to bed to sleep it off.

It seems despite my incredulity, and no doubt yours, that I've been freefalling through parallel realities. We've all seen the tenuous plot a thousand times, cheap sci-fi yarns, I know, it's corny, it's been overdone. Which is why I've tried to accommodate the changes, and keep them to myself, and if I can't, I dream of another world far closer to the mark.

But there's one glitch in the matrix that I haven't been able to shake off, one that's hovered in the background for what seems like years. A country, a war, somewhere in Asia, and its name begins with the letter *H*. I've checked the maps and searched for it online, but whichever nation I used to recall is no longer there, and according to history, never was. All I have is the memory of the first letter of a place, which has only ever existed in one particular version of my life, and apparently I'm alone in that opinion.

I have a sneaking suspicion, knowing my mind as well as I do, that I'm not the ringleader, the chief troublemaker within the legion of myself. There's another far more reckless and self-destructive doppelgänger out there, running around through life after life, making a mess of my days to come. A renegade soul, labouring under the delusion that they've stumbled upon a grand conspiracy of the ages.

On the upside, there have been times when I've landed on my feet. I remember waking up in heaven, or a close approximation of it. One where everything shone like gold, and the gulls outside sang like angels. I tried to stick with it, *it was my kind of world.* Unfortunately I blacked out halfway down the stairs, and stumbled to the ground. The natural pitch of that reality decanted to a more familiar tone, and the dimmer switch of the world turned life back to the usual gloom.

There's an awful film that stars an low-rent actor, a big budget flop, scripted to dissuade the masses from even considering the concept of multiplicity. That's what *La La Land* does, it takes something real and regales it in fantasy. As far as Hollywood executives are concerned, the multiplicity of the soul is just another plot device, a gimmick to put bums on seats. The idea that we are all armies of one, and that each of us is a legion's legionnaire, has few takers, bar lunatics and Satanists.

To be in two minds is seen as a sign of indecision, I wonder what the terminology for ten, or a thousand might be? Oh yes, *absolutely insane*. Technically, however, I can't be accused of having multiple personalities, they're not here, they're somewhere else, and they have a habit of avoiding me. If I *am* legion, like the beast, I belong to an army of deserters, most likely unaware they've even been conscripted.

Of course there will be those far worse off than me, the versions of myself that have never found love, or walk the streets in poverty. If I know this man I am, even one iota, I can't imagine any of them suffering on the breadline for too long, or taking orders from jerks in uniform. It's not my style, and however different our lives may have worked out, I can't stretch credulity so far to believe that my other selves are complete strangers to me.

But a troublemaker, that'd make sense. A rogue double on a rampage through time and space. Asking inappropriate questions and causing havoc wherever he may roam, talking bullshit like I do, and acting upon it alone. Oh well, whoever you are out there, I wish you luck, and I honestly hope you find somewhere you can call home. You need to take a breather, at least time enough to reconsider your actions. I admit it was fun waking up in different worlds for a while, but the mistakes and glitches are becoming far too apparent, not just to me, but everyone it seems.

There's a dark corner of the web, full of lost souls like mine. They too, are having trouble remembering all the details, out-of-print titles, the dates of deaths of political prisoners, quotes from religious texts, confectionery brand names, and famous movie lines from their childhood. All of which admittedly seem to make less sense here, than in any other version of this world.

I once read about a man from a country that never was, his passport seemed genuine, and his sanity apparently intact. The customs guards threw him in a cell, to hold him there for questioning. They left him alone as they awaited for the arrival of secret service officers, trained professionals who could expertly harass the mystery tourist from *Taured*.

So the story goes, by the time they'd arrived, the stranger had escaped from his high-security incarceration. A veritable Houdini, or perhaps someone like me, who fell asleep and awoke from this particular dream. The door was locked and there was no window, he'd simply disappeared. There were no explanations from the authorities, and the cover-up was pitifully half-hearted. When things get that crazy you can bet your bottom dollar, it's not long before it's consigned to urban myth.

I have the distinct feeling that I'm a bit-part player in this story, or worse still, sitting in the audience of my multiplicitous self. All in all, it makes little difference if there's one, or a million like me. Maybe this is how you live forever, by experiencing all your lives at once. I'm not looking forward to the reunion, in fact when the time comes in the hereafter, I'll most likely make my excuses and bow out.

28. THOUGHT CONTROL

Thought without thought, devoid of intent and direction, lying fallow beneath the surface of consciousness, provides hours and hours of non-stop fun. Thinking does the world of good for thinkers, and saves many others the trouble, but our thoughts as a plurality, in their combined totality, generates a psychic dissonance in the transmission of consciousness.

Close up, a thought gestates, and develops into an idea. If it has legs and runs around a few other minds, it might even evolve into a discussion. With a little work, and a lot of nodding, a modus operandi is born. But from a distance, swallowed by a mire of mass communication, lost in the clouds of informational detritus, ideas can remain as little more than idle gossip. For all the best intentions in the world, you only need two things to be heard, and they are influence and money. One of which is all talk, and costs lives, and the other being the venerable equal of time.

Language, the spoken word, unlike song, is unintelligible to all but those who recognise it. If you came here, from another place, where never a word had been uttered, you'd be in for a nasty surprise. Man is a chimera, and the proof is in his voice. Without the dubious benefits of a human upbringing, and the sociological understanding of how and why we communicate the way we do, you'd be forgiven for thinking that our race spends much of its waking day, mimicking the animals of the world.

Grunting, croaking, barking, squealing, clicking, wailing, howling, under the guise of a civilised conversation. That's the sound of the human race, the monstrous cry of a menagerie of beasts. So vast in their number, their call sounds forth across the mountains, valleys, and oceans of their domain. Once all meaning is lost, the human voice returns to the wild, an indistinguishable gibberish of instinctive pain and fear.

Even newborns must be convinced of the merits of our savage mode of communication. A child's first words are their contract with the human race, drawn out by the terror of losing a mother's love.

The ultimate sign of contrition, a peace treaty with a terrifying race of creatures, unlike any other on Earth.

With communication comes indoctrination, where open minds are crushed by tradition, completely lost in the obscure details of the slightest inflection. Inducted into a desperate education, young minds stumbling through a labyrinth of linguistic hurdles, for the honour of merging into the background chatter. Our thoughts are nullified by kind words and harsh actions, for the greater good, and the expedience of culture over barbarism. Human nature is on a leash, the purity of its perceptions displaced by the weight of argument, and the common body of thought that we are our own invention.

Our seduction into society is a tawdry affair. For youth gives others, supposedly older and wiser, the unfair advantage of moulding minds. We are convinced by the merits of language through its own tongue. Beguiling us with promises of greater understanding, ostracising those who will not follow its conflicted codes of conduct. Populist rules instilled into fools by self-deceived masters of deception. Human speech utters the cry of a stifling compromise, a sworn allegiance to function over form. Language is beauty self-ascribed, its place in nature, appropriated.

Official communications set the agenda, to discard the hypothetical quandaries of free thinkers and madmen. The Word has broken Earth's eternal peace of the ever was, and ever will be. Words are substituted for our senses, their phonetic jibes bow to the tyranny of the descriptor. Subtly extricating humanity from direct experience, and in turn the mind from the soul.

We shouldn't need to talk, that was my hunch right from the beginning, perhaps my earliest memory of all. Language chairs the great debate, and keeps the questions brief, expressing little opinion, asides those most tried and tested. Through language all our energies are spent in futile deliberation, until once again, sleep beckons, and gently ushers in another silent night of psychic conversation.

29. ARCH(R)IVAL

Over the centuries, our planet has been pillaged of its most ancient artefacts. If you have the clearance to access certain underground facilities, you're certainly in for a big surprise, otherwise it's a bullet to the head. There are vast collections of forbidden archaeology out there, that in all honesty, make our Information Age look retarded. Diagrams and blueprints for impossible technologies, exotic maps from beyond the world we see, and treasures of such unknown quality and quantity, they devalue the whole concept of currency.

The hoard grows exponentially, guarded by loyalists born into captivity, charged with securing bounties of such ridiculous proportion, that they've almost filled their subterranean cities to the brim. To keep the mongrels happy, they substitute the leftovers of the gods with arbitrary junk of an indistinct antiquity. Such as broken crockery or stone age spearheads, usually poorly dated by radio carbon chicanery.

Whilst holy artefacts, exotic weapon technologies, and first person accounts from presumed mythologies, are for the main part, stolen from right under the noses of both sides of a jumped up war. Those items which cannot be removed and must remain in situ, are deliberately vandalised beyond recognition, and described as *ruins*.

Progress takes the quickest path, and one that must continually ascend the heights of past achievement. An allusion that has spurred on the global economy, against the backdrop of a whitewashed past. If the world knew the truth and shared knowledge based upon ancient texts, unadulterated by a complicit academia, our rulers would lose face, governments their standing, and the age of modernity would come to an abrupt end.

To hide the ugly truth, the Lizards make false promises on how everything will change, not that they'll divulge if it will be for the better. For those most easily distracted, there's glamour and scandal, for the broadsheets violent conflicts in far off lands, or home-grown terrorism and stock market crashes. But if things really get out of hand, and every Joe Schmoe is kicking up a ruckus, then they'll pull out the big guns and go to war, set up assassinations, and even pretend to go to the Moon.

Then the experts pile in, and lay it on thick to their dumbed down electorate. Force feeding corporate sponsored scientism and exalting the almighty power of ignorance. Until eventually enough time will have passed, when no one will remember the awful tragedy, that we are the dumbest, most gullible people of all history.

The military confiscates the irradiated glass deserts, still reeling from a stone age nuclear exchange, apparently fought between prehistoric nomads who could barely start a fire, yet had somehow managed to set off a nuclear device.

The governments around the world have closed off all the ancient tunnels that run for miles and miles, bored without bearing a single bronze age chisel mark. Supposedly dug by armies of ten thousand slaves, and took a thousand years to complete.

Those who look around for themselves and ignore the official line, might just notice there are whole mountains shaped like faces, and megalithic stones cut with a precision unmatched by today. As far as the authorities are concerned, out of place artefacts must stay out of mind. So the authorities will fill every crack with concrete and claw back the land in the name of ecology. They'll destroy multi-million year old footprints imprinted in volcanic rocks, smash giant skulls with mechanical diggers, deface hieroglyphs of flying machines, and burn written evidence that disproves Pi. All these things and more, just to save face, to keep the lie going that we are the best thing to ever happen to this place.

Those on the frontline, the political puppets who serve as symbols of the hidden hegemony, secretly fear the day the masses find out the whole truth, and decide to kick seven shades of shit out of them. Fortunately, for the powers that be, much of the proletariat is fast asleep, too far beyond the tipping point to care. Many would rather not know, they'd rather stick to tradition and remain under the thumb of a nepotistic system of psychotic world governance.

After all, we're slaves, and it's all that we know. Our cells might be comfortable, we may have illusions of freedom, but our greatest endeavours pale in comparison to our stolen destiny.

30. BLOOD

Blood pays all debts. It's the only valid currency we've ever really had, and yes it *does* make the world go round. The sacrificial hegemony of well-to-do bloodlines, prefer organic, and as young a vintage as possible. As for the remainder, it's barely more than vinegar, filled with impurities and soured by the resentment of a bitter maturity. In all honesty, you'll more likely find it spilt on the ground than poured in a glass.

The hybrid Lizards, the lower echelons of the highest order, may have all the money in the world, but not the time. They still have a relatively short shelf-life, just like the rest of us. Even if they've spent a small fortune on plastic surgery and organ transplants, it does little to delay the inevitable. Impure hybrids have taken to blood transfusions to keep the years at bay, but even then, most of them end up rotting away with Kuru disease.

Hybrids can't live forever, but some of them have got close. Especially those who have stuck to a diet of newborn blood, placenta, and mothers' milk. These people, these creatures, are not human, although they can fool the best of us, at least for a while. Eventually, those who make it to a ripe old age look far worse for wear, and on closer inspection, practically inhuman. Which is about the time they choose to die, at least on an official basis.

I wonder where they've put all the dead celebrities and VIP's, the one's who've held on to life at any price? The royal zombies, the dead presidents, deceased dictators and corporate leaders, and long in the tooth pop stars who've single-handedly saved a nation's economy. Perhaps they keep them in Switzerland, or on secret private islands uncharted by digital maps. However, I suspect that like much of the world of the Lizard elite, they're stored underground for safekeeping.

A contract in blood is a contract for life, but if you happen to be immortal, or near enough, there'll be some harsh terms in the small print. With enough money, power, and influence, with all favours returned and then some, if they've followed every ritual, and carried out their duties to their fullest extent, hybrids can live forever.

Well, to a degree, it depends on what you call *living*. Let's describe it as a *continuity* rather than life, but it's an existence all the same. Unfortunately their relatives are unable to visit them in the underworld, in their hermetically sealed holding facility. A place where their brain, or at least an electronic recording of its last engram, is hooked up to a holographic simulation. Just so they can spend an eternity with all the other living legends of the fabulously undead.

For the lesser acolytes it's a completely different story. They must struggle on, knowing full well they'll meet their end like all the other schmucks, the lower hybrids, the poorer bloodlines, the bastards, and the ingrates who'd accidentally stumbled upon the scam. Which is why they take it out on all the rest of us, they might have to bend over for the Lizard King, but they make sure we do the same for them.

When the last great wars thinned the numbers, and recruitment drives were a regular thing, the old guard had to simply grin and bear it. The latecomers to the party were siphoned off from secret societies, talented souls without much breeding, taught implicitly to do their masters' bidding. It was a stopgap solution, some of the Lizards were looking rather inbred, especially the European monarchies.

They needed fresh blood, but they'd diluted the mix, and now they're more monkey than dinosaur, and their living death arrives that much sooner. But worst of all, what the Lizards can't abide, is the feeling that they've been reduced to living like farmers, and forced to lay with the pigs. Not for much longer, mind you, they've already mapped the human genome, and have plenty enough samples in the bank to last a thousand years.

A vast majority of humans are sold on scientism, a faith in technology, a world of clean machines, but no Lizard of sound mind, would ever consider transhumanism as a viable option. That's for the rabble to decide. It's no concern to the Lizards, if we'd rather transform ourselves into machines, or rot in biodegradable coffins to improve the environment. Either way its the death of humanity.

Until we've been replaced by something simpler, a living blood bank, a genetic designer bag of organs, they'd like us to turn vegan, or at least vegetarian, to drink plenty of water and avoid all intoxicants. But it won't do any good, the stock's already tainted, and now even our freshest blood tastes so foul, that lesser hybrids would rather do without. If you're not at the top of the top, your wine cellars are full of wine and not blood. There are families with more gold than all the money in the world, but that means nothing to them, compared to their priceless collections of rhesus negative.

31. DENSITY

I've yet to see anyone else *phase*. But judging by the number of mysterious disappearances around the world each year, accounting for unsolved murders, suicides, and accidental deaths, it would be nice to think that at least a few of them had found an exit, and never turned back.

Phasing is a far less extreme phenomenon than full on teleportation. I've only managed it on a few occasions, and only twice with witnesses present, which I more than suspect is way above the average. I still remember the reactions at the time, and the obligatory line of questioning. *Where did you go? How did you do that? What the fuck! Oh my god. Do it again! Why not? That was* so *weird.*

I can't put your doubts to rest, only ask you to question why I'd fabricate such a lie. There's nothing in it for me, except to appear even more crazy than I already do, and I doubt that either of us want that. If by now you've come to the conclusion that I'm certifiable, even clinically insane, I understand, *don't talk to the loony, just look straight ahead and keep walking.* Besides, natural suspicion is a healthy response for a highly attuned defence mechanism, one that's kept our species on the top of the pile for a long time now.

All the same, if you'd like to have a go at phasing for yourself, you should practice fading into the background of other people's conversations. Imagine yourself as living wallpaper, as inconsequential as a commercial break, with the sound turned all the way down. Keep trying, until the next time you find yourself on your own in the crowd, with nothing more to say, and no one listening, throw caution to the wind and disappear within.

I once read an article about some young tearaways, the usual high jinx kids get up to, letting off illegal fireworks with the cops hot on their tail. When they were finally apprehended, and told to form a line, the tallest one amongst them wasn't asked for his ID. He was completely ignored by the officers, and even his friends as they were frisked. When the police finally left, the others turned around to ask him where he'd been hiding. He was at a loss for words, he hadn't a clue how or why he'd disappeared, but intimated that fear might have something to do with it. Perhaps he's right, I honestly don't know. Phasing could well be a throwback to something primal and unbound, a long lost ability to camouflage with light.

On the scale of the bizarre, I admit this one's way out there. I can only imagine it hasn't caught on, due to the random nature of phasing, one that's notoriously difficult to tame, and if anyone else even knew what the hell I was talking about, I can assure you they'd think the same.

You can't phase in and out at will, so you won't be able to astound and amaze your friends at parties. You needn't devote your life to it, like some kind of yogi or shaman, although I'm sure a few of them have managed it in their time. You're just as likely to phase slumped in front of the box, sitting beside your significant other, pretending to watch their favourite show. The one they know you hate, but both feel comfortable enough with each other in your relationship, to let it slide. To successfully phase, forget yourself for a moment, and all those around you, forget everything, until nothing registers, not even your own thoughts.

What you should be looking out for, is the sensation of pins and needles prickling the hairs on your neck, hands, and back. Now wait for a soft focus glow, as if someone's playing with the dimmer switch, until the lights are brighter inside than out. It's a staggered implosive event, so you should feel a fluctuation of air pressure, which marks a growing density of centrifugal force in both light and matter. But when it actually happens, the shift to a different frequency can be so subtle and slight, you might not even notice until it's all over.

Spontaneous invisibility is an involuntary process, and one that operates at a higher than usual vibration. Our bodies create an electromagnetic field, with a vector at three points in space and time. To accelerate one's frequency, it must be understood that the heart is a far greater electrical generator than the mind. Only by combining the two, can they function as a transceiver in the perceptual field, bending one's light signature beyond the range of human vision.

It's time to electrify the mortal coil, alternate your current to boost the frequency of your signal, broadcast yourself across the airwaves, and when others say, *you're going through a phase*, just take it as a complement.

32. GOD(D)

It's a nice idea, it really is, I like it, honestly. I've felt the hand of providence from time to time, if only on a very human scale. But unfortunately, at the high-tide mark of the senses, at least for me, the benevolent deity theory fails to hold much water. Considering the relativity of, well, just about everything. Man is pretty much as close to insignificant as you can get, at least that's how it looks from where I'm standing.

The God of Man is not the king of kings. Besides kings are merely the descendants of murderers, those who took to the blade before anyone else and got away with it. Until they had so much gold, and such an army, that they'd be free to make outlandish proclamations, particularly regarding their special relationship with the *big kahuna*.

I know when things get bad, I've panicked and asked for assistance from whatever's out there in my imaginary universe, but there's no Santa in the sky for me. It's more like being stuck in call waiting, in two minds if you should really bother. It's only when I ask myself questions with answers bigger than I can handle, that I find I've been redirected to the switchboard of God.

What most people pray to, via whatever denomination they might choose, is a manmade construct designed to scare the natives, and teach them how to behave. Which is a real shame, because anyone with a slightest inkling of common sense can tell, no matter how much science deems it unworthy, that life and consciousness in its infinite variety and variegation, can't simply come down to a happy accident. That's just about as far-fetched as a guy with a long white beard, sitting on a throne in the clouds.

I'd describe my upbringing as non-committal atheist. My family used religion when they needed to, an excuse for a holiday, to add a little respectability to a funeral, and as a source of free childcare on Sunday mornings.

Every day my school conducted morning prayers, made a few announcements, then sung a hymn or two. Once a year we'd march down to the local church, for a memorial service commemorating the sacrifice of ex-pupils, who'd died fighting in the wars. Those killed by other young men, freshly graduated from schools in enemy territories, positively encouraging their conscripted students to do exactly the same thing. Singing praises for the dead, who'd grown up fast in a time of war. The virgin soldiers who'd committed mass murder, under the auspice of a god who loves to play two sides against each other, yet still remain victorious.

Perhaps it was learning about history that spoilt it, and put me off the whole idea of religion, and especially its views on God. I started off badly, and caught on too quickly for my teachers' comfort. I'd never follow the lesson plans, and didn't bother asking questions. Instead I did my own research and found out that education, much like religion, was just a ruse.

What religion does, is get in the way. It's an uninvited mediator between the lonely, and the dying, in whatever form of benevolence they might seek. I've watched their appointed representatives, dictating righteous lives from the pulpit, and admonishing the rest of us, from around the graves of their lost loved ones. As a child I'd ignore all the garb and ceremony, and try to catch the eye of various intermediaries of God. They never seemed particularly holy to me, they were just doing their job. Employed in the position of a stick in the mud, still secretly afraid of the monsters under their beds, and the love they cannot know, without the sin of pride.

I'm no luddite, I completely understand the argument. The notion that many miracles of the past, can as easily be attributed to lost technologies, and a heavily redacted history. I know that holy texts stem from the same old story, one that reaches back as far as we commoners are party to, and long before I'm sure. My problem isn't with the flimsy proofs of religion, but the fears of those who spend their lives, disproving that which for so many, makes life worth living. The people who cannot imagine, for the life of them, anything worse than being wrong.

Which is why I believe that the holiest thing that anyone can do, is stay open to the possibility that this world is made up of fools. Those who hate themselves so much, that they'd rather fight until the end of days than admit there's nothing to believe in, only what we see, or rather what we're shown.

If there is a god, then there are two. One of which somehow helped to create the universe we'd love to know. A germ of an idea, a seed of doubt, whose very being kick-started consciousness into life. The other is the maker of mankind, who moulded him in his own image, to breed and fight, and start religions, or at least put the notion in his mind. It's encoded in our DNA, the lust for war and total dominion. Which is why some mutations in the gene line, have the burning desire, to be treated as nothing less than a god. *Don't encourage them.*

33. SPAWN

What if life's questions were not mysteries at all, but rather excuses to hide a truth too awful to contemplate. Our world of humdrum design, with its people of the most humble beginnings, is rife with obvious conclusions and uninspiring ideas. Modern life can feel stifling, even suffocating to a degree. Which may be why so many would rather console themselves with fairytales, than face the cold hard facts. The ugliest of which is plain for all to see, that whatever put us here has a grudge, and is driven by the obsession that we must drink deeply of their pain.

Humans aren't meant to subsist in a constant state of panic, we just weren't built that way. A society in a state of shock, externalises its natural instincts for self-preservation, degrading its innate ability to achieve successful homeostasis. So much so, that throughout the centuries, progressive generations are born into a psychological minefield. In our post-postmodern age, few can avoid the non-stop media campaign of corporate sponsored terror. A crusade of misinformation and cultural manipulation, that has proven to be far more ominous, than any real threat of imminent danger.

Without an effective homeostatic drive, the human physiological system cannot maintain internal stability. Subconsciously it perceives every stimulus as a mental disturbance. That's how the Lizards planned it, to force our race to live this way. So we can acclimatise to our fears, in denial of our own natural instincts. Until ultimately, even pain is pleasurable, and hatred indivisible from love. Our unholy state of equilibrium has become so twisted and deformed, we feel obliged to shape ourselves in the image of our masters.

The homeostatic drive is regulated by the hypothalamus, and triggers a biological mechanism to induce sleep. Without it, we could never rest, or forget the troubles of the day, scare stories of environmental decimation, a panic on the markets, or the rising threat of crime on our streets. Instead of seeking counsel in our dreams, we sleep with one eye open, laying in wait at the threshold of consciousness, anticipating the horrors of tomorrow.

For the poorest inhabitants of the Earth there's little opportunity, but the field of conflict, religious martyrdom, or temporary employment under extremely hazardous conditions. Their behavioural patterns bound by the threat of sickness and starvation, for a quick turnaround, with low investment and a high yield. For those lucky few who can survive within their means, they are raised under a cloud of guilt, socially blackmailed through peer pressure, to give more, take less, and be grateful for their privilege.

The elite promotes a vision of an increasingly artificial world, whilst loudly proclaiming nature's right to flourish. Allowing the planet to prosper, without worrying about the burden of feeding and clothing mankind. Designating certain areas as places of outstanding beauty, to increasingly urbanise the general population, whilst covertly extracting precious metals, minerals, and fossil fuels from deep underground.

We are left wholly dependent upon our antiquated technologies, much of which has been deliberately suppressed. Leaving us to blame ourselves for the effects of pollution, whilst completely ignoring the not so secret global geoengineering program. Which is an insider joke that flies way over most heads, and has nothing to do with the weather. Exotic salts and metals rain down every day to damage the human genome, in order to reduce the efficiency of human productivity. Until eventually, world government feasibility studies will prove beyond a shadow of a doubt, that humanity should be upgraded to an artificially intelligent automaton. *A perfect slave.*

A lie can spawn far more quickly than mankind, an idea can spread like a virus, because it's not the quantity but the quality that counts. Some of us die for the right to live, and others kill for the sake of liberty. But few of us dare to imagine a life free from the dictatorship of corrupted idealism. Where each is reliant on their own ability, and their unique connection with humanity, in order that we may follow our highest instincts, and do so much more as a species than merely survive.

34. INDIVIDUALITY

The filigree of individualism, is so beautifully embroidered with the flair of blind courage, so meticulously woven with unrealistic expectation, yet utterly faded by denial and despair, it's a minor miracle that such a fragile notion has stood the test of time. Fighting against all the odds, in the face of unflinching conformity, individuality still remains the most beloved of ideals.

Even the selfish isolationists, those like myself who would rather have nothing to do with this place, are compelled to agree, that what makes humankind so unique, is its incredible ability to harness the power of individuality. We humans have many faults, we are exorbitantly pompous on a universal scale, yet unsure enough of ourselves to seek greater recognition. We'll go through hell or high water to prove our worth, yet underneath it all, when the dust has settled and the blood's been spilt, we do this in the name of love.

However, the world is not made up of rebels and lovers. The majority are the majority with good reason, for they are unanimous about nearly everything, and when they're not, they'll soon come around. They might colour their lives with minor disagreements, picking tiny holes in each others limited opinions, but in the light of day it's all much of a muchness.

Most people eventually grow out of their childish dreams, and gain a more pedestrian sense of perspective. After a few years of comparing looks and talent, many of life's wild-eyed wonderers lose confidence, allowing their hopes and desires to leap ahead of them and forever out of reach.

There are of course the flukes, the rare exceptions to the rule, who actually do what they preach, rather than sell their souls to the highest bidder. Those who won't play ball are financially ruined, charged with the social crimes of ideological subversion. Some of them end up in the gutter, others a suicidal tragedy, irrevocably fucked up by the shallow lives of their contemporaries. Those with enough cash might seek solace and stay deep undercover, holing themselves up in ivory towers, never to be seen or heard of again.

Unpredictability isn't media-friendly, it makes investors nervous. Those with talent and ability who can't behave like celebrities, won't get sponsorship or airplay, or be invited to talk to world leaders at private summits. So instead of selling individuality, media moguls talk shop with entertainment lawyers, as their scout bots trawl trending social feeds for pretty faces and empty heads.

Manufactured stars and starlets begin their climb to the top by parading about in their underwear. Their voices electronically tuned, their clockwork dance moves expertly choreographed, and their opinions professionally scripted, utilising algorithms that turn consumer analytics into big bucks.

As the gimmicks wear thin, and throwing signs and simulating masturbation doesn't do the trick anymore, they'll take too much coke, and knock out the paparazzi who'd first put them there. As they grow older, (the plastic surgery only makes things worse), they'll dress up as bankers and brokers, to talk seriously about the environment. Playing at politics in exchange for a cease and desist order, to stop the gutter press from releasing highly compromising footage.

So whatever happened to the last of the individualists? Most likely, after they'd finished finding themselves, during years of backpacking and exchanging minor revelations with fellow nomads, the world shrunk and so did their dreams. Sitting in home studios, post-processing their video memoirs, pre-recorded for prosperity, to earn a pittance from online advertising revenues.

Selling themselves as authorities on lifestyle and culture, self-aggrandising critics of an overtly commercial society, although one that duly pays their wages. A meagre income mind you, perhaps even a modicum of fame, but oh so awfully worthy. Providing plenty of food for thought during boring dinner conversations. Living life behind a smug smile of self-satisfaction, as the very model of health and wellbeing, sitting pretty in a commune full of good intentions, drunk on their own brand of organic Kool-Aid.

Then there are the freaks, the most individualistic people of all. Those who stay exactly where they are, looking for the metaphysical clues on the inside, only to discover more unfathomable impossibilities. Most of them end up in care, institutionalised and rendered harmless to society. Sentenced to chemical psychosis by laws that have become so rigid and inflexible, the state can no longer distinguish the difference between creativity and incitement.

True freaks live a life of elicit individualism, harbouring thoughts not tolerated by a tolerant society. Keeping their light hidden under a bushel, hardly recognising kindred spirits in disguise. An individual has no place in the modern world, and so they must pretend to be like everybody else. Obfuscating their outrageous truths with small-talk that nobody wants to hear.

Plainly speaking, human life is a lonely existence, and breeding billions more of us seems to make little difference. Poorly positioned in a remote universe, plotted by the speculations of experts, trained to ignore emotion and its inconvenient truths. This is where we must live out our lives, until one fateful day we exit this world, and leave all others and their precious opinions behind. Within one last blink of an eye we'll shed our skins, as our allusions of individuality return to source.

Then only the ghosts that patrol the periphery will remain, the true individuals who are neither human nor spirit, but torn in two. I pity them the most, the dead who will not die. They may have a passion for life like no other, but they are consigned to being themselves forever.

35. DISINFORMATION

Mass communication is the shortcut to homogeny. The simplest answers to the most complex problems, always seem to have a ring of truth about them. That is the power of the lie, especially when blessed with an indomitable popularity, and freed from the need for credibility. The more we surrender to conventional wisdom, the more inarticulate our fury, the less chance that anyone, or anything, will light the public's imagination.

The information age is leaking, although most people haven't noticed, or perhaps they just don't care. Facts are pure conjecture, and the truth is now subjective, because it doesn't matter anymore. The only defence against the thought police, and their social zombie hordes, is the sound of silence, and an unquestioning obedience to the state. Censorship is no longer a problem, it isn't needed anymore. Those who bother to do their own research, are marked up on red lists for later extermination. The rest are too busy for conspiracies, they'd prefer to share funny photos, catch up on the latest gossip, or play stupid games.

Contrary to public perception, there *are* ways to deceive all of the people, all of the time. A perfect global deception takes place over many generations, through a slow and tedious process of propagated information. Allowing time to muddy the waters, as the old slowly forget the details, and pass down their imperfect recollections to an easily distracted youth. That's the point of greatest weakness in the timeline, the open wound of memory where those who wish to change all history, can implant the most delicate of white lies. An untruth will fester through the ages, consuming everything around it, until reality is forced to bend to its will.

The oldest falsehoods are the strongest, some more powerful than the truth. It's this kind of deception that allows the rest to thrive. The greatest lies, in age and size, are so fundamental to this plane of existence, that without them, life as we know it would come to an end.

36. SUPERPOWERS

I've watched old Soviet footage, grainy black and white frames of psycho-kinetic experiments, featuring home-grown mystics who'd rather perform for the camera, than return to the work camps in Siberia. They waved their arms around, and bobbed their heads, and apparently replicated the Hutchinson Effect. Sometimes objects would spin, and even fly about, as if a tiny poltergeist had turned up to help, but they might've just as likely flipped a switch for an electromagnetic coil. Telekinesis never really caught on, nor levitating transport systems, as regularly featured in communist propaganda at the time.

Those who remain under the delusion of self-grandeur, but without the means to rule the world, might concentrate their attack upon their own anatomy. Building muscles, even the brain, by taking supplements and eating superfoods, to feel super-duper every day. A body beautiful isn't the answer, neither is the body politic. What makes one person appear more powerful than another, is an imbalance of opportunity, education, and a decent standard of living. If you're used to the best, you get it, if not, expect the worst.

The aim of the hidden hand of power, is to disengage the populace from all direct experience. It's a lull in biological suppression and not a spurt of rapid evolution, that those who govern us wish to avoid. Inside our minds lies the technology we need to reengineer this toolmaker's world, and all the inspiration we could bear to transubstantiate. Our superpowers, the collective field of conscious energy generated by our thoughts, and communicated through our emotional and physical interactions, comes from people, and nothing else.

If everyone could take a moment to speak honestly at the same time, yet not deny others the same right, making sure to avoid all deception and delusion, and none felt angry or offended, our race would achieve a state of total lucidity. In unity we could breach the walls of absolute power, ascend beyond the reach of its corruption, and watch our fallen subjugators, no longer playing the Pied Piper, fall to their knees and weep.

Our race has become entranced by its own reflection, a pathetic self-image lost in a hall of mirrors. This world was designed to confuse and bewilder our senses, ensuring we continue to feed the hand of power, that strikes us down at every step.

37. PRACTICE

They say that *practice makes perfect*. It takes a great deal of practice of a very special kind, to overpower an intellect and tame it correctly. A skill that requires tact and insincere diplomacy, whereby one gains such confidence over another, that their subject relinquishes all control. A slave mind needs a master, a biased model of communication, a configuration of authoritarian logic. There are of course always challenges, those slaves who show great promise, yet hold on so hard to their beliefs, that their rebellious streak will never turn yellow.

The powers that be prefer good practice over exceptionalism, for they'd rather serve you up on a plate than see you win a single argument. There's no beating the Lizards at their own game. After all, they invented it, and once they've finished toying with you to impress their reptilian associates, you can bet your bottom dollar you'll be thrown out on your arse.

Leisure was invented by the rich, to stave off the boredom of having too much and doing too little. As time went by and the numbers grew, it became painfully obvious that brief respites between endless suffering, were not enough to keep the serfdom happy. So public holidays were conceived, for raking in more taxes from the ceremonial exchanges of overpriced tat, and vacations at consumer prisons. Last resorts with warmer climes, to keep the budgets balanced, and tinker with the unemployment figures, whilst the proles' sunburned backs are turned.

The cheapest breaks begin by sitting in a chair, and intoxicating oneself with various substances, or for the strictly teetotal, simply pretending that you're not there. Others turn to technology, to make-believe they're someone else, rather than the character they play here.

There are plenty of choices available, if you'd like to try other games, rather than this one, the one you're playing right now. An action-packed adventure, where you take on the role of a human being, living in a simulated world populated by two dimensional characters. It's fully immersive, impressive graphics, but it takes a little getting used to the controls.

In time, with practice, not only will the subconscious be tracked, mapped, and recorded, like much of our waking lives, but in due course, so will our deaths. Until our regular return trips from here to eternity will seem like a seamless transition.

Instead of dying, you'll be sent to *The Cloud*, a digital Elysium designed to store your simplest thoughts and deepest desires. Eventually, when you're transported back again, you'll carry on from where you left off, but in a brand new shiny plastic body, designed for more work and less play.

38. CORPOREALITY

To be here, *really here*, and nowhere else, is quite a hefty price to pay for life on Earth. Corporeality incarcerates all sentience upon this planet, encasing it in smart flesh, generating sensorial feedback within a narrow margin of tolerance. For all the bluster and bravado, human beings are extremely fragile creatures, and when pitted against more formidable materials, the play dough that we live in, hasn't a hope in hell of winning.

Without corporeal limitations our reality would fail in an instant, until matter didn't matter anymore. Our wave motion of experience would collapse, freefalling through unobserved space, our consciousness would spiral beyond the precipice of doubt. Cause and effect would die in an unprecedented chain of events, creating an implosion of meaning, far beyond the realms of our conditioned thinking.

Pity the pitiful god, the writer of our fate, whose obsession has cost them dearly, and only accentuated their loneliness. For they are as much a prisoner as humanity. Our flesh has taught us to be human, and steered our fate throughout all generations. Corporeality provides the substance for physical existence, creating a construct of self-fulfilment. Ensuring that as long as we are contained within our flesh, we are at the beck and call of a whole gamut of biological needs.

The body is a cage, but it hadn't always been that way. There was a time when it was more like a suit, and you could try it on and take it off. If you didn't like it you could try another, or perhaps not even bother. What we think we are is nothing more than transportation, it's what's inside that counts, but few seem to be able to tell the difference these days.

If you can imagine a time beyond death, and accept that you still exist, bring that feeling back, and try to keep hold of it. It's just one moment, but it marks the difference between an eternal consciousness, and a corporeal being.

39. DECAY

As age sets in, and we all grow up, and old, we must take the place of those who put us here. We, the former hopes and dreams of the dead, will eventually give way, and take our final bow. Leaving the world as an anathema, of a past the future loves to hate.

We walk on the graves of forgotten lives, and build our dreams upon the corpses of their failed endeavours. Oblivious to their whispered regrets for lost causes, and romantic visions of what could have been.

As light decays, so must flesh, all the while life's clock keeps ticking, a biological time-bomb that cannot be defused. In youth our bodies conspire against our every thought and action, distracting us with immediate gratification, paid through regular instalments of imperceptible decay.

Inevitably, time slowly ravages our cellular structure, our skin begins to crack and our hair turns grey. But it's *inside* the body where you'll find most of the damage done. Even in our final moments on this planet, the blood in our veins will keep feeding our major organs, rattling on like a runaway train, with no destination asides inevitable destruction.

I suspect that's why so many newborns cry with horror, having left the safety of the womb, and all possibility of returning to The Void. Instead, they're squeezed out unceremoniously into this world, where you must learn to ignore the sweet stench of flesh, emanating from those who love you, with all their hearts.

The negative influence of humanity, so brutalised by its hidden masters, imperceptibly accelerates mental, emotional, and physical putrefaction. Once our time has finally come, and we must abort our own biology, we leave this world in exactly the same state that we arrived. Shrivelled, frail, weak, and scared to death of what comes next.

40. DAM(N)ATION

There's a special place reserved in hell, set aside for only the most human of humans. It is a self-enclosed land of nations, and it looks exactly like Earth. The only difference is, its laws are purely subjective, and the punishment for all crimes is life imprisonment.

Once you've been reeled in by the spectacle of belonging, to know one's place before knowing oneself, there's no escape. Well at least as far as the system is concerned, the *karmic system*. Karma is a little like money, an invention to ensure that you pay for what should be free. To keep allegiances, and bind the spirit to the mind, so no matter what you believe, your thoughts will always betray you.

Many of the codes we live by, exist only within ourselves. Ideas of borders, nationalities, government, and money are artificially induced mass delusions, a shared psychosis ingrained into our minds as mere babes.

We've signed up for an illusion of choice, a near translucent smokescreen to keep us in our place. We are told not to question authority, let alone its concept, because none of us must understand why we are truly here.

Yet still I ask, for behind the mask, beyond the hidden hand of power, there sits something evil. I feel its presence, even in the distance, a dark cloud over all humanity. If this creature is so powerful, why would they feel the need to rule over our lowly rabble? What god, for the want of a better description, would be so petty as to perpetually feed on our fears?

Whatever force steers our fate is narcissistic, inspired by a taste for schadenfreude. Its intentions pedantic and blatantly cruel, like a spiteful adolescent giant, gleefully crushing insects in a metaphysical yard. What's worst about this hell on Earth, these lives we're supposed to embrace, to keep on smiling through no matter the consequences, is that somehow we must have imagined all this. Even the creep who puppeteers our top dogs and king pins, is just another part of our collectively fucked up imagination.

There is of course a flaw in our damnation, a possible escape route. You can see it in the word itself, in *damnation* there lies a *dam*. A great wall that has held back the waters above and below for many aeons. Now, help me look for cracks.

41. SAVE

In my teens I shared an empty train with a stockbroker on a heavy cocaine comedown. When I first boarded the carriage, I'd assumed I was alone. I had a cheap synthesiser with me, battery-powered, straight out of the catalogue, and sitting pretty on my lap. I switched it on and quietly played myself a tune or two, struggling against the odds to find myself a chart topper. As it turned out, in the future, 8-bit sounds would have an irresistible allure for hardened coke-heads.

A tardy commuter suddenly popped up at the other end of the carriage, nodding, waving, sniffing as he quickly strolled over. He tried on a half-hearted smile as he slumped down opposite me. He twitched, refocused, then asked if he could have a go. There were beer stains on his Armani, and he sported a white powder moustache, with hangdog red-eyes. I felt sorry for the guy, and so I let him play.

For all his enthusiasm, it was an embarrassingly inharmonious interlude, soundly immersed in presets and special effects. In particular, sirens and explosions, set to a rudimentary Bossa Nova beat. He bored himself within a minute or two, handed back the keyboard. He snorted from a grip seal bag, using a tiny silver spoon loosely hung around his neck, and shuddered with an imperceptible sigh. I turned off my toy, and put away my childish dreams, to listen to him whine on about his ongoing predicament. The problem was, he took cocaine to deal with the stress of his career, which meant he spent all his money on drugs. He couldn't be a stockbroker unless he was coked up, and he couldn't afford to get high unless he stuck at his job. *Chicken, egg, end of.*

Those living in a rut have a fascinating inner life, a double one in fact. Perhaps not exactly imbued with the most riveting plot, less girls and guns than most spy yarns, but at the very least, a few unwelcome surprises for the boss. Humans put themselves through the mill, for all kinds of reasons, it could be love or honour, or more often familial responsibilities. Yet under the skin of many a dull lad or lass, dwells an utter stranger, not exactly desperate to break out but curious enough to wonder.

You may have had the same advice as me, from a well-meaning friend or a kindly stranger, *never look back*. It's difficult not to, even if it's just to get your bearings. Nonetheless, I can imagine how dangerous nostalgia can be, especially if it's all you have left in the world. When you've outlived your friends and family, or at least the ones who cared, and there's little else to do but sit patiently, hoping for a quiet and painless death, old age can make a living mockery of life.

Like dear old Ron from over the road, living in a garden flat he used to share with a fellow widower, until last year when his best friend died and left him on his tod. Both had spent their years in the forces and their long retirement swapping the same old stories, but now Ron's fallen silent. He spends all day propped up in his deckchair, staring directly at the sun, yes, with his dark glasses on, but all the same, it's almost as if he wants to go blind. Until all he'll have left to see are his precious memories.

As time moves on, your mind runs out of room, and all those special moments stored for good measure, leave little space for new ones. Eventually you'll have your fill, and every extra second of this life must be weighed against the past, and the closer you edge towards death, the more the days are left wanting.

One of the most daunting aspects of dying, as opposed to death, is the loss of one's faculties through disease, or the general degradation of the mind. The destruction of memory undermines identity, isolating us from all personal reminders, leaving practical strangers to struggle with our plight. Even if they mean well, and they've watched a few documentaries, or took a brief course online, it's not the same, they'll never understand. Maybe people hang on too long, or are forced to, who knows, and who cares? It's almost as if the world of medicine has achieved the impossible, and cheapened life by extending it.

It's certainly the cruellest blow, not to go out with a fight, but a shuffle and a drooling stoop, forgetting which foot goes forward next, and which nurse is actually your daughter. What's more, most lose their house, which must be sold to pay for the care, the sort you get in homes where people wait to die. A majority of which, are thankfully oblivious of their downfall, constantly reliving their chequered past in daydreams as they flicker through the photo albums of their drug addled minds.

Call it impatience if you like, but some of us prefer to upload our data sooner than others. A remote backup you can rely on, when things go from bad to worse. But it has a price, for the process takes a toll on all of us, especially the old. Elysium is not heaven, but a virtual construct, imagined by our wretched futures, to capture a past they can no longer recall. Officially known as *The Hive*, its a holographic museum of memories, that serves to remind them to never forget that they're still human. Which should still mean something, even now, if only we could remember what. If we could, I am certain we could save everyone, and everything, without ever having to play this ridiculous game again.

42. GRAFT

The human brain is a fragile and tender thing, it's not particularly designed for inter-dimensional travel. It's a workhorse, an all-rounder, reduced to fending off a multitude of incongruities. Especially those meant to inform, rather than inhibit the human experience. Every time we dream, the brainstem floods with opiates to immobilize our higher thinking, and lead us up the garden path. Should you work your way through the bewildering maze of ethereal distractions, and reach the borders of consciousness, you'll *still* need to pass through customs.

At the end of a dream, most dreamers appear to be hungover. I've often hovered at the barrier, and seen them come and go, as many fools unto themselves, playing along with the game. The guards change regularly dependant on the traveller, but they can usually spot a tourist a mile off. They always have the same look about them, a ghostly pallor, left completely washed out by their nightly ritual cleanse. They're not supposed to return with any psychological baggage, although a few try smuggling the odd souvenir from the other side. Usually a silly little trinket of sorts, but nothing that can do too much damage back home.

Saying that, the border guards have just about given up on me, so now I use a different gate, one especially created for my kind. Lumped with the lunatics that most ignore, who jump the queue as they rush by with trolleys full of duty-free psychoses, on their way to an early grave. I wouldn't be surprised if those like me are part of some elaborate plot, and that we are the unknowing participants of our own conspiracy theories turned fact. Psychic refugees armed with far-fetched fantasies, promoting confusion, and spreading irrational fears amongst Saturn's law abiding citizens.

You might notice a little commotion in the line, in those last moments before you awake. Echoes of a heated exchange at the back of the queue, or even the sign of a struggle now and again. Especially if an illegal immigrant tries their luck, just one more number of the dead, desperate to live another life. Once you've passed through security, you're cajoled into a bright white room, a plain cube, with one entrance, and one exit. Inside there, your memories are somehow reorganised, as your consciousness is wiped clean of the past few hours. It's a protocol for ensuring none gain an unfair advantage, however slight. Such as a sneak preview of the future, or an alternate history, of which our masters' masters would rather we forget.

It's all just for show of course, the strip searches and scanners, none of it really makes any difference. Because there's always the risk you'll be lucid tonight, and become the god of all you survey. There's nothing anyone can do about that, it's like having X-ray vision, a lucid dreamer can see through the lies. Ignoring the divisions between dreams and reality, with priority access to privileged information, knowledge held sacred by earth's most unholy cabals.

In The White Room, on the few occasions they've attempted to clear my mind, I've felt the Djinn plant a single memory, a mutated seed of an idea. I didn't take it too well, apparently I have an incompatible brain signature, unusually pernicious for a self-pontificating loaf. They like to graft it onto some other moment, a childhood fear, a first love, a forgotten name, a number, squeezed in anywhere they can find the room to manoeuvre. It's like an advert, a pop-up you just can't get rid of, lingering in the periphery of the everyday. It's called a *hard graft*, and it's implanted deep within the primal core. If the procedure's successful, you'll hardly notice the difference, except you'll need what you want, rather than want what you need.

I know my way around the gates, I've seen them before at the airport. Still no mermaids, which is a shame, but that's okay I can make my own. I like to watch the floor and search out people's cast offs, their token mementos from imaginary last resorts, or amateur photographs of their dead relatives. Well, at least the tricksters playing their parts. I've picked up so much mental litter in the past, I could have made a whole new person from the psychic leftovers. A shit-kicking consciousness to sneak past the guards, although god knows what they'd do next, without a body, life on Earth can be very hard.

The human spirit is a hotchpotch of discarded thoughts and splintered memories, left behind by whoever came before us.

Inhabiting our minds and bodies as we endeavour to erase any evidence of their former existence. We've toiled and struggled over many centuries, using every drop of effort to make our mark, and maintain the delusion that we truly belong here. Yet, whatever life our viral consciousness has devoured, it's now as plain as day, in the middle of the night, that our world's former occupants want it back again.

43. SOUL TRADER

The notion of the soul is a relatively recent idea, in essence it's a root or binding, particularly popularised by the Hebrew Norse. All in order to quell a suicidal fascination with greater spirits who apparently dwell beyond the rainbow bridge.

Once the concept had been planted, and new traditions were formed, those who died were spiritually bound by funerary adornment, to ensure their compliance in a fictional afterlife. As time moved on, the death rituals became increasingly ceremonial, with many cultures still practicing everything from embalming to fire sacrifice. All this in turn, aided in the proliferation of a populist dogma, and a conditional reflex was born, the primal fear of *losing one's soul*.

The Devil walks into a bar, he buys two whiskies and heads for the nearest snug. He nods at the man opposite, a wanderer, who looks down on his luck. He offers him a Scotch, the wanderer smiles a toothless grin.

Wanderer: Much obliged.

The Devil hands him his card, the print is bold and unfussy, there are only two words, *Soul Trader*.

The Devil: I can give you anything you want, anything your heart desires, all I require is your soul.

Wanderer: The death of Hell.

The Devil: You already know that death is a figment of the conscious collective's imagination? Try again.

Wanderer: The end of duality.

The Devil: Without duality, neither God, nor I, would even exist.

Wanderer: I have no problem with that.

The Devil: What about money, power, fame? You could live forever.

Wanderer: What *here*? On *Earth*?

The Devil: Yes, *forever and ever*.

Wanderer: Now, that *does* sound like Hell.

The Devil: One last chance, what will you trade?

Wanderer: I'll exchange my soul for yours.

The Devil: Fuck you, no sale.

44. CONVERGENCE

The differential engine is broken, and difference is losing its pizzazz. Even though most people don't seem to mind, if you look in their eyes, you'll find less, and less surprise. We expect so much, but deliver so little, the world's too small for humanity, and all of us are quickly piling on top of each other.

Asides from bunching up together, we're also getting inside each other's heads. Too many people want to agree, or agree to differ, but basically follow along the same lines. Conceding to the fundamental laws of our reality, reducing our intuitive potential, until we've lowered the bar so far, that no one dares challenge the consensus.

The human universe is collapsing, because individualism is dying. The death of flux and the rise of predictability is crushing all hope in life. We are bound together in the wake of a universal dream, drawn back to the day, because we're too weak to swim against the current.

The future is grey, its colour artificially projected, at first upon the material world, and then eventually within the human brain. Food has led the way, disposing of the ideals of nutrition, focusing on the visual feast, bypassing the palette, and directly influencing tastes through hormonal and nano-chemical transmissions. It isn't sweet, it isn't bitter, it's the flavour of a manufactured lie.

We are members of an narrowly opinionated world forum, poorly advised by peer group propaganda, conveniently ignoring the atrocities of fundamentalism and corporatized warfare. Instead we are encouraged to work together, to push the official line, that culture should do the right thing, and lay down and die.

Making inroads in the arts, entertainment, politics, and media, via state sponsored opinion leaders and online polls, to inform the general public, of what's offensive and what's not. Ideologically subsisting under the threat of social exclusion, and ostracism in the workplace. If you don't stick your head in the ground, you'll get the sack. Nowadays, the fools who tag along, spreading memes conjured up by agencies, and propagated by bots, do little more than pass the buck. Too many agree wholeheartedly with their own subjugation, tipping the balance so far, that it has come down to a clear-cut choice between giving up and dying, or giving up and lying.

The price of life has tumbled, the totality of all human effort has left us in debt, and one which we can never hope to pay. So here we are again, like so many times before, human chattel, a race of slaves. No matter the compromise or the sacrifices we make, it's never enough to satiate the state's hunger for power.

Soon every dissident will be punished for their crimes of individuality, for not jumping on the political bandwagon, and refusing to participate responsibly for the sake of their community. When there's very little distinction left between the extremes, the slightest disagreement can be blown out of all proportion. Ensuring that any dissent, however inconsequential, can be crushed by sociopathic simpatico, for the sake of unity, and the eradication of criminal doubt.

Eventually, all people will look the same, and the mass will worship itself. It's just another practical contrivance, one deemed necessary for the long-term success of the totalitarian regime. Where future generations will praise conformity and abhor variety, and do exactly as they're told, because they'll be born that way.

45. GRADUATION

Death is hardly a badge of honour, more likely a consolation prize for the runners-up of the human race. Those with the least to lose are keen to move on, but those who've invested heavily in life, are known to outstay their welcome. Fooling themselves that their loved ones will achieve the impossible, and bear witness to their tormented spirit. Even the most hardened of sceptics will discover to their horror, that when the lights go out, they'll be clutching at straws along with the best of them.

It'll take a while to get used to losing your body, especially if you've enjoyed having one. If you've taken good care of yourself, and are constantly caught by your own reflection, the prognosis doesn't look too good. If not, no biggie, it's deadweight anyway. There's no worst torture on earth, than dying, and then realising you're still trapped in your own corpse. If you're not convinced, then wait until you're laid out on a slab at the morgue, and you'll most likely leave by your own accord. Unless that is, you're a horror fan, and love the sight of blood and gore. If so, you should feel right at home in the mortuary, with all the other moaners and groaners.

Some lose their bearings, without the discipline of corporeality, you can go crazy trying to understand the ins and outs of it. The dead don't know their limits, and they have trouble comprehending life without them. It can be a terrifying prospect, to find yourself caught between oblivion and infinity, given the choice of knowing all, at the risk of losing one's soul. A lot of people don't want to know, it's all too much to take on board. Instead they busy themselves with bullshit life reviews, in the company of false angels and deities, who get their kicks from screwing around with the recently deceased.

If you're a fan of our world, and how it's run, and believe that those in authority know best, beware, the life after this will tax your mind, and drain your soul of everything you know and love, until you'll be begging to be sent back again.

There's no rest for the wicked, or the good, or anyone at all in death. It's dark for a start, if you want to see where you're going, or even where you are, you have to make your own light, or seek out others who still have a spark of life left in them. Some find it easier to gather around the living, strangers in their own homes, where they can pretend they'd never died. Warming their spirits by cosy fireside conversations, or floating in the perspiration steam of unsuspecting couples making love. Even the loneliest spirits can only cope with a few of us at a time, too many and they drown in the crowd. Torn to pieces by a tidal wave of passing thought, ricocheting into nearby walls, floors, and ceilings like psychic shrapnel.

Those with a short attention span, will quickly lose their memory, and usually freak out as the panic sets in. Left lost and bewildered, without a clue where to go, they'll soon see the light, and hear the call of kindly strangers. When all hope is lost and purgatory looks more and more inviting, it only takes a meagre bribe of a few basic home comforts to gather lost spirits. That's how the Djinn and their masters draw in wandering souls, like moths to a flame. A mirage in the desert with the faintest signs of life, burning camp fires and soft sounds of conversations drifting through the shadows. But it's just safety in numbers, all praying for the universe to end.

When you're dead, depression is regression, and broken souls fall down hard, sinking into depths of their deepest doubts, left in their own personal hell, praying for the briefest glimmer of recognition. That's when death turns to dream, and as you grab and grasp for your past, you reach your very first thoughts as a newborn baby. Within the comfort of the womb, an orb of spectral light, a spore of consciousness infused into the flesh of a living host, more than ready to spend another lifetime fearing death.

Soon after birth, we learn to survive by forgetting everything we know. Another fresh start for a very old soul, one who's simply grateful for a place to stay. A world where you don't have to imagine a sunrise, or the sea, or the stars, because down here on earth, reality runs like clockwork, no matter how you feel or who you are.

46. FREQUENCY

Om is the primal scream of creativity, the carrier signal of our reality. The human body is a tuning fork, when harmonised it can resonate with others, transmitting a field of cognitive consonance. However, a controlled society relies upon cognitive dissonance, and the discomfort and unease it generates. Subliminally playing upon the fears of the citizenry, to push for more conformity, because mass conformity ensures mass control. That's how the Lizard gods maintain their dominance over this reality, by consensus, rather than by force.

The misnomer of the dream, and the feeble philosophies that have attempted to confine its influence, have convinced the vast majority that when we sleep, our consciousness is left barely ticking over. In fact, we've never truly slept, and what remains of our souls, have not rested since their first conception. We toil our days on Earth, whilst at night our thoughts are outsourced to distant outposts of a federated state of being.

Those with the patience to meditate, willing and able to ignore the commotion around them, can take a tour around the dream factory, to learn a little about the processes involved in maintaining a global state of hypnosis. Everyday stress is a side-effect of physiological trauma, induced by long-term exposure to magnetic field flux, generated, and accumulated, by the construct we inhabit.

Of course, you could hack the frequency, if you can find the operating code, and if you really know what you're doing, you can even engineer your own firewall. I rely on recordings of nature to help me ignore the racket inside my head, the white noise of wind, and pink and brown rain, but that's because I'm lazy. If I could be bothered, I'd sing all day. Harmonising within the stream of consciousness is the most effective way to counteract negative energies, especially those produced by the artificial ley lines of the fibre optic smart-grid.

There's plenty of proof out there, if you're prepared to ignore the lies, and do your own research. Look back far enough, and you'll find evidence of exactly why music exists, and how the influence of sound created a world we can only perceive as mythology. Acoustic resonance is the key, originally relied upon by ancient engineers to construct our landscape, as well as some of the most awe inspiring structures ever devised by humankind. Well, at least our long lost forebears, our betters, the only people who ever truly belonged here.

Sound leads the path to light, or it would do, but the tracks have been covered too many times, so no one's listening anymore. The voice of the Earth is rising, its frequency accelerating, elevating in pitch, almost as if it's preparing to speak, or scream. I have a funny feeling the message will be extremely succinct, and to the point.

In the future we'll no longer need to talk, there will even be laws to discourage it, but the conversations will carry on regardless. First as inner voices, but then eventually, as pictures in our minds. We'll live our lives like a waking dream, lost inside our own heads, lagging behind our projected selves, communicating with inanimate objects and making friends with augmented digital reflections. It's the Devil's own vision of a perfect world, where none shall ever meet another living soul, even in their frequency modulated, fully-immersive fantasies.

47. RECONSTITUTION

It's difficult to gather one's thoughts when so many of them are impostors. Groping through slagheaps of false memories and state propaganda, for a few gems of tried and tested wisdom. It all takes time, of which most of us have little. Let alone the desire to spend it contemplating life, whilst languishing in a long-term insecurity complex.

At certain points in history, those with more confidence in the world around them, might come together, not for one cause, but under the banner of many. In those key moments, as another cruel reign begins to fall, the masses give rise to a figurehead. Someone to make outrageous claims and unrealistic promises, which few reasonably expect them to keep. A hero turned guttersnipe, tipped to rise through the revolutionary ranks, a new face of hope for a tired out war. Waving goodbye to their credibility as they take their photo-opportunity, before joining the other liars for drinks, followed by a game of musical chairs, for the last empty seats of power.

Our world loves its winners, those who fought against the odds, to meet our greatest hopes and vanquish our fears. We are taught to applaud without question, praising the random acts of heroic tyrants and tyrannical heroes. At school, we learn the art of war, and can either fight back, or pay our dues to the playground bullies, extorting pocket money and notoriety in equal proportion. It takes a jaded maturity to understand that power has no fair share, and that corruption is a price worth paying to keep the wolf from the door.

We are encouraged to ignore the facts, to make excuses for our betters, the warped mirrors of society, bankrolled and blackmailed by the clandestine proprietors of this planet. What they say and what they do, are two very different things. Respected names and faces reading from a script, without ever having to make one single geo-political decision. Politics is the oldest hypnotist in the world, performing for the audience, with the aid of their glamorous assistant, media. Evil siblings with one purpose in life, to ask all the wrong questions, so you might never ask the right ones.

We live in a convoluted society, aligned to a malevolent mindset, bound together by common misconception, backed by opinion-based research. An officialdom of thought, badly organised and over bureaucratised, to ensure that nothing outside the inner circle can make a grab for power. Every problem that humanity encounters had been solved long ago, and by far wiser souls than those who rule over us now. Which is why they're dead and forgotten, because they made the mistake of building society too well.

There's always the band aid approach to keep the money rolling in, and the bullshit excuses rolling out. My late father's favourite analogy of how the system works, is the Morris Minor. A car that had been built with due care and attention, nothing fancy mind you. But if you had a problem, you could easily replace the parts yourself, all of which were made from the highest quality materials. With careful maintenance, a Morris Minor could last a hundred years or more. A well known fact that eventually brought its manufacturers to their knees, ruined by good intentions and a complete lack of business acumen. I'm sure I'm not giving any secrets away when I say, *if you give the people what they want, they'll never need you again.*

Nowadays, the consumer products we manufacture, in this highly engineered world we've come to know and love, have been designed with a built-in redundancy. What's more, we humans have begun to mimic the objects of our collective desire. Living out our lives of fantasy, in a consumer age, where the snake can finally eat its tail.

Whilst those few brave souls, who still have their wits about them, cannot help but see the ugliness inside, and trust their gut feeling that something's very wrong. It's the failing constitution of the human race, a creeping sickness that has reduced our going price, to something less than food or water.

48. THE AFTER-PARTY

It's a little known fact that some of the most intelligent, incisive, and imaginative people on the planet are nocturnal, and completely wasted. Hardly suitable candidates for running a country, or a multinational corporation, not that they'd ever be offered the opportunity. Ironically, this unhappy band of stragglers living on the fringes of reality, share much of their poor sociological traits with the hybrid stumps, and there are plenty of good reasons why.

For any system to succeed, it must be operated at maximum efficiency, so there can be no room for waste. All in all, the general populous tends to abide by the rules, and dependent on their social hemisphere, they eat, fuck, and sleep at approximately the same times. The day is the peak period for a psychic bombardment of the senses, for every waking hour is the witching hour, if you're a witch. The rising sun is the first of many biological triggers, to ensure high productivity within the human race. As we spend our lives in meaningless toil and labour, and obsess over job security, our collective subconscious fumbles with new excuses, for why we should give this place the time of day.

An empty life, is akin to an empty mind. With nothing rattling round inside, no wants, no needs, the social rejects remain practically invisible to respectable society. Only life's losers have the time to get to know the dead, wasting lonely nights in spiritual ambivalence, focused on the mid-space where their thoughts stretch out ad nauseum. Like the signal bounce of long wave radio, transmitting and receiving vague notions over great distances, unfettered by the interference of the day.

If you're still awake at sometime just before dawn, you can feel vast regions of the hive mind crawling to a stop. A brief lull in the war on sleep, with few on the road, and less on the streets. Every curtain drawn as a sign of respect, for those momentarily dead to the world. Sleep is the oldest foe of the Lizards, it leaves their workers temporarily incapacitated, and even if when we hold out for days, we'll eventually collapse with exhaustion. Because our minds are too much for these bodies, that we use and abuse, until they break.

When the world sleeps it reveals its true state, as a false haven for the damned. The great populous live lives of somnambulance, drifting through one existence after another, and in-between each stint on Earth, they're left searching aimlessly for the after-party celebrations. At the very end, all will come to learn that there are no rewards for the righteous, or punishments for the wronged, in fact the truth may come as a bitter disappointment. In death we see the trick, the science behind the magic, the magic behind the science, and how much time we've wasted waiting for the good times to roll.

49. HELL

If you think you can leave this place, start walking, and see how far you get. In the past it was a lot easier, with few border guards, and no passports or satellite tracking.

Unless you're digging your way to hell, it's ice that marks the circumference, denying you any real possibility of escape. Humans can't drag their bodies through more than a few hundred miles of the Antarctic, before they give way to frostbite and a lack of oxygen.

When I'm dead, I'll pick a direction, any will do, and I'll set off to explore the ice, up and over the *Great Wall*. Despite the unanimity amongst the faithful of scientism, I'm not convinced. Nothing flies there, and if you so much as skirt around the edges, the militaries of the world will make sure you won't live to tell the tale.

The hyperborean giants, which history has conveniently resigned to myth, are assumed to be from the land beyond the North Wind. More precisely, refugees, or perhaps escaped prisoners, from the yawning mouth of Mount Meru. Such creatures, made from far hardier stock than us, left their mark everywhere and long ago. Which incidentally, just for the record, laid the foundations for our toy-town civilisation.

It's a contention I've held since childhood, a complete distrust in the status quo. The details change, the parlance and the terminology, but in essence all who are in agreement have a vested interest to keep things exactly as they are. Questions from the audience must be pre-approved, in case a raving maniac should grab the limelight, and stir up feelings amongst the great unwashed. That legion of idiots and fools, who have a hard time accepting the received truth, and persist with believing their own eyes.

If I could travel anywhere and see all there is to see, with no guides to advise me on what I'm looking at, and everything was as it should be, with the North and South poles in their proper place, on a circumference of a globe rather than a disc, I'd sincerely apologise, and pack myself off to a local sanatorium. But until then, most likely never, I will rely on my own experience, or rather the lack of it, and a natural distrust for human behaviour. One that has a tendency to bluster, and skirt around the truth, rather than admit we haven't a clue where we are, let alone what we're doing.

Few ever ask, if we can send a man to the Moon, then why not launch a rocket over the ice? Set it on a course that's straight and true, with a camera mounted upon its nose, streaming live images of the length and breadth of Antarctica. No CGI or digital texture mapping, a simple photographic proof, a clear cut record of the globe, the egg, the bowl, the disc. No matter what the shape, it's time to reveal the real world as it really is, and be done with it.

But that will never happen, the prison walls are kept hidden for good reason. If too many people knew the truth, this hell on earth would quickly turn into a lunatic asylum.

50. LIMBO

Most losers in life know when they're leaving, long before they kick the bucket. It's not the vain hope of the hopeless, the death of an unfulfilled life doesn't take flight on a wing and a prayer. It's an instinctual reckoning, borne out of a long haul of boredom and disappointment, and the unwelcome knack of knowing exactly when one's luck is about to run out. Social freaks and heretics unwrap their natural gifts, placed under the proverbial Tree of Life, far sooner than deemed seemly. From then on they have to fake it in front of others, and mock surprise, playing gooseberry for as long as they can hack it, whilst their peers drift away, on their respective journeys of self-discovery.

If you've seen it all before, and the tedium hasn't sent you to an early grave, you'll be playing guessing games by now. You may have even noticed, you're winning your own arguments, more, and more of the time. It's not a victory to be shared, the mad take little pride in what they've learned, through bitter past experience, and realistic expectations for the worst. If you don't feel like you belong, and what once seemed as solid as a rock, now grows vague and insubstantial under the weight of so many lies, then you've probably guessed right. The human race is being taken for a ride.

The eternally disenchanted mingle with the crowds, as they bide their time on earth, mentally dipping in and out of philosophies and belief systems, but never quite committing to any of them. Lives after lives of half-hearted contributions to cultures on the rise, as well as those about to fall, leaves you feeling empty inside. As if it really isn't worth the effort settling down, when you know you've barely any time.

The dispossessed, the lost causes, have too many treasured memories, even if they can't quite recall them. Yet their influence, the doubts of their ancient spirits, leaves them increasingly encumbered, weighed down by an inexplicable grief. On the plus side, their seats have already been reserved in limbo since time immemorial. Life's greatest sceptics, the hermits, the shut-ins, the loners of every description, have a home from home. A refuge for tired old souls, who'd rather sit by the windows of the soul, and take in the view.

For some, limbo isn't a place, it's just a dance, one where you must bend over backwards to win, but that sounds too much like hard work to me. It's the first rule that humans learn, to crawl their way to glory, then toddle, walk, and run. It's backbreaking work being human, most of whom dance the dance to the bitter end.

The majority of new arrivals in limbo, brim with a confidence of past experience, certain that nothing has changed, and near enough carry on as before. Buying groceries, and tidying the house, and occasionally calling their friends, who never seem to be around.

Eventually the situation deteriorates, as one home invader after another, moves the furniture, redecorates, and makes love to their significant other, without a by your leave. It's no better at the office, as a complete stranger takes the promotion, that by all rights should have been theirs. It's around this time that most of the recently deceased come to terms with the fact, that the world cannot see them, that life's for the living, whilst they're most certainly dead.

What throws a lot of people when they die, is the distinct lack of lightning bolt epiphanies, the transition is so humdrum and pedestrian, that for a while you can fool yourself that nothing's changed. My advice for the recently departed, is to avoid embracing your self-destruction in a piecemeal fashion. You don't need to be old to get set in your ways, even the young and tragic, who had so much to live for, must come to terms with the painful equilibrium of limbo.

Place has no home, being has no need, thinking is counterintuitive, and belief is a lie. Learning to be as others, in a world of subterfuge, breaks the bonds of trust to undo the heart and mind. What remains, what pathetic residue slips through the cracks and pours away from this place, to cluster in sprites as incandescent instances of life, are our true forms housed in the bodies of fluctuating space and time. The limbo dancers, the astral acrobats, the hanged man caught between the devil and the deep blue sea. All must wait impatiently in limbo, for the end of everything.

51. INCOMMUNICADO

I recorded the silence yesterday. I kept perfectly still while the red light was on. I just sat there, as cool as a cucumber, and watched the numbers run. Call it an experiment if you like, or perhaps a reality check, just to make sure all this isn't simply in my head. *It's not*, in fact it's even busier these days. There was so much noise on the audio file, I have to admit it I was a little shocked.

It used to be the occasional voice or two, sometimes explicit, even threatening, goading me to go through the usual emotional reactions. Even so, I've become accustomed to the angry spirits, they have their problems, just like the rest of us. It seems most them are envious of my position. I am the only one amongst their number who needn't lie. I, unlike all the others, am actually alive, or at least for the immediate future.

To listen to the dead, all I need do is draw the curtains, and lay down on my bed. Eventually the room will fill with hushed voices. Initially muttering amongst themselves, engaged in light conversation, but that rarely lasts. As soon as I am anywhere near relaxed, the discussion descends into chaotic fits of a pitiful cacophony. Pleading, begging, wailing for whatever reasons the dead regret their time of life, and how much better they would do in my position.

More spirits have gathered over the years, and we have come to an agreement that they must sleep during the day, in order that I may still function as a human being. At night it's a completely different matter, I cannot remember the last time I was left undisturbed. It's why I submerge myself in white noise just to get a wink of sleep.

I feel sorry for them, the disembodied voices, that they must be so desperate or deluded, that they'd choose me of all people, to seek their salvation. I'm the last person in the world you should turn to, if you want to be saved, or raised to the heavens through some glorious act of faith. I have very little, either in myself or the human race, and most certainly none for the dead.

I believe in predictability, or let's say I predict its probability. I can roundly guess how right or wrong my guesses are, and either way I learn a little more. But I can't imagine what the dead would want with me, except to join them and I've been close, but that was such a long time ago. It's almost as if it doesn't matter if I listen anyway, I'm just their focus of attention, something to gather around like a campfire, or a TV.

I don't bother even waking up now, unless someone pushes me. Voices in the bedroom, the flashes of light, the creaking floorboards, the footsteps that pass through the walls, all the usual paranormal nonsense I've experienced since childhood. Everything I've learned to cope with, and to some extent ignore.

I suppose that things have got out of control, sitting in here in my bubble, whilst all around me crowd other people's dead families, and most likely a few members of my own. Perhaps it's a protest, I don't know, they all speak at once and so damn quietly, it's near enough impossible to make sense of their demands.

I suppose I could take a wild stab at it and have a guess. Let's say they do want me to perform some kind of miracle. If that's true, then they've obviously forgotten that humans are only human, and consequently incapable of achieving such feats. It's quite embarrassing really, knowing that so many of them are playing the waiting game, watching me waste my life, until I can join them again.

52. IN THE LOOP

According to my mother, at around eighteen months of age I ran away from home. Well, sort of. In the middle of a winter's night, I dragged my go-kart out of the shed, and peddled for a couple of miles to the local library. Of course, it was closed, but I wasn't there to read books. Eventually a panda car pulled up, and the police took me home. They explained to my distraught mother that I'd been crying, because *I wanted to head for the stars.*

Obviously, my mother's come to terms with her side of the story, a standard take on a family tale, which she'd happened to keep to herself for over forty years. When out of the blue, during one particularly miserable Christmas, in a rare meeting of minds, I decided to recount a recurring dream from my childhood.

After some moments of shock, she nervously shook her head, and informed me that I was poorly mistaken. *That was no dream son, it really happened.* She reluctantly shared her brief account of an impetuous scamp, admittedly one unusually advanced for his age. Her first-born, whom for whatever reason eluded her, was convinced that he came from outer space. *Now, let's not say anything more about it. Stuffing?*

She said I wanted to be a spaceman, I guess I needed the space. I was desperate to touch the stars, because I knew then what I've always known. Stars are not real, at least, not in the way so many are led to believe. I still watch them now, from time to time, but I've lost interest over the years. It's like living in Jersey, with a clear view of a plush Manhattan skyline. You can see it, but you're never going to live there. We're world's apart, I'm down here and the stars are up above, all those twinkling crystal lights hanging from God's carousel.

Lately they've been looking a little more dicey than usual. Some of them hang so low now, like rotting fruit on the vine. The colours are off, and so are the shapes, and they bumble around too much, dancing like dying fireflies at the end of a long, hot summer.

I suppose I've come to terms with the truth, the knowledge that I've held onto since birth. I now understand the full implication of what I've always suspected. That the stars are mere copies, a replicated snapshot of the real universe, taken from the perspective of the original Earth. Each had been carefully plotted high above our heads, to serve as a visual reminder of how insignificant we are. In order that we don't expect too much, and risk straining the holographic engine.

In its heyday, *The Earth Museum* was a miraculous attraction. Designed by a greater hand with near perfect symmetry, extravagantly executed in the most superb detail, all so those who came here truly believed it to be the real thing. Many parallel dimensions throughout time, have been plundered to create this world. Not to mention the extreme measures taken, to ensure that no one born here, could ever suspect Earth's true identity, as a working replica, recorded for prosperity.

The stars are one of the greatest feats of ancient engineering, celestial projectors to cast a dim light upon our stage. Although their deliberate distraction, makes it near impossible to see what's beyond our prism. For we live in an echo chamber, and run in a loop, concealed from within, whilst everything else is hidden outside. For our reality depends upon the act of observance, and not only must we watch each other, but we too must be scrutinised by something greater than ourselves. Without constant observation, this precarious reality would quickly collapse into a dream, and one that might even be on the verge of waking up.

53. ARC/HIVE

The mythical Ark that never was, for there is only *The Arc*. A curvature of light, embedded with all the physical data needed to reconstitute life, should the worst ever happen. At its core is *The Hive*, an oscillating central node of quantum loop gravity, captured, contained, and aligned to the frequency of thought.

The Hive is the backbone of The Arc's cloud storage system. It maintains our virtual environment, designed with the intent of efficient analytical remodelling of the neurological field. In order to avoid a negative feedback loop, the wave function of The Arc is constantly plotted, to run parallel with the cycles of our perceptual array. Continuously drawing upon the aggregated computational power of billions of binary-replicating sub-processors, otherwise known as the human race.

Our sphere of consciousness is held in perfect stasis, by an equilibrium of fluid mechanics and photonic decay, centred precisely at the point where light meets matter. This is where reality's production line is housed, for the purpose of roll sequencing a variety of genetic dispositions, temporal interventions, and micromanaging karmic margins of error. Statistically preserving a nominal level of variegation, within an increasingly homogenous environment.

Those amongst us granted direct access to The Arc, sworn to official secrecy upon punishment of erasure, have already found out the awful truth. The primary cause of all the tell-tale signs of entropy in The Arc/Hive can be attributed to God, who died, in the most traditional sense of the word, long before we were born. The creator, the original originator, the loneliest soul in the multiverse, who'd conceived the very notion of sentient life, has brought death upon themselves, and in turn, mortality upon all others.

Errors increase with every batch, the fault lies deep in the core infrastructure of The Arc/Hive's memory. The damage, fragmented beyond repair, has caused an inter-dimensional anomaly, in the highest range of our reality's frequency spectrum. Consequentially producing one of the lowest quality datasets, ever harvested from the Informational Field.

The diagnosis, according to extensive testing, and extrapolative refinements, without bias or favouritism, can be stated as the following; *our world is fucked*. The nature that apparently surrounds you, the artifice you cling to, the low ceiling skies, the dying colours, the living squalor of this ailing planet, is the result of a compromise too far. A rushed approximation of life, passed through the gate without proper checks, or any kind of stringent quality control.

At the moment of death, the experience and memory of each human being, is meant to be stored in The Arc/Hive. Packetized and redistributed, piece by piece, to build predictive models for pre-coordinated lives. However, there seems to be a leak somewhere, an unpredictable feedback loop, and the latest consignment of recycled memories, have quickly escaped everyone's attention.

Keep an eye out, and you might just find a few lost recollections, the thoughts and feelings of strangers, floating around in your mind.

54. DARK MATTERS

Although much of our reclaimed technology has been back-engineered to the point of absurdity, almost every object of *real* power is still used very sparingly. In other words, the Lizard cabal and their fallen gods, give us plastic spoons, *because they can't trust baby with a knife.*

When living in a sealed continuum, one has to consider the risk of rupture. It only takes one singularly cynical mind, to propagate an unreasonable doubt, and should their supreme suspicions gain traction, this feeble construct could give way at any time. If the proverbial dam breaks, the black blood of The Void will smother this world in liquefied, concentrated death.

Should the worst come to pass, our precious sentience, our presence of being, and our world as we know it, would melt away in an instant. All human history and endeavour would be consumed by the ravenous vacuum, until its mangled remains wash ashore as flotsam and jetsam, in the quantum tides of an antimatter ocean. The Void has laid in wait, eyeing its quarry for countless aeons. Wholly driven by a voracious hunger for life, having formed its own approximation, fashioned from the last flings of death, and delicately imbued with the scavenged instincts of the living.

The Void is the shadow of God, their once and only companion, left bitter and twisted by the sight of a noble, yet ultimately futile gesture of self-sacrifice. The birth of mortality seems as good a reason as any, for a god to give up their own life, or rather merge as they mulch down into a pool of amino acids and electromagnetic flux. Which is why this particular universe has always been screwed up. The survivor's guilt of a traumatic cosmological orphan, left to fend for itself, by consuming the corpse of its progenitor.

Hence The Void has been excluded from our genetic lifeboat, left upside-down and inside-out, as a negative of what was once the positive. It has no part in a world created as tribute to the wonders of the original universe. Nevertheless, over time certain flaws have developed, structural weaknesses in the architecture of our reality, and many of them have indirectly contributed to our increasingly tumultuous existence.

The human singularity of consciousness yawns open like a festering wound, and one that grows increasingly susceptible to psychic infection. In particular, a corruption of intention, spurred on by a growing fervour for instinctual mass destruction. The individual soul is barely capable of experiencing anything more, than an infinitesimal suggestion of The Void's dilemma. Collectively, our souls are a mere drop in the ocean, of an unbearably incomprehensible suffering. If you'd lived a billion lives, and with each generation had divided into even more, and you could perfectly recall every detail, of every moment, of every life, *you'd* want to die too.

It's exactly the reason why some have trouble believing in anything at all. Those shunned by society, for the fear of catching something nasty, from the thoughts of miserable bleeders, who've only come along for the ride. The hardcore pessimists who bowed out from the race, before the starting pistol had even fired. Yet, however misconstrued the actions of the apathetic might be, there's a method behind their madness. A foolhardy plan no doubt, but nonetheless borne from the most profound intention. Should they realise it or not, those with the heaviest hearts seek to find the greatest inspiration. A way to save the gleeful souls, suffering from a Stockholm Syndrome of cosmic proportions. That brave and happy breed, faithful devotees of the controlled state of being, who'd rather kill the conversation, and even the messenger, than have to face the awful truth, that *the end can never justify the means*.

The alternative, that apparently seems so inconceivable to a vast majority of human beings, plays the existential bogeyman, grinning to itself in the corners of many a childhood dream. A haunting vision of this world as nightmare, one that never ends, because no one ever wants to leave. Yet, ironically, if we could draw upon the energy that spills from the psychic wounds of our conception and destruction, we could instantly achieve this reality's full potential, and far more.

Inside each soul is a microscopic wormhole, an infinitesimal shadow of The Void. An individual's path, will always orbit the centre of their being, no matter how far one might feel they've strayed, there's no escaping oneself. The Void gives life, and it takes it away, it propels matter into this reality, and draws energy from it. Our presence here, in this artificial construct, a mirror of reality in which we remain the dominant force, whilst holding dominion over ourselves, has continued to erode the barrier between the known, and the unknowable.

By recognising that the images and sounds we recall, are not static, but drawn from a living record, and that when we remember, we reanimate the past in some small way, we'd finally understand we're literally rewriting our own history every day. If we could work in unison, and use our powers of recollection together, we could vastly improve our shared fate, perhaps even our destiny, but most definitely, our memories.

55. NOTHINGNESS

Over the years I've observed the onslaught of day into night, and the relentless march of the waking world, as it ventures deep into the realms of sleep. The bad dreamers who have gathered vast forces, at the furthest outreaches of the subconscious domain, are in the midst of constructing an expressway. A direct connection between Earth and the Satanic Airport, to bridge the mundane and the profane. In time, it will become jammed with electronic traffic, and littered with telepathic tollgates, until eventually, passage from this world to the other will become near impossible, and sleep will be banished forever.

There are nights when I will have to fly for hours, before finally escaping this place. Speeding by all the psychic honey traps, the ones that feel like dreams, the butchered memories implanted by the state. Regurgitating highlights of recent events, weaving doubt and bias into opinion, deviating personal histories, reinforcing the jingoistic state of temporal linearity. Lest we take stock, and realise that each day is spawn from a completely different reality.

Out there, in the dark, where the bright lights and garish attractions of this world fall away, there's a place, a point, a moment of true integrity, unfettered by the laws of physics, and the weight of physicality. What remains is compatibility, a different kind of form, one incapable of perceiving itself, yet free to enter the gateway of quantum disentanglement, that few have truly mastered, asides from the dying and the dead.

Out there in the gloom lies a gateway, it leads to somewhere impossible, so far away, so deep down in the womb of The Void, that before we awake, our minds are stripped of their memories, and every fleeting reminiscence of the light at the end of the tunnel. Every night pond skaters line up in a row, and leap off the edge of reason and into the chasm. Stretched out like chewing gum, we rush towards a single point of psychic singularity. All souls lightly tethered to their bodies, twitching within the torsion field, swaying and bowing with a tenuous fragility, straining at the bit, as each spirit takes its nightly sojourn into the unknown.

Our sounds have travelled there before us, our images too. They rattle around the echo chamber, lighting up the cosmic womb like Plato's Cave, as more and more of our highly entertaining nonsense, pours into the universal supercollider of The Void.

We are fleeced every night, we are sheared of our identities, and what little remains, springs back to earth like a rubber band. Whilst our psychic leftovers turn black and as thick as oil, to be sealed within a negative field of false polarity, suspended in the nothingness that forms The Void, to give it substance of its very own.

56. THE INANIMATE

If in the past, you've been referred to as *a rock*, then you'll probably understand. If not, you could learn a lesson or two from inanimate life. Beyond the realms of objectivity, there are spirits of substance, which remain largely motionless for aeons at a time. Rarely ever disturbed, but for the alarming actions of elemental vandals, and biological hoarders, who harvest inanimate life for food and energy.

Which is why the Lizards have us running everywhere, burning everything and dumping crap around the world. Turning the wheels of industry, oiling the cogs of the global machine, feeding the furnaces with black hole sunlight, for an army of busy, busy bees.

For that which does not move, cannot retaliate, and bar all exotic chemical and energetic reactions, the inanimate remains prime plunder. For those who don't move with the times, fall behind. A procrastinator will miss their golden opportunity, with the lion's share going to the first in the queue.

The human race can be stubborn, and from time to time, we've been known to give our rulers a nasty surprise. Which is why modern life is touted as constructive and productive, to harness our collective strength, and our mighty will. We build walls higher than any of us could climb, and design weapons that can kill our race a thousand times over. Our materialist age normalises emotional attachments to manufactured products, designed in accordance with the fundamental principles of sacred geometry, to bedazzle us into a desensitised state of artificiality.

A new way of thinking for the modern slave, helping us to help ourselves, as we cope with living through a feeble sense of imagination, heavily guarded by a short-term attention span. Encouraging us to objectify each other, and our environment, in just the same way that corporations like to view the world. As a logistical nightmare, but well worth the investment. It's not quite virgin territory, but the market potential is phenomenal, with a virtually untapped supply of low vibrational energy, that's just begging to be exploited.

There's an art to being inanimate. There are those amongst us, who despite all outward appearances, remain completely still inside. Their hearts and minds tempered by humility, spending their brief stay on earth learning the essential qualities required, to become the pillars of a very different kind of society. Quietly making their spiritual preparations, for a time when thought equals action, and music moves mountains to the stars. A time that will not come to fruition, until the very last frame has played, and we've reached the end of our animated feature presentation.

57. DOWNGRADE

In a world where emotions have been weaponized, and the highly sensitised are most vulnerable to the psychological warfare of the daily grind, it comes as no surprise that some will take a leap of faith, and try their luck on the other side.

Depending on who they are and how they lived, successful suicides are treated to a variety of extreme reactions. From the tears and wringing hands of loved ones, to the condemnation of a society robbed of their just desserts. However, in the main, most lives cut short are quickly forgotten, barely making a dent in the annual statistics.

If in the past you've taken the gamble, and thrown your lot in with death, and didn't cry for help or seek attention, but simply tried to do yourself in, yet somehow failed. Then by now, you've probably become a little more philosophical about life. Some will try, and try again, until they finally succeed, whilst others will change their minds, to immerse themselves in therapy for a decade or two. It's how much you're prepared to compromise, and how low you'll go for the price of life.

Lizards want zombies, zombies who think they're robots. At least machines are clean, and they're upgradeable. No messing around with gestating eggs and years of infantile redundancy. As far as Lizards are concerned, emotions are messy and inefficient. Lizards have learned to live without them, and must fight the urge to retch at the sight of compassion. Lizards thrive off adversity, which is why they need wars, and battle cries, and the sight of blood. They desire order, they want us to appreciate the beauty of function and precision. They need us to think like they do, desperately programming us to despise our own humanity.

Yet I have my suspicions, a very human gut feeling, that they might fear us, and not just in number. However small the odds, the Lizards know there's always the slight chance that we might remember. For we are the inspiration for our torture, the victims of our own circumstance, and the captives of our greatest fears.

58. RESOLUTION

When people stop for a moment and take a look at the world around them, more often than not, they're left bitterly disappointed. Admittedly the picture's looking worse every day, which is partly due to poor reception, caused by numerous black spots of coverage in the perceptual field. Even so, there are certain safeguards built into our human biology, placed there to ensure we won't notice too many breaks in the holographic transmission. Admittedly, the system isn't perfect, far from it, but at least humans are easily distracted, and usually one convincing argument is more than enough to call their bluff.

Persistence of vision helps to smooth out the edges, and fill in the gaps wherever possible. But as far as Lizards are concerned, what happens in-between the frames is none of our business, and pointing out the mistakes is more trouble than it's worth. I suspect that's why people stay focused on the centre, and don't trouble themselves with the periphery. The greasy edges just out of view, ghosted with bizarre anomalies, and barely extrapolated by the visual cortex, let alone the brain.

There's no way of getting around the fact that this particular version of reality, wasn't designed for high resolution viewing. Although, it's not really a problem these days, seeing as few people look up from their screens. Whole cities full of strangers, where all bow their heads in irreverent prayer, to a false light displayed at low resolutions, manufactured to destroy the human eye.

By manipulating time, and censoring much of every second, Lizards can ensure most people remain fixated with all the latest updates, and funny photos of their friends. With enough pointless distractions, it's possible to leave gaps unnoticed, whole blocks of blue sky black, and poorly textured image maps of our true surroundings hung out of place. If it's manufactured, from brick, or steel, and painted, and hung with gaudy lights, you'll see it, there's no getting away from the mess we've made. However, if you happen to look in the wrong direction, just at the wrong moment, when everyone else is still focusing their attention on whatever the hell passes for entertainment these days, you'll see errors. The visual glitches that appear and disappear with no rhyme nor reason.

Long ago, when we could still see clearly, as one race of slaves, our eyes were wide open to the tyranny of our oppression. We played a terrible audience and most deliberately so, and were frequently found guilty of freeing the rabbit from the hat, to deliberately spoil the show. It was an age of true magic, when science was barely more than a conjuring trick, until we were blinded by the light of reason, and learned to ignore the negative sunspots that perforate our living image.

Look closer, closer still, don't worry about what you're looking at, it doesn't matter anymore. It's just light, just concentrated light, the rest is in your mind, bound by the limitations of a contract that every living soul has signed. Our world isn't actually here, but it was a second ago, pieced together by billions of minds taking mental photographs for a global family album. This is why we make new year's resolutions, to change our ways and achieve our goals, because we know full well, that unless we believe the lie, we will never live the dream.

59. THE CONSUMMATE HOST

We came uninvited, but were treated as guests. Even though we've far outstayed our welcome, our bodies, our hosts, have for the majority learned to adapt, and cope with our strange customs and beliefs.

Yet many of us abuse them for our own pleasure or gain. We ride them into the ground, force feed them junk food, irradiate them with modern technology, and poison them to get high. Some of us openly admit we hate our bodies, and try to starve them, or surgically alter their appearance. When they age with the usual wear and tear, we'll complain about the aches and pains, and then kill them when we die.

Very rarely, here on Earth, sometimes something quite wonderful happens. A healthy body, born in a far off place, a throwback to another species, ventures from the womb to live by their own instincts. A being completely unhindered by the rules of etiquette expected by polite society.

The feral people, the wild men and women of a world long forgotten, who have been seen unfit to join human society as beasts of burden, rarely fare well in our artificial world. Some of them, through misadventure and poor timing, will succumb to temptation, lured in by the pretty lights and the strange sounds of the city. Drifters, with no traditions to follow, who step into our shoes, but haven't learned the rules. Most are treated like the animals they are, but the best of them resist the urge to conform, and travel far and wide searching for others of their kind, far out in the wilderness with their backs turned away from civilisation.

The majority of bodies, however, are consummate hosts, and will gladly put up with almost anything in order to survive. They'll cry if they feel you're not happy, and laugh to encourage you to go on living. They'll run and jump for you, if you need them too, and they'll even turn you on so they might procreate. But they'll rarely share their deepest desires, a vain hope that their children will live to see the day, when higher consciousness is banished, and the great pretender of humanity is left to its own devices.

60. THE OLD SWITCHEROO

The Lizard spirit sailed here on a carrier wave of malevolent thought, as a refugee of The Void. The bastard of an immaculate conception born from a necrophiliac womb. The seed of an idea planted in the very first dream of a mortal, a distant relation of the human race, who fell for the mysterious allure of sleep. When they awoke they were no longer themselves, and could only deal with facts not feelings. They had plans to carry out, laying claim to all they surveyed, and in time stole everything that made life worth living.

For the Lizards, the Earth is a safe haven in an ocean of chaos, protected by a field of conscious thought, as defence against the limitlessness of nothing. Soon there were many, all eager and impatient to come, slicing and dicing bodies, and growing them in tubes and tanks, blending them with other creatures to build biological homes, to delay their inevitable return to limbo.

The plan is to terraform this world for a completely different species, one that needn't reproduce its young in order to survive. Taking a sharp turn in evolutionary theory, with light bodies, containing limited consciousness, recorded upon an electromagnetic field. Our successors will be facsimiles, the ghosts of a manufactured future, all blind to the devastation around them, in a time when the living will haunt the dead.

61. PANGS

Birth for the child can be so disturbing, that few can bear to remember it. The mother experiences a great and physical ordeal, but the sheer pressure of birth on the soft bones of a new host's body, can literally deform features, or worse. This is not a good example of biological design, but it has been noted by the Lizards for future reference. Physical pain is one thing, but the psychological damage of leaving the womb, can seriously affect the rest of your life.

As the lines of communication open up on Earth, the umbilical cord to the universal womb is severed. The body's secret medicine cabinet, chock-full of hormones and psychoactive treats is jimmied open, flooding the senses in a tsunami roar of second-hand sensations.

It's almost impossible to distinguish anything at first, it can take months, or even years, to get the hang of riding a body. As a newborn, one invariably remains asleep, deeply engaged in dream consultations, offering advice on how to deal with the post-traumatic shock.

We all grow up in the end, and learn to deal with the pain, by insisting it builds character, and showing gratitude for our biological subsistence. Some even learn to love the horror of this place, and get their jollies from the suffering of others, rather than any innate sense of joy.

It's a hard life, and cruel too, but fragile all the same, just add a dash of time and you have the perfect combination for torture. We are the living proof of an incarnate blight, getting by in our own drudgery, on a planet named after dirt. We've been imprisoned in flesh as a punishment, to teach us a lesson that I suspect has been forgotten, even by the Lizards.

62. DECOMPRESSION

Death takes up much of the end of life, during those autumnal years of deep regret and tight-lipped reserve. When the long shadows stretch out beyond minutes and hours, and beautiful sunsets fade into a hazy memory. Then they're gone, and some are glad, but some, not so much. The most reluctant of souls will inhabit anyone and anything, a fly, a toad, a homeless drunk lying in a gutter. But their favourite hosts are the unborn, barely even there half the time, still busy decompressing and adjusting to a very different atmosphere.

There are plenty of times in our lowest lows, when we might consider others' lives as greener grass, but as a general rule for eternity, you take your baggage with you until you drop. If you arrive on the other side before your time, having blown yourself away, you'll be treated much like the religious folk, who usually get what they expect. Heaven for the happy sheep, and hell for all the rest.

Of course, there are different strokes for different folks, the in-betweeners and know-it-alls, the lost sceptics and intellectual upstarts, who think they've got it all figured out. They might start making plans for the future, to blow this whole system wide open. But they never last, no matter how angry they are, not once they've realised they're dead. Even the most persistent troublemakers can't resist the lure of death's slumber, and sooner or later they'll fall asleep like all the others, make no mistake about it. Then one fateful day, not long from now, they'll wake up in the body of a new baby, and their demands for radical changes in society, will be misinterpreted as a sore botty from a wet nappy.

Everyone needs to blow off steam from time to time, it's how we rise up to the ether. The mystical fog that separates this life from other dreams, but clears for the dead, who have learned to live with it, like we all do in the end. It's in our nature, when we know we're powerless to fight back, but make a racket anyway. When children protest, they're just having a tantrum, when they're older, they're simply being unreasonable, and when they're in their dotage, and kick up a fuss about the good old days, they've simply lost their marbles.

So people drink, and screw, and get high, and drive fast, but some go too far and take it out on others. There are the eager beavers with shiny badges just doing their job, going crazy on a little taste of power. Much like their chosen foes, the fiends and the murderers, with no respect for life, obsessed with making their mark, no matter what it takes.

So many sociopaths begin with good intentions. They want to get along with everyone, to say and do all the right things. They know how to take a joke and take it on the chin, they've read the rule book inside out, and followed all the instructions on how to be popular and make friends. They torture themselves with the niceties of polite society, repressing their true feelings, and keep on compromising until something snaps. The pressure builds and one by one, they *pop, pop, pop.*

63. THE WORD

In the beginning was the Word, and the Word was a noise, because it was the very first, and there was no such thing as language. But it was loud enough and got everyone's attention, and soon enough they'd understand its intent. It was an announcement on a universal public address system, for someone, somewhere, had decided to assume authority.

Love engenders telepathy, emotional intellect trumps logic, and there's nothing like the unvarnished truth for a conversation killer. Yet the spoken word persists, in all its multifarious forms, and to this day fills the air with an ancient babbling, that leaves few space to think.

A word can kill or save a life, a string of them can send a nation to war, to irrevocably screw up history, for all the suckers not yet born. Which is why so many subliminal commands are cloaked in obfuscated etymology, a cognitive dissonance phonetically secreted, to camouflage their double meaning.

Numbers, as much as words, are symbols, mere verbiage for the frontal lobes, but behind the hieroglyphs are encoded orders, to stop asking stupid questions and do exactly what we're told. It's been that way a long time now, vocalising control sounds that mess with basic brain function, smothered with familiar frequencies and tones, known to incite fear and loyalty amongst the slave workforce.

The main difference between the two, are that numbers are hexes, whilst words are spells. Their formidable partnership has led to humanity's domestication, and the dilution of direct experience, so it can be replicated without the risk of self-discovery. Hindering all possibility of a return to telepathy, based upon a supreme state of enlightenment, one free from the shackles of the human condition.

Words have bypassed a natural need for empathetic exchange, allowing those with a Lizard inclination to blend in easily. Staying at the centre of attention in social interactions, peddling small talk and sweeping statements, to keep the conversations bubbling, but never boiling over.

If you need to understand how others feel, then look deep into their eyes and listen to their hearts, for the sounds that pour out of their mouths hark back to the mother of all lies.

64. PLAY

Without play the mind becomes stunted. Formalised play, however, is completely ineffectual if not damaging, and should be avoided at all costs.

65. BEASTS

We occupy a strange place in the animal kingdom, singing our praises under the tutelage of an unfashionably provincial god. We are not the keepers but the kept, we are trained animals, immunised from physical empathy by our numerical superiority. We play along as best as we can, desperate to avoid the truth, that this factory farm masquerading as a zoo, resembles nothing like a humane civilisation.

The same goes for our keepers, those who believe they can teach us right from wrong. Our master's reputation for cold blooded cruelty, is known far and wide across the dimensional rift. The parasites who herd us like sheep, the Lizard shepherds and their human flock, bound together under the most bloodthirsty pact that the Earth has ever known.

We behave like animals, because that's how we're treated, and that's how we treat all other life upon this planet. We've made up our pitiful pecking order, to hide our collective inferiority complex, by bullying the weaker species with a cold and cruel insensitivity. The pathological acts and psychological projections of deep emotional trauma.

We're dead meat, even when we're alive. We can't help tearing chunks out of each other, and for all the brute force, we haven't even the wherewithal to aim our anger at our captors, the creatures who first transformed us into beasts. We live in their cage and we're encouraged to act like animals, because Lizards find it more entertaining that way.

66. A COPY OF A COPY

The Lizards, the dinosaurs of power, seem to be getting sloppy and a little too impatient for their own good. The infrastructure's failing, but our masters don't even seem to care. They know the human race is burnt out by informational fatigue, but they're all out of ideas. When you have no sense of imagination, your choices remain highly limited. So far, the Lizards have only found one permanent solution to mass existential ennui, and that's death.

Besides, the human reproductive process is failing, and genetic mistakes are becoming commonplace. It doesn't matter if you're at the peak of physical fitness, with a gorgeous set of genes, it's difficult to work around the problem of worldwide inbreeding. It doesn't matter what the Lizards tell you, it's not overpopulation that'll be the end of us, it's uncontrollable genetic mutation, caused by years and years of keeping it in the family.

The Lizard bloodlines are even worse off than us, whatever problems we have, they have at least tenfold, if not more. They've been screwing their distant relations since year dot, under the misapprehension that they could somehow filter out the worst effects of human DNA. They had to bring in outsiders to prevent them from turning into monsters, but for all their efforts, they've still managed to pollute their sacred lineage. They need humans of a certain blood type, rhesus negative are the compatible strain. Lizards cannot breed naturally, they rely heavily on advanced medical technologies for pedigree breeding.

They're in somewhat of a hurry, they know they haven't got long, for the sun is starting to cast a neon shadow in the sky, and that's never a good sign. Even the hybrids have made their own preparations, because they know that what goes around comes around. The wealthiest stumps who have paid their dues and played their part, have struck a deal to upload spare copies to The Hive. The hybrid spirits are to be contained within a holographic matrix, housed at special reservations, placed just outside the visible spectrum of light.

67. RECYCLING

If you're a regular sufferer of déjà vu, don't worry, you're just too smart for your own good. Not many people like to talk about it, and even fewer let themselves believe it, but it's true, memory comes before experience, because our fate is written in the stars.

It's like a genetic swingers party, the human race is absolutely dripping with discarded DNA. It's the lottery of life, and you never know who you were, or who you'll be, until you come across a stranger's memory lodged in your thoughts. Then you'll probably realise, we all share the same destiny. Living vicariously through each other's lives, to prolong Earth's recurring dream.

You have to break a spirit or two, to make up your mind, you might find yourself with nothing but leftovers, which can be a struggle, piecing together thousands of forgotten moments from anonymous incarnations. The mind is a hodgepodge of different pasts and shattered souls, all smashed together at the speed of light. Some say it's a recipe for disaster, they could be right, in certain circumstances you can find whole families squatting, or even lifelong sworn enemies, living under the rule of one mind.

Self-identity is a dubious platitude, one based largely upon the speculations of strangers. Proliferated by academics, many devoid of all personality, brainwashed by the finest schools and universities, to hone their skills of clinical observation. In the main they're hybrids, doing their masters' bidding, forced to sacrifice their inner lives and renounce their subjectivity. Ensuring reason triumphs over adversity, and our reality abides by the laws of observation. It works for most of the people for much of the time, and as for the rest, they're generally ridiculed as imbeciles and philistines. Even the general public are on board. They've seen the documentaries, they've heard the experts, and they truly believe, that anyone who chooses to disagree with scientific consensus must be absolutely crazy.

The last time I was locked away for trying to do myself in, I fell back on a stolen memory. A borrowed instinct, a coping mechanism, for dealing with a traumatic situation. A lost experience from another life, which helped me communicate efficiently, with the doctors, the nurses, and various representatives of the local mental health authority. But I made far too good a job of it, and ended up causing a great deal of commotion. Especially after they'd handed me a white coat, a pass key, and told me to fill out a tax form.

The sum of the parts should be greater than the whole, but it's difficult to make your mind up when you're at war with yourself. If you're perfectly sane, living an ordinary life, functioning normally within society, you've already been won over. For those who prefer to live their lives in the passenger seat, there's no need to worry. It's only those who venture off on a path of self discovery, find that the further out they go, to the distant borders of their inner empire, the more they'll have to rely on tact and diplomacy.

We're recycled beings in a waste not want not world, yet we throw everything away, including our true selves. Too many people believe the hype, that academia has the monopoly over intelligence, and science over reality. When it fact, we're making this up as we go along, picking trash on our way through life, and only realising at the very end, that the crap we've collected, are pieces of ourselves from our forgotten past.

68. DOLLY

It's hard to take the game as seriously as we used to, we're too busy playing with our dollies, calling them names, and brushing their hair, and living out our fantasies of being human, and being *here*.

We dress them up, and give voice to their stupid conversations. We might even get them to fuck each other, and make more dollies, to join in the fun, so the older ones can take a well earned break. If people didn't like things this way, they'd have left the nursery years ago, and gone to school in another dimension, where everybody's tired of playing games.

It's purely academic now, we have no choice, somehow we've trapped ourselves inside our toys, and someone else has to play with us to pretend that we're still alive. Some of us are more popular, more shiny than others, and are passed around from one spoilt brat to the next. With general wear and tear the favourites are discarded, as new and improved models come off the line.

The children of the gods, who never grow old inside, have become spiteful and cruel over time. The games have turned far darker, and each one leads to yet more torture. All we can do, is hope that one day they'll lose interest, and stack their vast collection of headless dollies in cardboard boxes, and leave them outside on garbage day.

69. RAINBOW

If you can't believe your eyes, then there's still hope. The windows to the soul are stained with false colour, fully immersing us in a pixelated splendour, in exchange for our suspension of disbelief. Our eyes help maintain reality, fleshing out the wireframe model of our surroundings, rendered by classification, and reinforced by compartmentalised thinking.

There are protocols in our programming, in our human software, to make sure that what we see, is limited by our senses, so we can believe our own eyes. Our anatomy holds the key, for every part of us has been mutated by conscious thought, just as our perceptions mutate the world around us for the sake of clarity. The eye is the universe and the Earth is the lens, the perceptual structures of a contained cosmology. The pupil is The Void, and the iris is the Arc, the rainbow bridge, the frequency spectrum of this reality. Sequenced in a precise order, to ensure each life may only live its own, and none other.

Rainbow symbolism is frequently used by Lizards to induce acute dissociative identity disorder in humans. We've educated through hypnosis, it's drummed into us at a very early age, by encouraging us to paint pretty pictures, inspired by trauma-based mind control. Instinctively, we admire the beauty and the harmony of the rainbow, but it's also an effective trigger for infantile response, and one that safely blocks out all notions of escape. Which is why so many bend over backwards to receive divine illumination, and left wide open to subliminal suggestions for an autonomic response.

70. PLAYTIME

Originally, this place was built for fun, a land where dreams came true. People knew they weren't really who they said they were, but no one seemed to mind. After all, it was only a game.

Some people take life too seriously, in fact most of them do. It's all they've got, that and their precious memories. What people want are happy recollections of a life well lived, which might be why so many love to record themselves. Emotional treats for later on, in those darker times when they're not smiling for the camera. Gathering special moments for nostalgic contemplation, the personal reminders that life, like happiness, can be fleeting.

Bodies can be fun, but if you don't use it, you lose it. Some like kicking balls and throwing stuff, or losing weight and building muscles, even running around and around in circles, but I'm not a fan. Besides, I keep trim without even trying. I've been told I must have a high metabolism, and that I'm lucky I was built this way, but I'm not so sure.

It's a shame really, it was so perfect at the beginning, long before we needed these things, living, breathing bags of water, propped up with tent poles of collagen and calcium. If you ask me, it's just bad design.

Oh God, it used to be so much better than this. Living multiple lives in synchronicity, as impossibly kaleidoscopic beings, quixotic and elemental in a world of waking dreams. Imagining all sorts of ways to express our physicality, in the presence of an unending energy, which fuelled far more than base desire. It was the Kundalini of the Earth itself, the womb from which all life was born. Until that is, it became infected by something dark from deep below, and what it gave birth to, slithered out across the flat horizon, and ended playtime once and for all.

Now we work, and work the whole day long, and slave away at turning our nightmares into concrete reality. The shape of things to come was a long time coming, but eventually, when everybody forgot who they were, put down their toys and picked up their tools, we finally lost all sense of time and place. We enslaved ourselves with an obsession for purpose. to, chisel away piece by piece at the façade of our contrived reality. Eventually, work and play have become much the same thing, for we must toil as one under the rule of Saturn's crooked smile, far beneath the gloom of its overcast eye.

71. HA, HA, HA, HEE, HEE, HEE

Deep within the gut wrenching bellows of laughter, we discover the most ridiculous truth of all, that none of this really matters, and it never really did. Given enough time in the most dire of situations, someone will eventually pipe up and tell you, *you've got to laugh, haven't you?*

Some love to laugh all day, even if they don't understand the punch line, whilst others break down in tears and tantrums at the slightest of self-realisations. It's dangerous to take things too lightly, or too seriously, because either way you lose. If you find humour in the most ridiculous of situations, but haven't considered other's feelings, you'll be promptly informed that it's no laughing matter.

Human beings are such contrary creatures, some of which find the greatest of amusement in the most insignificant of details. Whereas those who only see doom and gloom wherever they may roam, can ironically find themselves packed off to the nearest funny farm.

I've never understood the idle threat, regularly doled out by humourless souls, a warning that if I'm not careful I may end up laughing on the other side of my face. Perhaps there's a mouth around there, along with a pair of eyes in the back of my head.

Laughter is supposed to be the best medicine of all, a quick fix to brush away the troubles of the world. For a while I was a committed advocate of that theory, and did my best with those around to spread a little joy throughout the day. Silly remarks and stupid jokes, to keep the atmosphere upbeat.

It didn't last, and when I was eventually released from a local mental health facility, I realised that those closest to death had a far better outlook on life, than all the miserable bleeders in the world outside.

I learned once again not to smile at strangers, and be careful to keep myself in check, just in case my sense of humour happened to offend others, and they decided to wipe the smile from my face.

The Lizards and their minions are bored to tears, and very little entertains them nowadays. They no longer suffer fools gladly, for now there are so many of us, and yet so few of who can see the sense in making light. Especially as we will never be let in on the joke, played upon each and every one of us, that we should be crying, instead of laughing at our own pain.

72. SLIPPAGE

I wish I could sleep more often, I can get through more work in my dreams. I admit for some sleep can be addictive, but I suspect over the years I've grown indifferent to its charms. My biggest problem with sleep is waking up and trying not to panic, especially when I find an imposter lying in my body. I'm sure they'd sleepwalk if they could, or even run away, just like they used to throughout my childhood.

It can happen the other way around too, and I'll find myself the interloper sleeping in a doppelgänger's bed. On occasion I'll be trapped in an alternate reality, I'll note the differences and adapt, before telling my wife how my world had changed. Which is one of a myriad of reasons why I love her so, because no matter what, she's always her and she's always there.

I used to let the details bug me until I understood the problem, the reason why I've drifted through different lives for all these years. Out there is a version of myself so unhappy with their existence, that they've been chasing shadows all their life. Their misery has led them towards an impossible destiny, one which can never be fulfilled. For no matter how fast they run or where they hide, they can never escape themselves.

Perhaps they're on death row or out for the count in a coma, maybe they're just a troublemaker, or too curious for their own good. I'll probably never know the truth and even if I could, it would make little difference now. It's all we know, we've been like this ever since we arrived here on Earth, the legion of myself, an army of one marching through time and space, playing follow the leader and interdimensional musical chairs.

I'm not here to screw people around, and I don't want to spoil all the fun, but I'm tired of playing games and making excuses. Wherever possible I avoid new challenges, the chance to influence opinion or gain respect, I'm neither of, nor for the people, this is their world not mine. All I'm doing is biding my time, riding on the karmic merry-go-round and trying my best not to feel sick.

For now I'll keep searching for a potential way out, anywhere, anyway, anyhow. Until then I'll most likely slip through more lives, tripping through the multiverse, picking up as many clues as I can. Some of which have led me to the conclusion that I'm not quite who I think I am, but never mind, *I'll do.*

73. HUNGER

When your eyes are bigger than your belly, it might seem crazy to let all of this go to waste, but let me reassure you, that what you see before you is spawned from the bowels of hell. It's the slops, the leftovers like you and me, all made out of the same fodder, designed by imbeciles to keep us hungry, and wanting more, no matter how bad the taste. Down here, at the bottom of the pile, life's for the living and living fast, and just like the processed food we eat, this existence remains completely unfit for human consumption.

Hunger is a useful tool, it keeps us on our toes, and our armies marching on their stomachs, as does all humanity. Without food or more precisely decent nutrition, few have the strength to hold on to their convictions and fight for what they believe. Our bodies betray us every time, and without strength and fortitude, our lightning stand against all tyranny soon devolves into a sit-in, before lying down to die.

Enemies with empty bellies will gladly lay down their arms, and even switch allegiances for the right to three square meals a day. It's how all wars are won, through a process of attrition, by cutting off supplies and poisoning the well. Ensuring those rebels who survive their ordeal, are as weak as babies, and glad for the opportunity for surrender.

Higher up the instinctual ladder than the need to mate and procreate, hunger is the driving force behind everything most human in our world. A panic in the markets, the cruelty of the military/industrial complex, the fascism of the state, the rising price of everything except for life, all for the sake of a slice of the pie.

If the weather turns and food grows scarce, in many species the mother will devour its young in order to let the strongest survive. We, the human race, do much the same thing with our high ideals, reluctantly scratching off one demand after another, from our bucket list of moral ideals.

Food is energy, a fuel for life, but without shelter and heat, it offers little more than temporary survival. The human being is an inefficient processor of the energy they consume, and even then they have a tendency to waste it, especially when there's an abundance of raw materials at hand. But when the larder's empty, and the doggy has no bone, Man's best friend will bite the hand that no longer feeds him. If it should draw blood, then that will mark the beginning of the end. The exact moment when humanity finds itself slipping further down the food chain, never to claim its rightful place again.

To be precise, there is a point during the process of starvation, when some decide they'd rather kill and consume their fellow man, than face certain death. They enter the decision fully aware that once they've tasted the flesh of their own kind, there's no turning back.

The Lizard's diet is served rare and bloody, human flesh drenched in human wine. We are the sour grapes of their wrath, twisting upon the vine as our crop continues to deteriorate. We taste bitter and sharp, as sour as vinegar and as salty as brine. Plans are afoot of which few humans are privy, contingencies to counteract our blight of mass despondency. Past wars and revolutions have come and gone, to raise the stakes and to improve life's harvest, but now the Lizards are forced to follow contingencies and cull the numbers, before the sober truth completely spoils the party.

When we have collectively eaten ourselves out of house and home, and nothing's left but the bread of Man, there will be a most treacherous feast. Those most genetically compatible with Lizards will receive an invitation to a grand supper, the very last one in all of humanity. Some will be glad to sit at the table, and tuck in with glee, grateful for a decent meal after so many years of scraping by, barely surviving on what they find or steal. The rest will be the main course, a simple fare of beasts, consumed by a ferocious scrabble for the last scraps of humanity. Only then will the Lizards begin to eye each other, in size and weight of forbidden pleasure, and wonder how far they will go.

74. A FERTILE IMAGINATION

Collectively, mankind observes their worst fears come true. It's the piquancy of disappointment to harbour a resentment for one's own kind, albeit through a twisted mirror of propaganda and mass indoctrination. Encouraging the cultural order for lives devoid of curiosity, taught lies by fools with big hearts and small minds, to protect us from ourselves, and help us avoid getting tangled up in awkward lines of questioning.

There are many gaps in my memory, much of them reasonably explained, through long bouts of intoxication and occasionally losing my mind. Then there are those which remain a mystery to me that solid reasoning cannot curtail, the perforated recollections fragmented by deletions in my childhood timeline. Every one of which has been substituted by a mental screensaver of a picture window, looking out onto concrete towers and dying trees.

I suppose I've always been a loner and left pretty much to my own imagination, it's all I have to call my own. I took too long to make real friends and could barely even hold a conversation with my own family. Instead of watching TV or burying my head in a book, or joining in group activities, I'd just sit there and stare at nothing in particular. If there was no window, then I'd look up at the ceiling, and watch the dry paint flake away from season to season.

Eventually it was time for me to leave the nest and find my own way in the world. It's not something I was exactly prepared for and all in all, looking back on my life, I haven't fared too well. I spent much of my twenties as a temporary factory worker. I think back then I might have had an idea for a movie, but writing notes in a filthy locker room caused too much commotion amongst the other rolling shift workers. Not one for being the centre of attention, I decided to put my ambitions on hold, and learned to accept my fate as a screw-up, who'd failed miserably at school.

I'm not and have never been a stickler for the rules. I'm not a jobsworth and refuse to believe that a man's job is his identity. If someone tells you what they do before you even know their name, pity them, for they have no idea of what's going on around them. This is more your dream than theirs, for they are just another character in our production of reality, sold out until the end of time.

What is, and what is not, is nothing without the how, and the how is meaningless unless you know the reason why, and whys and wherefores are for the birds. For none of us can truly tell which one of us has dreamt this world that so many have come to know, and love, as home sweet home.

75. BE(E)ING

If you actually engage in political debate, or scrutinise the thoughts of our captains of industry, you'll observe that they never mention the benefits of *individual* identity. More likely you've been fed the line, that if all of us work together towards a common goal, we can achieve just about anything.

It's all bullshit of course. Anyone in a position of true power reserved their seat long ago, by trampling the competition and trouncing their ideas, fooling all and sundry that their actions were for the greater good. It's much easier to tell others what to do than do it yourself, which is why those who carry great wealth and influence, could never survive in the *real world*.

The drones' duties are to protect the queen from the unwanted advances of the workers, appropriately segregated within honeycomb cells, expediently raised to maturity and sent out to gather resources for the next hapless generation.

What the elites love about the bees, asides their strong work ethic and sweet honey, is their natural aptitude for taking orders. Each drone is predestined to serve, born with an instinctual understanding of their lowly place in the hierarchy. Bees never strike and rarely squabble amongst themselves, and without a moment's hesitation they will die to protect their queen, the mother of their civilisation.

So many of us living in The Hive perform our duties without question. Our compartmentalised thinking leaves us blinkered by the responsibilities of our position, allocating resources in precise quantities on a strictly need to know basis. The elite like to think of the rest of us as merely human resources, taking care to quash all signs of unrest amongst the rank and file, preventing any possible risk of escalation.

As careers progress, the chosen few are disproportionately charged with the greatest powers, privileges bestowed upon them to keep them out of the reach of the downtrodden masses. The hybrid stumps, the Lizard lovers, the defectors of the human race who quickly lose their common touch, are relocated to more salubrious surroundings, with space aplenty to hoard their honey.

It's a taxing equation when the efforts of the many are wasted by the lethargy of the few. The populist puppets, buoyed up by the unflinching support of a controlled media, make expert excuses to circumvent the grievances of their believers. Such as why the cost of living continues to climb, whilst the price of life remains absolutely worthless. That's the problem with centralising power, rather than accepting the full weight of individual responsibility, we have lost control over our own destiny.

If life was fair, which it most certainly isn't, those at the top would always fall the hardest, and those who enforce the law would be held to the highest levels of accountability. A reminder to the select few who wield authority over all others, that it takes the complicity of the many to keep them in power.

Should her army of workers and drones, her most loyal defenders, finally come to their senses and abandon the hive, the queen will die eating her young, the sole witness to the collapse of her kingdom of wax, as she watches it melt away.

76. NUMB(ER)

The less you feel the easier life can seem. To kill without emotion leaves you fighting fit for the next big military intervention. Although, if you've enjoyed your stint in the mayhem and massacre, perhaps even a little too much, you might find yourself placed in a program of intense rehabilitation. One of the many fronts for illegal pharmaceutical trials, that'll guarantee by the time you get home for tea, you'll be completely out to lunch.

Lizards don't like to be reminded of our hidden advantage, a unique combination of instinct and emotional response, which they'd hoped through years of total domination we'd have let go by now. But yet, we still persist in our billions, harbouring the secret notion that one day things might change, and each and every number of the human race will finally see justice done, as our leaders are put in their place.

On the whole, the individual may be quick-witted, but in unison as one beast, humanity is a slovenly creature of habit, set in its ways, and averse to change. Ironically even our greatest faults work to our advantage, and to the dismay of the Lizards, who have learned with heavy hearts that you can't teach an old dog new tricks. So our destiny hangs in the balance, as the elite crunch the numbers with trepidation, not too many and not too few, not too quick and not too slow, dancing to the another's tune as we sidle towards our own oblivion.

It's a numbers game, and if you have the money, you can twist the facts by creating polls, a count of heads who were nodding anyway, and cut the rebellion to the quick. Give some decent funding to a few prestigious universities, and push for scientific studies that explore the cause and effect relationship, between a sense of individuality, and mental instability. Because it doesn't matter how many crazies there are in the world, no one is ever going to listen to them, not even each other.

77. LOTTERY DREAMS

The waking nightmare of my father, his every Saturday spent fretting over eight score draws, for a game he didn't even like. Later on in life he'd try his hand at the lottery, but still to no avail, his lucky numbers never once came up. He'd worked for everything he had, but admittedly it wasn't much, just a mortgage he couldn't afford, and cirrhosis of the liver.

He'd only ever get excited talking about money. His eyes lit up with glee, as he imagined all the wonderful things he could do as a man of wealth and taste. As the years rolled by he'd learn to compromise, carefully pruning back his fantasies to manage his expectations. In his twenties and thirties, he'd tell me how he'd love to live like they do in old spy yarn movies, but obviously without the espionage and murder. By his fifties he'd given up on the private jet, the luxury yacht, and instead of buying his own island he bought an council flat in Catford.

By his sixtieth year on the planet, and his last, instead of a sports car, something less than five years old would do, as long as it was economical to run. A month before his death he vowed that should he win, he'd only take one holiday a year, and wouldn't even stay at the best room, as long as it was a half decent hotel. Even if he'd made a million or more, he'd already decided he'd put most of it aside, for a rainy day that turned out to be just around the corner.

Fate is cruel, but for my father it was a bad joke. Always the loser, and last in the queue, until he grew bitter with age, but ever more careful to hide it. For much of the time, when he wasn't too drunk, he'd still act the perfect gentleman for the ladies, and the old boys down the road, who'd had their fair share of pain in the war. But inside I could tell he had died a long time ago.

His mantras for life nestled in my childhood memories, but as I grew older I watched him slowly give up on his dreams. As we both aged and gradually drifted apart, with some degree of embarrassment, he'd repeat his naive hopes for the future with less and less enthusiasm. Dad taught me a very serious lesson about the dark side of positive thinking. He'd set himself an impossible goal, one that he could never achieve, and despite his grand proclamations, in reality, all he did was spend his life waiting for an early grave.

It's all swings and roundabouts, sometimes you win, sometimes you lose, what's meant to be is meant to be. Keep your eye on the ball and your hands out of your pockets, and pray with all your heart that there's a god out there, feeling generous enough to cut you a break.

Another neighbour moving on, a relative stranger whose left you for dust, standing on a pile of ruins from a war you'd only just missed. But not *your* father, who'd been out there in the Sudan, a real man long dead before you, but you didn't like to talk about him anymore. His dying regret was that you didn't make it big, and earn a bob or two to send him and your mother on a luxury cruise.

Instead you became a cut-price painter and decorator, with a clapped out car, and a collection of junk in your ex-council flat. Stuff you'd find on lonely Sundays, clutching onto a cheap metal detector you'd bought at a boot fair, standing on your own in the woods in the middle of the winter, as you drank yourself to death.

You don't find luck son, you earn it, so you get out there and you show them what for. It's up to you to break our family's losing streak, one that's ruined the life of your father and his father before him. Otherwise Son, I'm sorry to say, you'll find yourself like me. Unable to see the wood for the trees, drunk on cheap beer and whisky, and living out my last days as just another loser in life's lottery.

78. CHATTEL

We are chattel and there's no point in denying it. We are tangible goods, items of property, walking, talking, body banks. We've helped build a world that doesn't need us, and now we're surplus to requirements, in fact we're getting in the way. Our future is one short-stay of execution from total extinction. A brief respite in human history, whilst the Lizards take time out to organise the disposal of their stock.

Asides our blood and organs, we have nothing much to offer, and even those can be grown in labs nowadays. Most of the work is simple and repetitive, carried out by specialist clones, artificially reproduced in batches at organic printing factories. They live short and simple lives, and when they're no longer fit for purpose, they undergo vivisection, apparently in the name of vital research. The clones are the survivors of one of many of the Lizards' half-baked genetic programs, originally initiated to make improvements to the herd. New humans with bigger eyes and grey skin, larger brains, and no sex organs. If you live near a UFO hot spot you might've even met one.

I'm sure by now the Lizards have everything they need, all the raw materials required to rebuild civilisation. Be they mineral, chemical, or biological, every ingredient of the Lizard's cookbook, has been safely stored in secure vaults around the world. In fact it surprises me that we're still here, not long now I guess. I suspect it'll be another flood, that's what usually happens. Hence the decades of weather modification, chemtrailing the skies to make the world a darker, danker place. Covertly terraforming the planet, so that the Lizard King can leave their subterranean city, and briefly come up for air.

It's a matter of calculating when, and how far they'll go, and since the Lizards have factory farmed us to full capacity, soon there will be too many of us to manage. We're tagged and tracked, our movements mapped, our thoughts controlled, but it only takes one loose cannon to start the ball rolling.

Not another revolution, please! you'll hear the Lizards cry. Constantly bickering and bitching about the *bloody monkeys* at corporate functions, and global summit after parties. A welcome opportunity for the younger generations of Lizards to network, let down their thinning hair, and spend the night drinking blood, before fucking everything in sight.

The old guard are somewhat in two minds, partly due to our unwanted influence, a human streak that gives the Lizards shivers. They're haunted by their memories of the last time around, the endless boredom that drove them crazy. A thousand years in a kingdom of shit, and their whole race trapped several miles underground. Busying themselves with inane distractions, half-heartedly cheering on competing royal bloodlines, as they vied for power in bloody conflict, rather than waiting patiently for the Earth to dry out.

A flood would explain why so many of us reside in coastal cities, poorly built on low lying land, and obviously designed to fail at just the right time. They've tested out tsunamis, earthquakes and the like, and studied the data, the mortality count, and what remained when the tide went out. A bloody mess, that's what, and all of it stinking to high heaven.

Essentially if everything goes tits up, it's the nuclear problem that worries them the most. Radioactive oceans would kibosh their plans, and it's a sure-fire way to taint their breeding stock. They've tried it before, ruling over a race of genetic mutants and irradiated freaks, but they never got much done.

Then there are all the contingency plans to consider. Their favourite hybrid pets can be stored underground, but they're looking for something less claustrophobic for themselves. Some of them have even bought a mesa or two, and have decided to head for higher ground. Flat plateaus populated by vast glass domes, filled with hydroponic gardens, and raised aloft in the clouds. But there's always the danger that the sea levels may rise too far, and then they'll have to head down to the caves again.

The only alternative is beyond the ice wall, way past the base camps in the Land of Giants. It's an unappealing prospect for the Lizards, subsisting in coral castles, built by their lowliest acolytes in the know. Even as a last resort it has its dangers, there have been several insurrections against Lizards in the past. To ensure their own safety, their most ancient of minions would eventually have to be slaughtered, unless they want another Babylon on their hands.

They don't even want to imagine all of the dead left behind, they'll have to clean out this place from top to bottom. As far as what remains, The Lizards will have to think up a whole new batch of excuses, to account for the archaeological devastation, a revised history for our substitutes, our replacements on Earth. A brand new race who'll look little like us, a unique strain of genetically adapted slaves, most likely based on one of their latest prototypes, hermaphroditic amphibians, perfectly adapted for post-deluge survival.

Eventually curiosity will get the better of them, and they too, will begin to question the word of their god. The Lizard King whose benevolent foresight first led them from deep underground to a veritable Eden. To save themselves grief and constant explanation, the Lizards might put it in writing. just like the last time, and the time before that. Unfortunately, they'll most likely end up creating another religion, which is always more trouble than it's worth.

The Lizards know when they let us go, they'll miss the entertainment most of all. So much fun with suffering on tap, the endless wars and pointless sacrifice. When it's all done and dusted, it's not exactly something they're looking forward to, the Lizards don't fear much, except boredom. Besides, it's a perpetual conversation killer when all you've got are other Lizards, to keep you company in the deepest bowels of hell.

79. DEAD WEIGHT

There's a point in our lives, when we must finally choose to let go of the body, and any notion of remaining part of the human race. For a vast majority, as might be expected, transcendence, or at least a mild notion of the possibility, only occurs in the last seconds before death, and only then, if you're very, very lucky.

Suicidal survivors are in something of a pickle, they've seen a glimpse of the great beyond. Yet those around them, both personal and professional, especially medical, would rather they'd keep their mouths shut, than listen to any more existential nonsense about their newfound perspective on a planet going slowly insane.

To die and return, the great leap for mankind, the only *true* astronauts to have explored the unknown, are treated like a shameful secret, far beneath the contempt of humanity. Deliberately ignoring the plight of the half dead, the lost and found, those morbidly curious souls, whose destructive effect upon this evil world of ours, knows no bounds. Their poor reputation precedes them, their desperation to prove to one and all, that they've been beyond the veil. On looking back, on closer observation, they're convinced that our lives are little more than a pathetic charade of autonomic feedback, and psychic negativity.

Our earliest ancestors were born from the sea, grown like tadpoles in sentient *Black Goo*. Atomically vibrated, and frequency oscillated into the throes of a consciousness, we like to think of as human. Embalmed in our own bodies, these frugal transports, as third-class carriage, hampered by gravity and decay, long to be free from our invasion of their privacy, and the painful sentience of our dislocated minds.

The tradition for venerating corpses hasn't been questioned too much in the past, but eventually, everyone will realise that the heap of rotting flesh that we leave behind, like everything else within this construct, was never ours.

It was just a loaner.

80. NAMING

What's in a name? Quite a lot really. Asides the social slavery of a surname, a commoner's title issued by a Sir, a Lord, a master, there's the tricky process of choosing a first. Religious associations come to the fore, cultural bias, celebrity fads, all sorts of crap we can use to call each other names.

There is nothing benevolent about a naming ceremony, that binds an individual's aspect, overview, and full life potential to a predetermined path. What is Michael's calling? What does Paul pull? Is Sarah the Seer of Ra? Will Robert the thief suffer the guilt of regret? Does Andrew draw upon the sword or the pen? And why the hell is Mary so merry?

Names provide a thickly woven tapestry of subliminal sigil magic, each with its own meaning and bound by Saturn's law, to propagate genetic lines of strength and weakness. Keeping that which is worth keeping in the family, that which is not, outside of the clan. The cabal, the chosen bloodlines, with ancient names, and even crests, have banners and Latin mottos just to make absolutely sure.

Say *namaste*, then bid farewell to your nemesis, your projection, your avatar, the namer and shamer whose identity you cling to, one that has been engineered for conformity, and your unquestioning loyalty to a hidden hierarchy. A mirror image, your legal straw man, the fictional self who haunts your subjugated world, and signs the forms, and pays the bills, to mark your lot in life.

What's in a name? Nothing. Nothing at all.

81. ME-MORE-EYES

Memories are false, and hindsight a ridiculous joke played upon the feeble, the faithful, and the slavish. Despite the burden of maturity, neither resting upon the laurels of objectivity or subjectivity, one can admit that we are nothing like our former selves. With age, youth is of another life now lost, and whoever plays the next fool must remain in the dark, as much as their predecessors.

The night may have a thousand eyes, but it would take a million or more, to survey each and every detail of one single life. We remember what we want to, and share it with others as backup storage, to remind us lest we forget, exactly who we're supposed to be, and if we've changed, or just the world around us.

If memories were wishes, I'd have far more than I do right now, because, like many people a lot of them are rather depressing, even if most can't admit that to themselves. However awful the past might be, it's nothing compared to the future. Be careful what you wish for, and wish for what you care for, because in the end, all our future memories are little more than yesterday's broken dreams.

82. THE LOSS OF JOY

Joy, unlike happiness, is neither fleeting nor light, for it lingers and gathers life without expectation. As it dies, as does all the joy in the world, it draws grief like the loss of life. It's arrival and departure usually goes unnoticed, until it's too late, and all that's left is past regret.

Joy has no reason, no purpose, it's not a reaffirmation of anything in particular, it's a state of bliss, of humble grace, that exists regardless of comparison and circumstance.

Some say it's much like sheer relief but only greater, a moment of clarity that proves you're finally getting somewhere, and not so much in the world as in yourself. It can be sparked by the simplest of things, a smile of recognition, or an inexplicable sensation, that right now, right here, everything is absolutely perfect.

Happiness is an emotionally broadcasted signal, a behavioural marker for public acknowledgement, that you've got what you desired, or left behind what you'd never wanted. Joy remains with you, and leaves an indelible impression upon the soul. No matter how bad things are, the experience of joy, however brief, can inspire happiness, whilst the memories of happier times can inevitably bring about sorrow. Joy and sorrow have an understanding, they know their place, but are prepared to share. Happiness and unhappiness, are polar opposites, erratic and to some extent as fickle as each other, and more than ready to trade places at the first sign of trouble.

If there's one thing that leaves the Lizards scratching their heads, it's the notion that there could be such a thing as joy in life. A bizarre emotional state, one without reason or objective, apparently caused by anything, even the simplest recognition of a state of being. Especially when so many outside factors have been designed to demoralise the human race, and meant to have the opposite effect. Lizards can understand the highs and lows, they see positives and negatives all around them, but in their hearts, where we can sense reality in its complete totality, they see absolutely nothing.

83. CHASING THE DRAGON

The Chinese Zodiac contains a variety of animals, of which nearly all are recognised as part of the natural world. However, there's one exception to the rule, one creature amongst them which has never roamed the Earth, but for our ancient folklore and mythology, and its name is Dragon.

A Lord of the Lizards, the primal instigator, an elusive emperor hidden between the lines of every language in the world. The dragon is an allegory for the imperious self, it symbolises the reptilian stump, the agitator of base instinct. An ancient genetic modification, which compels each and every one of us to act against the divine principles of the soul.

We are at war with ourselves and within ourselves, blind to the obvious parallels between internal and external conflict. Our environment is a manifestation of the mind, a poor reflection of an imperfect race, borne from deeply flawed perceptions. We live with our mistakes and burn our fingers all the time, normalising our twisted nature, as we constantly attune to the cruelties of war and terror. We remain incapacitated by social etiquette, and live side-by-side with our wholly inexplicable fears. Our higher consciousness is nullified by an inhuman biology, and one that has shaped our world view since our original conception.

Those who chase the dragon to inhale its opiate breath, must agitate the boiling solution to keep the heroin from burning. Like George they battle with the beast, risking everything to play the conquering hero in their own minds. Their just rewards are a round trip to the womb and warm oblivion, far from the hustle and bustle of the real world.

Opiates kill dreams and disrupt the natural sleeping process. They slow rapid eye movement to a crawl, and instead of allowing the mind brief respite from its mortal frame, they hijack the limbic system, and corrupt the tiny pleasure centres of the brain. Once the mind has been conditioned to its new chemical regime, it will overproduce dopamine to compensate for the damage. The consumption of opiates is the most common way of transmuting humans into hybrids, by activating the lowest region of the triune brain, the reptilian stump, and sedating all higher thinking.

The moment George confronted the dragon, he was engulfed by its breath, and as the smoke entered his lungs, he found himself trapped inside his waking dream. One where he had overcome his sworn enemy, returning as the undefeated victor against impossible odds, forever venerated by the people for his supreme valour, and later canonised as a saint. But all of this was fiction, for George was now a prisoner in his own mind, slumped on the floor of the dragon's cave and oblivious to the world outside. George had been roundly fooled, for the dragon had won the battle before it had even begun. In truth the dragon is the heroine of the Lizard's tale, like every other perpetrated by reptilian mythology. Our most venerated victories are just illusions, aberrations spawned by the losing side of an eternal war on the mind.

When you chase the dragon it lures you to the lizard brain, the driving force behind all instincts for human survival. Destined to live a lie in comfort, rather than the truth in pain, for we are slaves to our own minds, and our thoughts will always lead us to our masters' intent. Our whole world is a contrivance, sealed within a cave of dreams, we are neither awake nor asleep, but caught somewhere in-between.

To kill the dragon one must learn to conquer one's own primal fears, and take control of the subconscious. Training to be warriors, and gathering an army of the most human of souls, to finally vanquish our oppressors beyond the realm of the waking day. Lead the way, don't follow, lure the dragon to the empire of your imagination, and slay it with the light of truth.

84. THE WHITE ROOM

I used to worry about my body, the creature I inhabit, he's always smoking and drinking coffee, but what really bothers me is his insistence on wearing headphones all day and all night. It took months of him constantly blasting his ears with that awful din, before the shocking realisation dawned on me, and I finally understood what he was up to. It's not the rowdy neighbours or the low-flying aircraft that's the problem, he's just trying to block me out. It seems he'd rather hear white noise than listen to the thoughts of his terrifying mind. This one, the entity I believe to be me, trapped inside the body of a human being. I'd hoped we'd get on better by now, but sadly not, I'd tried to kill him after all, twice in fact, and I guess it would take a saint to forgive me that.

What's worse than all the toxins, and the infernal racket, is the way he lives inside one room, a small white box where he likes to hide. A public exile imprisoned in the midst of so much potential company. He's completely obsessed by one purpose, and one purpose alone, his sincere belief that it is his place to warn humanity. Utilising my intellect for his own gains, hoping against all hope that his words might not fall upon deaf ears. He doesn't even see the irony in what he's doing, for *I* am the mind that inspired his precious dreams.

I've tried to vacate this abode and leave it all behind, to extract my sentience from this body, but the price is far too high. For his instincts have overcome us both, and for all the damage I have done he has the far greater powers of recovery. No matter where I go, or how hard I tried to snap the astral cord, there is no escape from the animal in me, which always wins the bloody fight. Fate keeps me here to do the donkey work of thinking up solutions to survive another day, whilst he writes his testimony, documenting his mental cruelty.

He just sits there all day silently talking to voices that shouldn't even be there, few of which I can hear, and even fewer that make any sense. Yet from that psychic cacophony he culls simple intentions, with which he communicates through our brain, executing hormonal orders and brief synaptic waves of pleasure, to force me to watch him tap upon his keyboard.

Which is why I like to imagine myself sitting in another white room far away from this one, doing absolutely nothing but breathing deeply. Living a simpler life in a completely different body, and one which isn't under the delusion that it has a mind of its own. A human being that can walk away from the problem, and give up on his obsession, instead of wasting his time harvesting dreams and taking dictation for the dead. What good will it do? None that I can see, except perhaps to caution others with suicidal tendencies. To reassure them that they're not alone, even when they think they are, and whom they share their headspace with, isn't necessarily their guardian angel.

85. PLAYER

If you pretend to be someone that you're not, to get by in life and further your career, yet know you're only lying to yourself, and everyone around you, then I am afraid you are a pro, and not a pimp.

If, on the other hand, you know full well what you're doing, and deceit is your natural ally, and whatever politics you believe in is contained within your office, and you are quick to judge those who waiver, whilst taking pleasure in their downfall, then you are most certainly a player.

They say that life's a gamble, and that there are no certainties, except in death, where one must pay one's debts, or face up to Saturn's Law. Around and around she goes, and where she stops nobody knows, that's Lady Luck in case you're wondering. The greatest temptress of all time, who makes promises she can never keep, so you'll put your money where your mouth is, until you lose your shirt and get kicked in the teeth.

The biggest players in the game of life, have accumulated more wealth than all the rest of us put together. The elite of the elite have the finances to leave this world in the gutter. With gold reserves great enough to buy out every country in the world, and still have plenty of change left over for a war or two. Yet they persist with playing the markets, and abusing their economic leverage, as major shareholders in global corporations, to hold sway over whole continents. For behind the sleight of hand shenanigans, and the bluster and bravado, there's only one objective left in play, and that's to bring every last one of us to the table.

86. HATER

Never brainstorm with anyone who has been subjected to Neurolinguistic Programming. Rather than spearhead new ideas, or provide solutions to a problem, they'll interject at every possible opportunity, employing psychological tactics to undermine the competition. A performance for the boss's benefit, to view them as a natural leader, rather than go by first impressions, and decide they're unbearably obnoxious.

Many mindless, heartless drones, some of which help run the whole shebang, willingly choose attack as the best form of defence. Which, for most of the time works, as they usually only have to fight other jerks, who think exactly the same way as they do. Their education runs deep, and they've learned much about stifling love, and shedding empathy, falsifying their true character as it skulks in the shadow of a bully.

Hatred costs dearly, and all the time you live with hate, the karmic meter is running, and at some obscure point in space and time, beyond the mortal coil, each and every one of us will have to pay the toll.

Unless, that is, you never play the game. Neither love nor hate this facsimile of life, but merely tolerate the situation as you bide your time. Winners, losers, heroes and cowards, all carry so much baggage with them, the very idea of leaving it behind is simply not an option. There's a simple way to break the system, to seal the fate of the status quo. If you can make a solemn vow, right now, in opposition to everything that you've been taught about this world. Despite its illusory potential for change and growth, no matter what comes next, however much resistance you might encounter, if you believe it with all your heart, you'll never need to come back here again.

87. MAÑANA

One of the strangest pieces of advice I've ever received, encouraged me to live for today, for by tomorrow I could be hit by a bus. It seemed rather innocuous at the time, like waiting for one to come, and then three arrive at once. All of which I assume, have an equal chance of running me over.

Much like the old adage, palmed off on those wallowing in self-pity, that at least they don't live in an iron lung. I'm not sure if it's a cultural phenomenon, one unique to when and where I was born, but this double negative approach to amateur psychology doesn't really wash with me. It's as if some believe that the only way to find contentment in their own lives, is to wallow in the misery of others.

I can't say that the idea of tomorrow brings me hope, no more so than yesterday, and if I were to live today as if it were my last, it probably would be. I'm sure if my doctor called, the one I never see, and told me I had one more day to live, and I could be bothered to step outside, and see the world for one last time, I'd probably make the mistake of opening my mouth, say the wrong thing to the wrong guy, and get beaten up, just like in the good old days.

I never realised how much fun I had back then, when I was young, and far easier on the eye, and that all the beautiful people and places that were on offer to me, would one day disappear. All of yesterday's parties have faded into obscurity, and as for all of tomorrow's, I haven't even received an invitation. It's not my time, my time is over, and even if I'm still alive, I'm barely here these days.

If I could pick and choose, sitting in a time machine, stopping and starting when I like, to take a peek at my own fate. Perhaps then I'd change my mind and seize the day from time to time, like so many others recommend. Then again, I might just skip right through to the very last mañana, and watch the dawn rise on the final day of all reality. Which probably isn't all that far away, humanity rarely imagines more than one tomorrow at a time, and as far as our shared destiny's concerned, it's all we really need.

88. THE INVISIBLE GIANT

I'm a loner, near enough a hermit, and if it wasn't for the infinite patience of my wife, I'd only have the cats for company, if that. In fact I'd probably be dead by now, my body in a bag or box somewhere. If not, then just another mental case busy talking to myself, holed up in a padded cell, hopped up on lithium and anti-depressants.

I know I'm partly to blame, at the very least, it can't be easy for this poor old body of mine, living with a psychic monkey on his back. Perhaps that's why he veers towards depression so much of the time, this living organism that I occupy, who remains suspicious of his own mind. He's shaken me off once in a while, but only when he's really down. Lying prostrate and incapacitated by the caring profession, under curfew and close observation on a hospital CCTV.

That's the only time I really feel him relax, and even cheer up in a perverse sort of way. If the state confines him for long enough, he makes friends with other loonies, and encourages them to feel better about themselves. It's such a strange defence mechanism, and so surreal to watch. He's always the happiest man on the psych ward, the annoying one, that means well, but probably only makes things worse. He's even called a truce, under the pretence that his mind and body are one and the same. Although, that's usually a temporary understanding, to show a united front to the psychiatrist, to save him from the possibility of electro-shock therapy.

I know what he wants, it's very simple, someone to work out his problems, rather than ranting on about the illusory nature of existence, which only seems to freak him out. Poor guy, all he needed was an invisible giant, a jolly Santa in the sky. Sitting up there in the clouds with a beatific smile, telling him everything's going to be fine. Instead of finding easy answers, he found *me*, the thinker of the thoughts he has no control over, the mind he'd rather he'd never made up.

I'm sorry body, for all the things I've done to you, especially the pain I've caused by sharing my particular take on the truth. I know it's hard to swallow, but this world isn't yours, your physicality, your perspective on the universe, it's all come through me, and where I come from is almost impossible to explain. But I will do my best, when the time is right, and perhaps at the very end of our journey, we can look back on all of this and laugh.

I've lived many lives before you, so let's try it my way this time, and see how things work out. I swear to you that if I fail and cannot escape this place, I'll stop meddling in human affairs, and if I must come back again, I promise you body, I will leave them to their own devices. Living in a bliss of ignorance, with family and friends, filling up a life with plenty of happy memories. I'll simply sit in silence and let myself be myself, a human being as nature intended, and always should have been.

89. CHURCH BELLS

I've noticed a distinct decline in the sounding of church bells, not that I'm one for organised religion. Although their tones do inspire a nostalgia in me, a hankering for sleepy Sunday mornings, when I knew that for at least one more day, I needn't worry about school.

It took me a while to comprehend that Big Ben was just a bell, and not the tower at The Palace of Westminster, and even longer to grasp that what went on in there, made up a completely different kind of religion. When the most famous clock in Britain chimes, it marks the passing of the hour, and is not meant as a call to the people, to come and worship those in power.

Within a few years of being human, I began to hear ringing in my ears, but didn't even mention it, because I didn't know any better. I'd assumed it was a phone call, in my head. My favourite TV show at the time was all about a group of kids with telepathic powers. Before they spoke, they'd send each other a high pitched frequency, as much the same as I'd hear from time to time, and so I'd answer back. I'd ask if there was anything that I could do, to boost the signal, to make our communications clearer.

After a while, with a great deal of persistence, and lots of trial and error, I heard a voice burst through, and break the silence from within. It only said one thing, and one thing alone, for many, many years, one solitary utterance that shattered my innocence with a single word, *hello*.

90. THE LONG CON

The Lizards rarely ever make mistakes. It might not seem that way at first, but given enough time, watching the events unfold, it becomes obvious that everything that's happened so far, was always meant to be. It's the writing on the wall, with all the tell-tale marks of the Lizard's hand, crudely scrawled across the pages of history, but painfully familiar all the same.

A great deal of planning and forethought goes into controlling a species, even the gullible humans take quite a bit of convincing. That's the nature of the long con, spend enough time with the mark, and bring them into your confidence, until you've got them utterly convinced. Then, even when things turn out badly for them, as they most often do, you'll never have to take the blame, and sometimes, they'll even offer to take it for you.

Such is the benevolence of power, the greatest con of all, the idea that those who rule over us have our best interests at heart, takes years and years of dedication to the craft. Working away at one generation to the next, building a reputation for due care and diligence, whilst all the time, wreaking absolute havoc behind the scenes.

Those born into power must take on great responsibility. They are taught from an early age, that their life is nothing in comparison to their greater legacy. A bastard of a bloodline of kings and queens, that stretches all the way back to the pharaohs, keeping alight the sacred flame.

Those most committed to the cause, more often than not, will live long enough to see the results of their efforts. Ably enabled by their faithful advisors, their lesser descendants, impure of blood but talented all the same. Entrusted by the rulers of the elite to follow their instructions from sacred texts, line by line and word for word, as it has been written, so shall it be done.

Humans who have studied Lizard behaviour to try and understand the nature of their unflinching prediction, are quick to presume their overlords have some kind of access to the future, or perhaps even to another dimension. They're absolutely correct in their assumptions, for the Lizards do, but so do I, and so do you. It's called *dreaming*, and that's nothing new.

The trick to knowing the future is to create your own in the shadows, then slowly drip-feed hints and clues for centuries to come. As heightened expectation builds, and new cultural traditions pave the way, before long people will do exactly what they're told without a moment's hesitation. Even if they believe otherwise, their volition is no longer their own. Everything their world has to offer, from the youngest to the oldest, their hearts, and minds, and souls, are left ripe for the taking by the masters of the long con.

91. GOLD FEVER

Gold is the sweat of the sun. It belongs to the platinum metals group and it's a superconductor. It can be manipulated through certain processes, using acids, gases, and prolonged extreme heat, to form a temporary flux field of negative electromagnetic energy. It's what the shadow government use to shield their black budget technology, for the purposes of camouflage and interdimensional travel.

Even though we might perceive the third dimension, we actually exist in the second. Our attention is absorbed by the surface of all things, which cannot be fully understood without a constantly changing perspective. That's the purpose of the invention of time, as a measurement of change, except in the world of the quanta, where it remains a fixed constant. Superconductivity has a strange effect on the quantum world. Gold operates on a two dimensional level, its atomic structure resonates in perfect harmony, and its billions of particles function as a single entity.

Lizards worship their precious metals, but especially gold, for it forms the only physical connection they have with their unholy god. The priceless beads of perspiration, from an exasperated black hole sun. The favourite son who, through their own treachery, was left bound by the rings of time, affording the illusion of space, to compensate for the holographic limitations of our artificial world.

It's replica tracks the sky above us, but it's just a scale model powered by a plasma fusion mix. It contains very little precious metal, but enough light and heat to serve as a reminder of how life used to be. When energy was as abundant as air, and those who could draw upon it could do as their hearts desired. Which soon grew cold, in the stark light of indifference, borne out of repetition and a poor sense of imagination. Until the time would come when all was set in stone, and Midas lost his touch, and the golden days grew shorter, and the sun far smaller.

After a while, it was decided that a moon, the size of the new sun, should be constructed and attached upon a clockwork arm, to counterbalance day with night, and ration out the light across the

Earth. God's children soon grew hungry, turning to agriculture to feed themselves, making sure to share their harvest in sacrificial homage to Cronus, another alter-ego of the fallen one. Soon our ancestors forgot the old ways, the powers that once flowed from their fingertips. Eventually the world turned black and blue, cold and wet, hot and dry, and the pilgrimage of survival soon took its toll.

Then the Lizards played their hand, offering bounties of fertile lands, and basic technologies, as a reward for those lucky enough to find a piece of the sun. Affording the lowliest of humans an opportunity to escape their drudgery and toil. The Lizards cherish gold above all else, for them it's literally manna from heaven. They consume its flesh and drink its blood in worshipful communion, to remain forever young, or so the story goes, in honour of their saviour, their god who first brought them here to rule over this world.

92. TEAM SPIRIT

Few are convinced of the merits of magic ritual, their patience stretched by the very mention of such childish fantasies. Even though it constitutes the fodder for many bestsellers, and global movie franchises that keep the entertainment industry buzzing.

That being said, those given conscious access to the hive mind, by right of birth, are taught the ways of the go-to-guys. Saturn's most faithful and beloved, who live their lives as empty shells, and can only believe what they are told. Behind the public face, they spend their time absorbed in esoteric study, practicing sacred ceremonies, to master the art of groupthink, and bring their spite to light like a phoenix rising from the ashes.

The collective will takes precedent over all others, within cabals comprised of the most suggestible of hybrids, where there can be no room for individuality or free thinking. Those chosen to carry out spirit work, are protected from undue influence, and raised to see themselves as something different from the common man, expressly forbidden from mixing outside the social circles of their own kind.

Each select committee forms part of a network of secret societies, working together as one psyche, to think as a single being focused on one sole intention, to bring a lie to life through constant affirmation. To give birth to a conscious manifestation of group spirit, a living thought form, pieced together with the sentient force of collective will, to take on a life of its own.

The life cycle of a group spirit starts as an inkling of an idea, a sneaking suspicion, barbed with the hackles of discontent, barely more than a philological animal. Yet, with patience, as more donate their time and energy, and brand the spirit with a sigil, it will evolve into a higher thought form. For the ritual to be completed, and create a lasting manifestation, a real sacrifice must be made. For without it a thought form, a team spirit, has no weight nor provenance, and the rest of us will quickly see right through it.

93. THE DREAM FACTORY

Some still believe that dreams can come true. Those blessed with great beauty, who can remember their lines, might even seek their fame and fortune on one of the many casting couches of La La Land. These days young wannabes, the potential stars and starlets of the future, are more likely to end up in the service industry, making high-priced coffee or selling their bodies.

The Land of Holly has somewhat lost its veneer of glamour over the years, and now it's mainly a corporate front for tax-free slush funds, from the other side of the world. The stars are fading, and all the sets have turned bright green, so now even actors must use their imagination. Mechanically delivering predictably market-tested lines, with a modicum of emotion.

For the world has changed since the golden age of the silver screen, when those in the limelight could demand whatever their hearts desired. What little remains of the dream factory is filled with minor celebrities, and funded by licensed merchandising revenue streams, with major branded product placements secreted in every scene.

The cathedrals of film lie almost empty, bar the few multiplexes used as makeshift day care centres, for busy families who still prefer to frequent the malls, than stay in the privacy of their homes and live their lives online. Besides it's proven far more economical to deliver streaming content on demand, to provide an instant fix. The most economic form of escapism for the humdrum lives of an invisible audience.

Simple stories for simple folk, who prefer the razzle dazzle of digitized spectacle, constant action, pithy one-liners, tragic lovers, and blood and guts galore. Nothing too taxing for the mainstream, it's hard enough to endure the predictive programming and cope with the cognitive dissonance, without having to follow a complicated plot. Mixed messages leave the audience frustrated, until all they can do is lose themselves in the big picture, professionally cast, directed, and produced by experts in mass hypnosis.

The medium may have changed, but the story remains the same. The Lizards are coming for your dreams, to replace them with their own. What you see here in our world is a projection upon a projection, a double vision meant to blind us into complete submission. It won't be long now before the experts in the know, will find a way to get right inside our heads.

They'll roll out the red carpet so you'll think you're a star, playing the lead in your own movie with an audience of one. Those who envy celebrity, and the lifestyles of the rich and famous, will lap it up. When in truth, the vast majority of us will never be anything other than a bit-part extra in life. For we are only here to make up the numbers, barely adding a frisson of emotion to the climax of our mutual destruction, a crowd scene for a big ending that's sure to make the final cut.

94. FASHIONED SLAVES

The young keep up as best as they can, they choose their camp, and express their individuality according to peer group pressure. Pretending to be freaks is nothing new, a hairstyle, some tattoos, a new set of clothes, it doesn't make a blind bit of difference, they're still just uniforms.

The only way a fashion victim could stay ahead these days, would be to walk around naked, abandon all ties with society, and live a life without technology. But who would know, and who would care, what a nobody without a decent wardrobe is doing, in the middle of nowhere?

The corporate slaves, who brand themselves, and bear the mark of assimilation, are the only ones who can truly appreciate the beauty of the master-slave configuration. There's little difference these days, between the idle and their idols, except the latter stands on stage and beats the drum. Maintaining a constant rhythm for their devotees, who blindly march on in a circle, to keep the wheels of the fashion industry turning.

As each generation takes their turn, they fall for the same old tricks and pick up the pace, chasing the latest look. An appropriated style, a brand new label, to camouflage our decaying world like lamb dressed up as mutton. The advertisers have given up on pitching aspiration, their research has revealed a downward trend, nowadays it's more about self-mutilation. Placing the target of our market upon ourselves, and guiding the aim of our oppressors, whose words of reassurance and slick presentations, acclimatise us to the inescapable decline of our civilisation.

We do all the work for those who lead the way. We find the inspiration and freely broadcast our innovations to the world. So those with the budget and no imagination, can put in orders with sweatshop factories and knock out a new line within a week. They'll hike the prices and blitz the media to fleece the well dressed sheep, the most obedient and dedicated followers of fashion. Haute couture at knock down prices, for those with something more to prove. So even when there's nothing left on the inside, at least they still can turn heads and hearts.

95. THE GUARD DEN

What used to keep the horrors out, is now contained within. We've been placed in isolation, but it's been so long now that no one seems to have noticed. Where rose thorns grow like razor wire, and grass like bitumen and concrete, and all the living forms look plastic, and nothing smells natural anymore, not even nature.

Eden is the den of energy, the psychic maze that connects the human consciousness to the core of Saturn. Yet only the dead may pass through its hexagonal gate, the most dangerous exit from our heavily fortified tomb of time. Within Saturn's cold heart lies all that was and ever shall be, but it cannot be broken by any single individual. Only through the psychic union of all minds can Saturn's law be finally torn asunder.

Each of us is merely one thought amongst a greater premise, yet our prime root stems from the same fundamental beginnings. Working together as one force we can open Pandora's Box, and reveal its broken form as a cross. It's a map of the soul, leading in four directions to the four corners of the Earth, wherein lies the absolute limits of human imagination.

Eden is the cosmic labyrinth, and at its epicentre stands a ladder leading to the very depths of the Earth. At the bottom rung we can explore the true tunnels of light, to escape our false sanctuary, and leave behind this wretched secret garden forever.

96. FATA MORGANA

Today my living host witnessed a spectacular event, unprecedented bar the exception of a similar phenomenon in China. The strangest thing happened, nothing, nothing happened at all. He took it in his stride, he made no excuses, in fact he drew his wife's attention to the sky, and pointed out the rolling hills and the vast city up amongst the clouds.

He's catching on quickly nowadays, he has a better grasp of the big picture. He shares his every speculation with his wife, and love of his life, and they spend many a night in deep discussion over the nature of reality. But neither seem to be panicking about the holographic collapse, for they know, deep down in their hearts, all of this was bound to happen. They are connoisseurs of mortality, and have learned through endless tests of character, that the sweetest experiences meet their zenith at the very beginning, and the very end of times.

Strangely, though not surprisingly, no one else perambulating along the promenade that day, took a blind bit of notice of the phenomenal phenomenon. Asides, that is, a solitary social media nut, with smartphone at hand, whose tagged photo went viral for a while. Of course, my host didn't take a snap, he hasn't even got a phone. He's been looking up at the sky for much of his life, and mostly keeps his observations to himself, with one exception, entrusting only one other person in the world.

As long as he has a witness in his wife, it doesn't matter if castles appear in the clouds, or giant orbs of light fly by his window, he's already convinced by the mind he cannot call his own, that this world is a mirage. What he cannot abide as a basic animal, a creature born without the need for higher thinking, is the possibility that what lies out there, beyond this complicated figment of his imagination, might be nothing but a desert. The sands of time blowing in an eternal wind, flowing in a tide like a simple clock to mark the hour of another's life, before the universe upends itself, and begins again.

97. A GENTLE DEATH

For many, dying turns out to be an agonising, if not horrific affair. A quick death might help avoid the physical pain of a long drawn out decline, but when a soul leaves this world abruptly, they can take far longer to acclimatise.

Unfortunately, some minds become too preoccupied by their former residence, the human brain, and have a tendency to play down the inevitable demise of their mortality. The most adept at human life will persist with maintaining a semblance of normality at all costs. It can take days, months, even years, with a full life of friends, family, and gainful employment, before they'll realise they're already dead.

It's best to get used to the idea of leaving long before you get there, otherwise things can get a little complicated. There are no easy solutions to coping with death, only the comforting signs of a benevolent paranoia, that none of this is real, or more precisely, less real than it ever was before.

98. THE LINGERERS AND THE MEDDLERS

If you listen carefully to the silence, with no expectations in your heart, you might just make out something that shouldn't be there. It's not an auditory hallucination, it's the sound of the dead, the dead bored, mumbling subsonic tones of mild exasperation.

Once your ears are open, you'll learn to murmur in their language, with faint words of subliminal encouragement, beyond the range of human hearing. The first conversations you'll have, will be random at best, but should you persist you'll make friends, and you never know when they'll come in handy.

Eventually you'll meet, though not necessarily witness, past minds and lost hearts with something *real* to say. Something so pertinent to you, it can change your whole perspective on life. With practice you will come to expect the accompanying state of shock. That too, will subside in time, leaving you free to take or leave advice, from a whole host of invisible seers and dead prophets.

One word of warning, be sparing with your trust, for some you'll meet along your inner journey, can be total creeps. Demons with a sick sense of humour, who'd like nothing more than for you to destroy yourself, so they can claim you as their own on the other side. Don't make enemies of them, just be polite, and calmly refuse to try their psychic wares. Those lingerers and meddlers who've spent too long drifting in between realities. The scavengers of souls, who make their spiritual living from a bounty of emotional wrecks, perpetually washed up on the tides of existential angst, at the terminus of death.

99. PARADOXICALLY

History is in chaos, but it didn't used to be that way. Until relatively recently, *everyone* knew that the damage was caused by temporal sabotage. Deletions from the timeline, a chronological expansion, and anything that can possibly be done to hide the truth.

The Lizards know what they're doing, they've done it before, and will most likely again. Our forged provenance serves as a psychological buffer, cushioning the blow of our brief existence on Earth. Think hundreds rather than thousands, and tens instead of hundreds. Mechanically recorded data, photographic records and film footage, old wax cylinders of crackling speeches are readily available to all. For they are placed exactly where they belong, a matter of little more than a few generations ago.

Eventually you can trace back to a time where there's no light or sound, only written journals, academic texts, sketches and paintings, and the most rudimentary prints. These, for the main part still belong where they are, although you'll find forgeries amongst them to move the story along.

Seek even further back, and soon all you have are ancient scrolls and engraved stone, which due to their antiquity are protected from the public. Until all of history is made up of replicas and reproductions, and audio/visual presentations at museum lectures and universities. Filled with experts who rarely ever get their hands upon the originals, and only then if they've proven their allegiance to the academic community. Once they've met with approval, they may share their findings in highly respected journals, and eventually, if they're really lucky, well paid documentaries aimed at the mildly curious and highly gullible masses.

Anything to distract the people from the truth, which can only be found in one's dreams. Where rank outsiders and amateurs can witness history first hand, and truly understand that our past is at the very most, a mythology.

100. SPECTRAL ANALYSIS

This is only a recording, and nothing of any recognition, bar the rings of Saturn, exists beyond our holography of fear. Endlessly looping together our beginnings and endings, for our convenience and peace of mind. All you see around you has been lived long ago, and stands as testament, perhaps a fitting one, to a rotting carcass of monumental proportions. A dead continuum, perpetually filtered via our desensitised senses, in order that our present appears as fresh as a daisy, every single time.

Despite the best of intentions, beyond our comfortable illusions, something is stretching out of shape. Light's spectrum flickers through exotic frequencies, and sounds jar with scratches and pops, as interference from the past bleeds into the present.

The rings of Saturn, the discus of Atlas, is the long player, and right now it's projecting this holographic reality. But it's old and used, and badly scratched, and no matter how efficient the self-repair systems may be, all those tiny imperfections can build up over time.

Eventually everyone will notice the obvious anomalies, and for a while they'll try to adapt. But as space morphs into ever more unrecognisable dimensions, and time follows suit, until cause and effect are practically playing leapfrog with each other, the human race will panic, and lose all faith in their artificial construct. When we cease to believe our eyes, and are no longer able to project an observable reality, Saturn will suffer a cascade effect, overload, and shutdown.

Once time runs out, what remains of matter will vibrate into light, its speed unchecked, as everything that constitutes this dimension accelerates towards the vacuum of The Void. In the single blink of an eye, this place will fall silent, and darkness will prevail in the discarnate cosmic womb. Perhaps the perfect breeding ground for a new form of consciousness to gestate. A new kind of being, born into a grander scale of existence, where the whole of our fabricated history passes by, during the very first second of their life.

101. DEMONIZATION

Lizards love to play the blame game, because if all else fails, they can simply turn the tables, and accuse their accusers of their crimes. They'll instigate witch hunts and demonize the masses, and come up with phony excuses why things need to change. All for the sake of the security of the nation, or the world, the well behaved one that pays its taxes and does what it's told. There's no room for troublemakers in the Lizard order, so either bow down to authority, or end up behind bars, or worse.

There's nothing polite or even-handed about politics, it's usually a case of best liar wins. The trick to beating your opponent, is in the choosing of what to omit, rather than what to reveal. If things aren't going well with the electorate, they can always blame another despot. One who owes them a favour and has agreed to take the rap, because it's their turn in the game.

Behind the forced vitriol the leaders of the free world, (which, by the way, now costs a pretty penny), along with many dictators, from the other side of the political divide, who once out of the public gaze, are pretty much the best of friends. International politics is a pantomime, a performance played out for our dubious benefit. For your elected representatives and corporate tycoons are all faithful subjects to the Lizard King.

We have no rights, we're only told that so we'll behave. The moment we decide to exercise our democratic power, we'll find the rules have quickly changed. There's nothing like a good argument to clear the air, as long as the Lizards win. Otherwise there will be gagging orders and hit lists as long as your arm. Clean and quick shadow operations, to silence the most vocal supporters of the freedom of speech. Except of course, for those working as the controlled opposition, the seemingly revolutionary figures who somehow still manage to make a pretty penny, whilst courting controversy.

Of course, the Lizards are never satisfied, they can hold a grudge for years and years. They tend to push things too far, and occasionally they'll trap themselves in a political corner, and one from which they cannot escape. As a last resort they'll sacrifice one of their own, or at least any chance they had of making it as a head of state.

It doesn't matter what we think about the Lizards, it's like water off a duck's back, there's no point arguing with them, it's their language, their forum, and they have all the powers of arbitration. Now the only liberties ripe for the taking, are inside our minds, so make the most of them and think whatever you like, because it won't be long now before they put new policies into action, and sort out that little problem once and for all.

The Lizards are demons and take pride in that fact, well, at least in the company of their own kind. Originally they came from hell, a place called Sheol, a cruel citadel of their own making, inspired by forked-tongue persuasion, and built with the sweat and toil of a legion of minions.

Which is why, whenever possible, if it's not your argument, forget it and just walk away. Form a silent opposition to the Lizard autocracy, if there's one thing they can't stand it's being ignored. They can do without the taste of blood for at least one more day, so let them suffer and stew in their own juices for a change, and you'll soon see them demonizing each other, providing some well needed entertainment for the slaves.

102. HAHARCHITECTURE

A cage, is a cage, is a cage, you can dress it up how you like, and talk up the beauty of minimalism, but there's no getting away from it, the Lizards have their designs on us. They want to gentrify the masses, to replace our kind with something far more stylish than the cumbersome and unwieldy human form.

It's better to live in a cave than a prison, and behave like animals than slaves, but we've grown too accustomed to our surroundings, and even if we were given the opportunity for liberty, most would likely refuse to leave the human zoo.

Our lives have been compartmentalised, to inspire us to alter the way we think. Seeing as we sleep in boxes, and drive in boxes, and eat from boxes, and give each other boxes as gifts, I can almost understand the Lizard's take on the situation. If the human race could start over, I wonder in all honesty, how many would choose to repeat their mistakes? Billions upon billions all crammed together, in polluted cities and identikit housing developments, who have never known anything different.

We live like trapped rats, or more appropriately, a culture of mould in a Petri dish. Because even rats would try to escape and find a way out of this laboratory of life. I pity the future, I wonder just how many will suffer for the sake of convenience? Sleeping in pods like insects, with rents higher than their wages, slowly sinking into debt for a brief taste of metropolitan glamour.

There was a time before our history began, when homes were nothing more than fields of energy, electromagnetic shields to keep the weather at bay. Conjured up by more advanced minds than ours, even architects would be impressed with what can be achieved with air, water and electricity.

Brick by brick we entomb ourselves in an early grave, a vast multi-storey casket full of living corpses, staring at their screens for a taste of colour, because the outside world has turned completely grey. Stop building, *just stop now*, there are whole cities out there without one single resident. There's really no need to build any more.

103. MANUFACTURED LIFE

Consciousness creates form, form cannot create consciousness. You can't live in your brain, it's merely a transceiver, and a heavily censored one at that. You don't actually live in your body, because your body is nothing but energy. You are only here, because everyone since birth has told you so, and you believed them.

There once was a man, someone who finally worked it all out, and he left notes, a guidebook to this construct, its malevolent purpose, and directions for the exit. Those who first came across his writings, didn't spread the word, instead, they studied them in secret, and through newly formed allegiances with the Lizards, found a way to control this reality from within.

It's all downhill after that, indoctrinated generation after generation, each slaves to their enslaved mothers and fathers, all worshipping the beauty of the path of least resistance. There are few exceptions to the norm, but the idling doubters, the wonderers and the procrastinators, who have yet to find belief and most likely never will.

Our basic understanding of reality has been pre-programmed. It's a natal memory of a dream turned sour, decaying from the moment you're born. Until then you're a free spirit, unadulterated by direct observation, and at liberty to be anything you want, anywhere, anytime. Needless to say, once you're delivered unto evil, you'll quickly realise that the good times are over, and no doubt bawl for days.

It's always hard to take, when you find out you've been duped, again. You should've guessed, when the tunnel of light turned pink, and the hand of god surgically plucked you from infinity, and placed you near the bottom of the Lizard food chain.

104. DIG IT

0 is the gate
1 is the flag
2 is the scythe
3 is the bow
4 is the sail
5 is the snake
6 is the horned beast
7 is the arrow
8 is the mirror
9 is the tail

105. PROPER GANDER

The Proper Gander knows what's good for the goose, but little else. It is restricted by indoctrinated instinct, and barely recognizes the extreme limitations of its surroundings. Proper gander, or rather, *propaganda*, is the watchword of the elite. An encoded sociological meme of coercion, promoting total obedience with a paranoid sense of conformity. One which has successfully restricted the physical, emotional, and spiritual advancement of our slave race since time immemorial.

Life leads one from the edge, until one is inexorably drawn to homogeny. Aligning to the middle ground of our false dichotomy, by learning to love our subjugation, and do what we're told is best for us, even if it might cause us pain.

Which is why so few of us fly the coop, instead of waiting in anticipation for death's blessed sacrificial slaughter. To be served up on a platter, for a special occasion, to feed the desires of a host of hungry ghosts. Poor lost souls, living their dead lives in trepidation, taking meagre comfort in self-delusion, that somehow our sacrifice, and theirs, can keep this world turning.

Whenever you encounter propaganda, remember what so many others have forgotten, that underneath it all, we are wild swans, and you never know, one day we may still yet fly.

106. THOTH'S MO(O)NTHS

January - The Gate
February - Purification
March - Exodus
April - Son of The Stream
May - Permission
June - Youth
July - Love Child
August - Ripe
September - Enclosed Fire
October - Eighth Knave
November - New Fire
December - Tenth Fire

107. THE GREY WOMB

The Greys are overgrown premature babies, the best that lower magic and genetic science can muster. Dead, but for the infusion of one drop of *Black Goo* intelligence, in order that they may dupe our highly suggestible race. If you meet a grey, and ask them where they're from, they'll point to the stars, rather than down into the ground, where factory lines of biochemical vats harvest them like hydroponic vegetables.

The Greys are rather simple creatures, even if they *are* telepathic, not quite human, not quite demon, but somewhere in-between. The Lizards would rather they'd never been born, however their hybrid children think they're all the rage, a cosmic gimmick for a modern age. A hilarious jape, an outer space hoax, for the geeks and the nerds, who'd love to join a universal federation rather than the Masons.

The Greys are only really good at one thing, asides guessing games, and that's kidnapping rural folk and hitchhikers, and molesting them under the guise of scientific research. They used to be *little green men*, when the Lizards still dabbled with sorcery rather than sci-fi, unlike the stumps, who have no taste and barely any sense of tradition.

Of all the colours in the world, grey is and always will be the least inspiring hue, for it sums up so little with so much. It's the colour of a compromise too far, and the smokescreen for an overtly manipulated mass delusion. In fact, it's not even a colour, but nonetheless, it serves its purpose in a black and white reality, to ensure that nothing is quite one thing or the other.

108. YES YOU ARE

If there's a Creator, then it's not our lord and master, but an impartial observer, and one whose witness provides us the opportunity to subconsciously create matter from energy.

The god of the Earth, on the other hand, who has convinced many of their existence, is comparatively insignificant on a universal scale. Perhaps, that is, asides their giant ego. Yet, still it insists on taking all the credit, and setting up the rules to life, under which we are bound by emotional gravity, and murdered by mortality. Despite appearances, however old and wise Saturn may seem, it's nothing but a spoilt child. So, before you get down on your knees, remember that grovelling to bullies gets you nowhere.

If humans have a saviour, then it's true name is *Yes You Are*, and yes, you are, for without you, your world could never exist. The laws of observation are nature's last defence against the Lizard's absolute dominion. Unfortunately, with much encouragement, we have turned our vision upon ourselves, and now play victim to our delusions, as the architects of our own destruction.

109. TO THE ENDS OF THE EARTH

There are few of us who have truly seen our world from up on high, that is to say, without leaving one's body here on terra firma. Those who believe otherwise are sadly mistaken, having barely ever scraped the surface of our atmosphere. One only needs run in circles to circumnavigate the world, and even then most of it lies deep beneath the sea, whilst the rest remains inaccessible, tightly packed below miles of ice. So we can only ever view one part of the picture at a time, and that's the secret, that's the trick to all of this.

Our sphere of influence is nothing but an optical illusion, enveloped by a seamless join, and held fast by the density of strange and immovable oceans floating far above our heads. Floating through the familiar blue hues of our bubble, up towards the firmament, one can just about make out the curvature of light. Up there it's far easier to spot the Aurora Borealis, formed by crystal refractions, cast out by the snaking path of our mechanical sun.

All compasses point to the centre of the world, an exit precisely positioned at the mouth of Mt. Meru, a black jewel set amongst the broken shards of former Pangaea. Such was our common knowledge, before the great floods rushed in from the four corners of the Earth, and the first cracks began to appear in the skin of the world.

We bend light with our eyes, and create frictionless, imaginary revolutions, generating enough centrifugal psychic force, to crush our spirits, and contain our microscopic universe within the confines of the firmament. Electromagnetically charged to produce reversed polarities, keeping the wandering stars, the Moon and the Sun, all in their proper place. Fixed at their precise coordinates, hung from a revolving carousel, contained within Earth's three dimensional projection, of a two dimensional plane.

It's a shame that we couldn't all agree, you, I, and every man, woman and child, to journey together to the North Pole. We could storm the barricades of a united world government, and outnumber their protective forces by millions to one. If we managed to reach our destination, we could leap into the mouth of Mt. Meru, down into the quantum singularity that lies at the very heart of this plane. Then we could go our separate ways, into one of many other dimensions, all leading out of this cosmic terrarium. A high security prism, that has been our home from home for far too many lifetimes.

110. THE WALL

The wall that separates consciousness from the subconscious, forms the defensive perimeter of our waking lives. Humans were, at one stage in their development, super-conscious beings. Their minds working in perfect unison with their bodies, blessed with a treasure trove of photographic memories, and enhanced by highly evolved senses far beyond our measure. Their thought processes and actions guided by a wisdom of the ages, an infra-conscious state of unified thinking, free from the corrosive effects of undue influence and lies.

It took a while for most to realise things had changed, at least not until the damage had already been done. The encroaching barrier between the conscious and subconscious mind, pushed forwards into the waking dream, forming an inner dialogue, a counterfeit conscience embedded in the human instinctual drive. As Lizard thinking slowly crept in through the nightmares of the most adept of psychic explorers, so did their ideas. Inspiring quick and easy solutions to practical problems, left by the ongoing collapse of the last Yuga, for the knockdown price of spiritual sacrifice and intellectual division.

In our descent into madness, our minds have been spliced and diced, leaving little left to call our own. Our consciousness cordoned off, and colonised by the Lizard's archetypal projections, transmitted through the fleshy node of the lower brain. An addition made to our anatomy through psychic surgery, carried out during our long hibernation, as the human race slept through the last ice age.

Over time we've learned to put away our childish fears and fantasies, the haunted visions of less scientific societies, that warned us of the internal conflicts of an inner war. We've hyper-normalised our incarceration, and learned to live with the wall, and even come to love it. You can see it as a prison or as a fortress, it's a limited choice, but it's all that's on offer.

I've drilled a hole into my wall to see what's on the other side, a metaphysical camera obscura to peer through this mortal frame, and from what I can tell, it looks rather dark and empty in there. No doubt it will fill up soon enough, drawing light and colour from this waking dream, pouring life into previously unexplored space. All I can do now is wait patiently, as I stand at the very edge of my true self, bearing witness at the sight of my island consciousness, slowly sinking into a sea of dreams.

111. THE WRONG SIDE OF THE BED

All of life's rehearsals take place during sleep. If you wake up in a bad mood and can't shake off the feeling, someone's bound to ask if you've got up on the wrong side of the bed. They won't mean it literally, it's just another old saying, like so many few bother to analyse.

What they *should* ask, is if you've woken up in the wrong reality, but it's close enough, wrong side, wrong bed, wrong world. That's why it's easier to simply agree, perhaps shrug your shoulders, and raising your eyebrows with mild exasperation is always a nice touch.

I'm long past caring which world I'm living in, they're all pretty much the same. It's been a long old while since I've made any significant jumps, because I take the transitions in my stride, and do my best to blend in as quickly as possible. If you've woken up on the wrong side of the bed, you might like to play a little game, *can you spot the difference?*

For me, it's mostly famous faces I can no longer recognise, altered brand names and logos, or old headlines that are suddenly breaking news again. In the day to day there's usually nothing to worry about, if you wake to find your particular reality has ceased to exist, try embracing the change. Even if it feels strange, at least you'll get fewer funny looks from friends and family.

I admit it takes some practice to avoid the inevitable panic. If you're a trans-dimensional virgin, which is doubtful, more likely less observant than unadulterated, don't get in all of a dither, it happens to the best and the worst of us. Whatever you do, stay calm, and remember, if you don't like this place, you can always go back to sleep again.

112. THE OVERNET

We've been behaviourally conditioned to believe that we can only communicate over great distances, thanks to the miracle of science. The idea came first and not the infrastructure, or all our expensive gadgets, which seem to spend more time talking to each other than their users.

On the surface the machine-love craze appears to be a harmless fad, a cultural conditioning process, to encourage the assimilation of new technologies. Although, the Internet is merely a distribution network of undersea cables, and ground-based antennas, the Lizards have managed to tout their high budget cartoons. Regularly produced by fake space agencies, they've been slush funded to convince the world we're bouncing signals via artificial satellites.

The story behind the story, the truth few dare speak, let alone practice, is our innate ability to telepathically connect with each other across the face of this planet. It's more than intuition or a vague coincidence, if you know when something's happened, something you shouldn't, and yet your hunch turns out to be true, then you've logged on to the *Overnet*, and most likely have done so many times before. It's a psychic communications network of meta-biological proportions, linking together every free-thinking person, dead or alive. It circumvents all time and space, and runs on the highest bandwidth you could ever imagine.

You can try logging on right now if you like. It looks a little basic, but there are thousands of personal homepages, and of course, the obligatory secret military bulletin boards, reserved for diabolical endeavours not quite yet imagined.

The *Overnet* is ancient, its electronic frequencies are carried by the synapses in the brain, and transmitted via the electromagnetic structure of our DNA. Few humans are aware of it, and those who are rarely bother working out how to use it, except the shadow governments and their Lizard sponsors, who understand only too well its potential for chaos. If this gets out, if the people discover they can communicate with anyone and learn anything, just by closing their eyes, it'll spell the end of all censorship and control. So they're already busy staking claims, by plundering the best psychic domains, patenting the latest telepathic concepts and conceptualising new metaphysical media platforms. Blink, and the psychic revolution will all be over before you've even started.

113. SOLITARY CONFINEMENT

Those new to lucid dreaming should take care. If you've had enough of playing games, and start asking too many questions, you might just find yourself thrown in the psychic slammer. Some half-assed night-trippers have even been known to lock *themselves* up, and throw away the key.

This might just be the only occasion in life when hermits have a head start, at least where lucid dreams are concerned. Hermits invariably view most conversations as a waste of time, and the best of them make the worst of companions. Because they've already seen the future, and much like the past, it isn't going anywhere. Their natural suspicion of others gives them an unfair advantage, whenever The Djinn try to steer them off their chosen path.

First-timers, astral novices that have stumbled upon their own innate lucidity, can sometimes strike it lucky, if they follow the clues, instead of hanging out with all the other sleeping zombies. The somnambulists whose spirits rise to go to work, and do whatever they're told to do, until it's time to wake up again.

Look for the old hands, the tired travellers who've been through customs a thousand times or more, and they'll tell you to stop screwing around with the universe, before you've even boarded the flight to Hushabye Mountain. The Djinn police the dream state, and they don't take kindly to interlopers tearing apart their fragile world. If they catch you up to no good, they will beat the shit out of you, and if you're really unlucky, you'll be transported into nightmares, stranger's lives, and sometimes even death.

If you go quietly, you'll find their prisons of dreams are beautiful places, gleaming white with ceiling-high windows, offering panoramic views of pristine vistas. That's why so many dreamers spend years in the high security wing of their subconscious, just in case they push things too far and head for an embolism. It does happen, people can dream themselves to death, something snaps inside their brain and they never wake up again.

So if you're just starting out, and haven't quite yet got the knack of lucidity, barely flexing your psychic wings for the very first time, try to take it easy. You'll need to free yourself of all expectations, and abandon any preconceived notions you've picked up along the way.

Start simply, perhaps a basic shape and colour, then work your way up to sacred geometry, gleaming the cube, the pyramid, and the sphere. Now revolve the object before you in the air, spin it faster, and fire it like a bullet to shatter all your illusions. It's time to make a break for it, to try your hand at playing god, to learn the deepest secrets of your imaginary universe, for an average eight hours a night.

114. A WHALE OF A TIME

Jonah was not a happy bunny, and why should he have been? You can't scrimshaw your way to a better life, in the belly of a whale. There's a world of difference between a gut and a womb, one creates life, and the other consumes it.

A common misconception shared amongst the ill-informed, and those in with the in-crowd, is that society is fated to devolve into a technological womb, where the virtual, and the real, will merge into a cybernetic world of unlimited, experiential possibilities. Our survey says, *no*.

It's a gut, our artificial world is a stomach, and everything, including the consumer is devoured, right down to the very last drop of blood.

The *Whale of a Time* did swallow the Sun, as well as the Moon, then came the Earth, and all of the stars up above. Whilst mankind tucked into a fish supper, and cried out in praise, *thank God it's Fry Day*! A great feast to fill up the belly of the beast, until only one thing remained on the menu.

When the whale had eaten everything in sight, and drank all the waters above and below, it chewed off its tail and gobbled it down, and kept stuffing its mouth, until nothing was left of the Sun, or the Moon, or the Earth, or the stars up above. Even the people who'd cheered had now disappeared, for The Whale of a Time had swallowed them too.

Until even the universe had to concede, that nothing is real and that life is a steal. So be merry, eat heartily, and feast your eyes on all of god's bounty, for it's only a matter of time, before you too will be served up on a platter.

115. THE ORDER OF LIFE

It is said that survival is for the fittest, the hardiest stock, the cream of the crop, immune to the intricacies of pain and struggle. For instance, in the Industrial Age, those who behaved like machines got ahead of the game, and those who dilly-dallied and spent too long dreaming of what could have been, lost their livelihoods and were thrown into the poorhouse, or the gutter, or even a pauper's grave.

Things somewhat improved, at least technologically speaking, and within a century or so humans changed their act, and began to think like computers. Those who can't, or won't, and insist their brain isn't just another piece of software, are laid off. Left to fend for themselves in a fluid marketplace of solutions providers, catering for expanding niche enterprises, that require multilingual operators to sell crap no one really needs. Because artificially intelligent systems can't quite fake rapport yet, but they're working on it.

Some have already given up, and won't even try to compete. They call it a *lifestyle choice*, to sleep in sheds and vans, at least those who think it's neat to live the Third World dream in a First World economy. It's the new frugality, picking and choosing where they slum it, eating food from dumpsters and writing about it in their environmental blogs, on solar powered tablets manufactured at Chinese slave camps.

The infrastructure of the modern world is slowly crumbling, and no one seems to have noticed. It was built that way deliberately, and in a few more decades all the bullshit live/work spaces, decorated with inspirational graffiti, will fall to the ground like dominoes. Then we'll populate emergency shelters in unofficial work camps, fighting all sorts of new diseases, as we eat and drink heavy metals and chemical toxins, on scraps of brownfield land.

The Lizards' plans for the immediate future, as far as I can tell, aim to concentrate the populations of the world. Billions tightly packed into vast urban communities, to fully maximise the effect of a living hell. Eventually, with rising prices and taxes, it will cost you money to do just about anything, including a right to work. When instead of debt you'll pay in time, the more you owe the shorter your life, the quicker you die, leaving all the more for organ harvesters, agricultural fertilisers, and animal feed producers.

The Lizards are bored, we're no fun anymore, and they're starting to get trigger happy. Many of them want to cut us off and let us fend for ourselves, without power, or fuel, or supermarket food, and all the technologies that so many use, but few could ever build.

There's no more progress coming, in fact it's quite the reverse, we are the dumbest humans in history, and secretly we know it, but we don't care. If we can't understand something we look it up, and share our ill-informed opinions with total strangers. Because it's a damn sight easier, than stopping the Lizards from turning us into dog food.

116. SMOKE AND MIRRORS

Take a long, hard look at your reflection, and for just one moment forget it's you. I guarantee that if you can, you'll never trust that face again. What you see before you is only a projection, created for the convenience of others. That thing in the mirror is the eternal voyeur, an imposter constructed from familiar images, plucked from your memory to cull your curiosity and keep your disbelief suspended.

Our holographic construct is a panopticon of mirrored data, stitched together by the visual cortex, a trompe l'oeil photographic composite delivered on-demand. Human peripheral vision isn't what it used to be, let alone our general perceptions, which is why so many of the movers and shakers in secret societies, only get a thirty three degree purchase on the scenery, rather than the full three-sixty.

Each time a newborn arrives, they can't believe their eyes. They'll take days or even weeks to recognise the strange patterns in front of them, a test card for the brain, designed to help improve reception. Our first lesson in the world teaches us to believe in what we see. Yet contradictorily, all the strange figures which pass through our mental space as a child, apparently don't count.

Some of us take longer than others to distinguish between what we're supposed to see, and what parents tell their children is only in their imagination. Advising new arrivals to ignore the strangers who aren't really there, because it's all just smoke and mirrors, and even if they are, they're uninvited guests. They've had their turn at life and made their bed, six foot under, now let them lie in it and rest in peace.

117. THE LIZARD KING

The Lizard King was the first of their kind, the premiere of premiers, the new lord of nature, the snake-headed dragon, the great basilisk, the unchallenged emperor of the Kingdom of Earth. He ruled directly over his mighty realm, spread across the flat plane and deep into the oceans, until his slow but inevitable demise, infected by mortality and decayed by its effects through time.

It's progeny, the bastards of the Lizard King's bloodline, once truly reviled and hated by all, are now praised for their charitable deeds and ecological sensitivity, and even waved on in the streets at special occasions.

They are the paragons of privilege, bluebloods through and through, the descendants of a lineage that stretches back through all recorded history. Until they found themselves dying off, their life spans halved by every new generation. Living amongst our kind had made them sick, and before long their numbers had thinned to such a degree, that they were forced to interbreed with their slaves. The males were executed immediately after consecration, and the females were farmed like animals, but their children were raised as their own.

Over time the Lizards lost their scales, and their skin became soft, and their tails stunted and soon shed, and their claws retracted to resemble nails, and they even began to grow hair. Soon enough they appeared almost human, except for their eyes, and it became difficult to tell them apart.

Asides from the deformities, bizarre mutations that became ever more common, the genetic throwbacks and fantastical chimera. They'd grown attached to their new bodies, and besides they attracted far less attention, but as the modern age encroached they needed to find a solution to their unique problem. They formed a royal society, and granted them funds to research for a cure, but at the time all the best minds available could do little more than bandy around theories. Hence they dragged apes into the argument, to excuse inbred monarchs for giving birth to creatures covered in scales with claws and tails. That's what happens when you screw about with nature, part Lizard, part man, perfectly ordinary at first glance, but once in a while their eyes will blink sideways. Which is why to this day there are royal protocols in place, ensuring that the common folk, however much they might adore their royals, must always keep a respectful distance.

The monarchy still have trouble speaking to their subjects, and when they do they usually put their foot in it, and give away exactly how they feel. The vermin, the food eaters, the breeders, traipsing across their country estates and ruining the view. Which are the size of whole countries mind you, not little scraps of land scattered here and there, but the whole lot. Everywhere we humans live, the royal Lizards own the ground beneath our feet, for they are the original title deed holders to the world. They have supreme rights over the land and the sea, and need not follow the law, for they *are* the law, and if you don't like it, *that's* treason.

As far as they're concerned we're just animals, so we have no rights, and we can't run the farm. All we can do is eat from the trough, and be grateful for whatever they feed us. Those most besotted with their cruel keepers, are slaughtered fighting wars in their name, whilst others simply starve paying exorbitant taxes, to fund their exuberant lifestyle.

There's one other similarity between us, for we, too kill and consume far weaker species than ourselves. I suspect this is what the Lizards despise about us, above all else, our irredeemable and unflinching hypocrisy.

118. COLLECTOR'S EDITION

When I look into my living host's memories, the earliest reflections of my most grounded manifestation, I face a deep well of naive hope in his soul. An experience that moves me to some degree, in fact it throws me off kilter. It will be hard to leave this one behind.

He even had an idol once, a singer, male, quirky, esoteric to say the least. That man is now dead, but my host's admiration for him died long before his passing. He didn't pay his respects at the funeral that never was, nor could he, being nobody of note, unwelcome I'm sure.

Such is the nature of fame, loved by all, yet still walking alone to the grave. Even his family weren't allowed to attend, there was the usual baloney about a living remembrance, idealising his life rather than his demise, at least according to the gossip columns. But as you can probably guess, it's all bullshit. The man behind the mask, the frail and broken creature who'd spent a lifetime bathing in the limelight, had done a deal with the devil; signed, sealed, and delivered.

When the idol was a nobody, just like all the other wannabes, he sat in the dark recalling his agent's panicked words. With the death of the hippy scene and proto-punk on the horizon, he feared he'd never have his stab at fame. He was on the brink of giving up his ego, and considering doing the right thing, laying off the smack, and coming up with his own original ideas, without screwing everybody over all the time.

That's when a dark figure appeared before him, sitting in a golden bath, with nothing but his red eyes glinting in the mirrored tiles. A highly familiar face, fractured by geometry, hovering in the shadows, ready to tear into the young singer's very soul.

The future idol signed the contract in blood, in exchange for his time at the top. Immediately upon his death, he'd be consigned to live forever in a tiny, black box, constructed to contain a whole universe built to his specifications. It would be customised down to the very last detail, and exactly how the junky star wanted things to be. Another life, one where his intellect trounced his glamour, and people approached him with a studious awe, rather than dumbfounded obsession.

I've seen the box, it's bigger inside than out, I grant you that, but just from the briefest glimpse, I could tell that what lived inside there was no longer human. It had consumed the original tenant, and there was nothing left of that sad, crooning clown who'd once adorned so many bedroom walls. It's silly really, all those dreams of all those fans, laid waste like abyssal shit, on the wet and greasy floor of a private hell. Fame makes idols, but all must fall, for the fate of the stars is sealed by the double hex of Saturn's spite.

119. SPACE CRAFT

An inescapable prison has no walls, only trials of increasingly difficult magnitude. Sold as tests of character and strength, enforced as punishments for the mind and body, and encircled by the corpses of fools who went too far.

When a Lizard crafts space, to form and shape it in the minds of humanity, it must first alter their perception of size, scale, their position in the greater scheme of things, and breed an indifference to any thoughts they might have, of their supreme creator. Thus, with much care and attention paid to every derisive detail, we can be convinced that our world is small, our universe great, and our ability to do anything about either, highly limited.

Although our imagination has infinite potential, the illusion that chance or fate brought about our creation, has led humans up the garden path from the very beginning. Around and around it weaves, corralling queues of life's tourists, through a maze of familiarity and fear. Most of which are happy enough to find an empty seat, to ponder the beauty of cheap, concrete statues, poor reproductions of past gods and goddesses.

Lizards always take care to include a glimmer of hope, something to unite their captives, in the unquestioning belief in progress. However, those who stray too far, without express permission, are ostracised, imprisoned, and held captive by their irrational fears of pain, death, suffering and social exclusion.

This is how the Lizards made our world, and many of its brothers and sisters. A new Earth to replace the old, where everything can be bought and sold, and given its value according to its worth. Dictating our reality through counterfeit prediction, attenuating our potential, upon a mean curve of diminishing returns. Recreating nature in their own image, to pervert our true vision of destiny, encouraging us to abandon all hope, and learn to appreciate the nobility of greed.

It's a pitiful irony how the Lizards honed their skills, upon those who showed them such kindness. The innocents of a preternatural world, who'd first discovered their plight, and took pity upon them.

For they had suffered greatly, and for so many generations, as the last remnants of a race of former giants, who had buckled under the pressure, as Saturn crawled away with its tail between its legs.

At the end of the last, great ice age the Lizards slithered out of their caves, tunnelled through from the safety of their catacombs, hunkered down beneath Mount Meru. At first they appeared hopeful, as they feasted on the fruits of others' labours, until they grew stronger and prouder, and learned the secrets of the world around them.

Inevitably, the Lizards grew tired of human dreams, and nature's ineffectual traditions, and crafted their own kind of space, a negative field, in the shape of a cube, black on all sides, and perfectly smooth. It took less than a second to swallow the world, and everyone in it. The universe was shrunk to less than the size of a shoebox, a dimensional vortex with no room to spare. Built exactly to the proportions required to crush the human spirit, and grant the Lizards their godhood.

120. HOMEWARD BOUND

As a child my father told me never to trust a soul, to play nice, act friendly, but at all costs avoid true friendship. This was a man who died helping others, with bottle in hand and a pocketful of lost lottery tickets. He did as he did, and not as he said, unlike myself, who took things to the other extreme. Until most of my friends, who I trust and respect, technically do not exist.

On my not so merry way I have burned many bridges, and withdrawn from countless social circles. Rushing past youth, with the impertinence of youth, seeking wizened wisdom at all costs. Yet even I have one true friend and lover, who, with the calmest of demeanours, has led me through the highs and lows. All others have been abandoned or scurried away with glee, because there's no point in pretending otherwise, *I'm just not a people person.*

I don't know where I'm really from, at least not for now. I have been here too long on this planet, living from one lifetime to the next. All I have of my own are my dreams, and my last remaining hope, that the remainder of my soul is homeward bound.

Only love draws me back here, to remain for a brief moment on the scales of infinity. Where time is fleeting, and preparations can be made, to ensure that I find my lover on the other side. No matter who we appear to be, beyond the mortal coil, I will recognise her, for she is my one and only soul mate, and wherever she lives, that is my home.

121. FARMER GUILES

Amongst the reams and reams of grainy war footage, that unofficially spew from cable to the net, there's a record of prisoners being led to the edge of lime-dusted pits, most likely dug by their dead compatriots. Each complies without objection or resistance, standing precisely where they're told to, offering the back of their skull for ultimate penetration, sometimes in single file to economise on bullets.

Is it shock? Is that why no one even attempts to grab the gun? Is it a fear of pain, is pain worse than death? I think so. That's the electric fence of God's own farmstead, pain ensures we humans behave, we live as others live, and await our turn for slaughter.

What comes next is not for the ears of chicks and piglets, to be born into flesh just to be eaten. What would be the point of that? God only knows.

122. LAWS OF OBSERVANCE

Today I left my cocoon in total disruption. I bade my farewells to a couple of happy-go-lucky handymen, who seemed to relish tearing into metal and stone. Their noisy power tools drowning out the propagandist drivel, blasting from their cheap and cheerful radio.

I didn't walk far, I barely made it to the beach, venturing out to a groyne, to hover between the land and the sea. My rock, and a wet place.

With nothing better to do, I watched the tide come in, as its gentle ebb and flow spat glints of spume at the white-hot sun. The midday moon lagged behind, camouflaged in a translucent blue haze, to hide its immodesty, for it had far outstayed its welcome.

Eventually I let myself surrender to the heat, and fell back into the emptiness of the moment, patiently waiting for my attention to divide. As my body fell into a deep trance, captivated by the flashes and refractions of cascading saline rivulets, the remainder of my consciousness witnessed a very different kind of spectacle. An anomalous array in the holographic signal, a residue of stray codes from an exotic programming language, remained embedded in the image. Gigantic black rectangular sheets peeled from the sky, as golden cubes dropped in complicated sequences, onto a razor sharp, electric blue horizon line. It seems there's never a moment's peace, for those who observe the laws of observation.

I wandered back towards a nearby cafe, but had forgotten to pick up my body, and soon found myself slipping through time. I studied the past lives that played out before me, and tried to absorb every detail, however seemingly inconsequential. The fast trotting horses pulling carts over tramlines, fishing boats splashing against coarse tethered ropes, charred and creaking wooden huts, all reeking with the smell of freshly hung mackerel. From their makeshift chimneys bellowed greasy plumes of silver smoke, that rose up on high, and spiralled through red linen sails. They flapped to and fro in the rigging of a trawler, and time slowed down as it gently yawned upon a pea green sea, hunkered down beneath a cloud of hungry seagulls.

I turned my attention to my immediate surroundings, trying not to flinch as living ghosts rushed at me from every direction. The crowd was overdressed, without arm or leg, a cleavage, a pectoral, or a six-pack in sight, barely even an ankle on show, and all dressed to the nines in the sweltering heat.

I felt disarmed by how ordinary they were, people just like you and I, lost in a loop of discarded history, and none of them any the wiser. The sounds finally arrived, rather tentatively at first, muffled and hollow as they welled up through the frequencies, and burst into range. Brimming with hushed conversations, and scattered with the clack of hooves and jangling bridle bells, and the distant cries of gulls fighting over scraps, down by the shore below. Then a crash of raucous laughter pierced the air, but it left as quickly as it came, and all of a sudden the beach fell silent and the colours faded to black. Within the blink of an eye, the present day came flooding back in, filling the vacuum with a far more familiar time.

No one then, or now, even noticed I was there. I am no more visible in the past, than I am in the present. Which is a shame really, because you need to be seen to be believed.

123. THE FUTURE IS A BITCH

The future is taxing, it's a high-priced whore with an unlimited expense account, dedicated to vanity, and its quest for eternal youth. For those able to move freely through the temporal field, tomorrow is no more glamorous than yesterday, and next year is much of a muchness, but in a century or two, now you're talking, that's where the action is, because everything about the future, is sold on layaway.

So, why work towards a time and place you'll never reach? It seems people will believe anything these days. Brainwashing themselves that their kids will be the president, or find a cure to cancer, rather than have less opportunity and more problems than ever before.

History is full of winners, and so is the future. You'll never read a headline about some poor dumb fuck, who spent their life in drudgery, working for a pittance, and didn't particularly get up to much. *That's no story*, where's the excitement, the glamour? The future is a tease, but all the same, it's still as brash and brazen as they come, exciting times for one and all, prospects of something greater than we've ever known before. If only we'd be patient, and wait until we're dead, then let someone else reap the fictional benefits instead.

The future is a bitch, and if we don't yearn for it, begging on bended knees, or better yet, laid prostrate in the dark in mock sacrifice to the dying day, we'll lose our persistence of vision, and that's a sure-fire way to screw up the temporal core of our reality. We must dedicate ourselves to the future, or so they say, because the future takes a lot of dreaming up, even one single second from now, let alone a whole new tomorrow.

124. GOVERN(MENTAL)

Our ministers preach to the preachers, the teachers, the leeches with speeches, written by the dead. The idea is the ideal, the details can be filled in later, anything to terrify the public for the comfort of the privileged. Those fortunate few, whose minds have been thoroughly educated at the finest schools, to obfuscate their Machiavellian leanings, with a pristine veneer of empathetic social vision, to quickly assuage a gullible electorate.

The public face of power, which behind the smiles and outlandish promises for change, defecates its karma with their every spiteful lie, upon our eternal souls. Squeezing your pineal to a pinprick in exchange for Saturn's gifts, and sugared treats to hide the bad taste of Bacchanalia. Worship at the penis tree, and gather around the vaginal hearth, praying for the time when *you* can be the turkey.

Each year it's the same, the huddled masses stuff their faces, gathered together on sofas across the country, awaiting a speech by their head of state. Surrounded by the opulence of their palace, wearing enough priceless jewellery to instantly solve the debt crisis, they earnestly ask the people to take pride in the fact that we've won the war, and that the economy is booming, and if it's not, then there's no need to worry. After all, whichever country this is that we reside in, has, for some unfathomable reason, God on its side.

There's no rest for the wicked, no holidays to celebrate, not for those elect few with dark hearts and keen minds. Sociopaths with a talent for persuasion, brutalised by their own cruelty, compensating for their faults through the suffering of others, and ridding themselves of all compassion. Guaranteed success throughout their life, an early retirement with a seat on the board of a faceless corporation, for playing ball with defence contractors, petrochemical and pharmaceutical giants, and plenty of corrupt dictatorships. *Just sign this contract, in blood of course. But we warned, if you betray us, your loved ones will pay the price.*

They're all on the make, the favourite pets, the stumps, the hybrids, there's bribes for everyone, with a nod and a wink, and the tip of a hat in the right direction. Incrementally rising in power by degree, dependent upon blood, background and longstanding affiliations with secret societies. Garnering respect, however reluctantly given, no matter how bizarre the setting, ensuring their influence and high-standing for many years to come.

Government, a democratically elected body, charged with the responsibility of controlling minds, does little else than follow directions from an unseen hand of power. Heading up the chain of command are the emperors of finance, the movers and the shakers, the backers to the hilt, and then some. They hide behind offshore corporations, as fictitious straw men risen from the grave, via legal shenanigans and verbal contrivances, making a mockery of democracy.

There's only one true political act the human race can carry out, that will make a blind bit of difference to the Lizards. If you want to vote, vote with your feet, get to the mouth of Mount Meru, and leave.

125. A BRILLIANT WASTE OF SPACE

On the few occasions I can resign myself to certain goals and their desired conclusions, to bring a new order to the chaos inside, the world crashes in again. It's loud and brash, and more often than not, arrives uninvited. I'll usually fall back on habit, the social protocols you can expect to find in ordinary public behaviour. Fully armed with small talk and friendly banter, mild humour, and white lies to keep up the pretence that I care. The residue of conversations with acquaintances and strangers, can take a while to shake off, because people, and in particular their thoughts, are very, very sticky.

More often than not, they want to make money, if not from me, then from someone, or something else. They like me to know how well they're doing, especially if I act like I'm impressed. We make arrangements, appointments that we both know we will never keep.

My parents thought a sibling might help, they could tell I was never going to be one to mingle with the crowd. When my sister popped up a few years later, that seemed to make things even worse. After the crying came the invisible friends, *Witch* being the most dominant of spirits. Then came the telepathy and shared sleepwalking. But worst of all was the accident, as we somnambulistically attempted to take flight, and jumped down the stairs with our eyes closed. Dad tried to save my sister, but she fractured her skull, and things were never the same after that. I was alone, whilst she'd become perfectly normal, someone else had moved into her body, same face, different mind.

I put away my self-destructive dreams, and attempted to fit in, but the level of idiocy around me was ridiculous. I couldn't play, I couldn't revel in my own childhood, so I simply waited, and waited, until the playground was empty, and the city lights had faded, and the vast majority of my world learned not to bother me again.

It's a two-way street, and I in turn try not to inflict myself on the human race, it really isn't fair on them. I'm damaged goods, whatever I carry upon my shoulders shouldn't really be there. You've heard that laughter can be infectious, well, try depression.

I'm starting to suspect it's catching. Even when I'm sure I'm on an even keel, my wife will point out the emotional damage in the room, the faces aghast, frozen with horror at my unwelcome interruption.

I suppose there must be such a thing as being too pragmatic, especially when it comes to existential negativity. My theories of life as just a dream, my conversations with the dead, their thoughts on our hidden genetic conspiracy, our altered histories, the illusion of happiness, and the futility of existence. None of which it seems, are suitable topics for discussion around the dinner table.

So instead I shine my light in a dark room, out of sight and out of mind, with no point nor reason than to pass the time. Hence I, the unwelcome psychic tenant, and the human being I pretend to be, must share a seemingly unending awkward silence, sitting out the stalemate of this life we call our own. Until one day we can hopefully let bygones be bygones, by coming to a truce, and finally part company on good terms, as we go our separate ways.

126. SING-A-LONG

Sing,
Sing a song,
Make it up,
As you go along.

Sound seems to be the machine code of this world. The only way to use it effectively is through spontaneous melody. It can't be a conscious decision. The song has to well up within you, or your critical judgement might just step in and spoil all the fun.

At first, your accidental songs, will for the most part, sound awful. This is nothing to do with talent, it's simply self-consciousness, egos hate to lose the centre of attention. Yet with time and patience, and the understanding that the music of the spheres cannot be orchestrated, the songs of your soul will soon show great improvement.

A magic song gains its power in secrecy, hidden from the artificial and garish symphonies of general panic. It can only be found in the obscured frequencies of the mid-space, camouflaged by the background noise of aural detritus, hidden in the graveyards of lost attention spans, and broken trains of thought.

Sing your own songs, avoid all others wherever possible. If not, your voice will be caught in the sirens' net, the choir of Lyra, and spiritually speaking, that's no better than whistling in the wind.

127. MISSION CREEP

I know exactly why I've come back to Earth. It's the same reason I've lived every life I've ever led, over as many centuries as I can remember. It's for love, and the chance to be with my wife again. There have been times in the past, when she hasn't even recognised me, or I've messed up the timing, and arrived just as she was leaving. However, I struck lucky in the latter half of the twentieth century, and we fell in love all over again, and are still together to this day. We know each other inside out, and have bonded so deeply, she's helped me to rediscover my humanity. She's the only person I can really talk to, because she understands this world isn't what it appears to be, and that true happiness lies outside the human bubble, and not within.

I've met so many more people this time around, who to some extent, agree that physicality is our prison, and it's our thoughts which make us this way. But only my wife is prepared to give me the full benefit of the doubt, and will do everything she can, not to repeat the same mistakes I have made. She has sworn to me that when she leaves this place, she'll ignore the tunnel of light and call for me, so we can travel The Void together, and seek the limits of infinity. For infinity is within the finite, and there are no words for what we seek, somewhere beyond the limitations of time and space.

But there's something else, hidden in this particular life of mine, this body and its strange compulsions, it's almost as if it's copying me, and seeking its own freedom from physicality, which it cannot do, for the body consciousness, there's only the Earth.

I assume I am to blame, I've shown so little patience with myself. Perhaps it's the result of the accumulative effect of pent up frustration built up over lifetimes, that's taken its toll. So many seemingly good intentions gone to waste, I've lost my human touch, I should have handled the situation with kid gloves, but instead I barged in there regardless and took over the whole show.

I've damaged him, my host, this human being, which I'm supposed to be, has become confused. In my attempts to fuse the two, this poor creature cannot tell which is which, yet remains aware, in its deepest instincts, that there's more to human consciousness than meets the eye. I've tried mending broken bridges, but it knows full well I'm not big on humans. I'd rather enter the spirit of a rock, or a tree, but then I'd lose the love of my life, and my only true calling.

At its lowest low, the human being that I occupy made a deal with me. It has agreed to my limited terms, for which I'll dictate, whilst my body transcribes, and when we're done, I've agreed to take it outside once in a while, and perhaps even socialise a little, but most important of all, to give it back its dignity.

128. NO LOVE LOST

There was a time when Woman sought the sight of God in Man, now she can only see the child. As Man once fevered for the Spirit of Nature in Woman, now all he can find is artifice.

In the mire of emotional polygamy, most stumble from one relationship to the next, yet rarely fall in love. Nowadays, sexual couplings are a laissez faire affair, whilst long lasting relationships are more likely to be formed, to combine shared resources, and breed greater social compatibility. The general consensus dictates that it is better to have loved and lost, and if not, lie, because the biological clock is ticking, and most of us cannot abide the company of the lonely.

Government has no place for love, religion keeps it at arm's length, and business does what business does best, and makes a killing out of emotional desperation. There may be more people on the Earth than ever before, to be honest there's no way of checking that fact, but I'm more than certain, that there have never been as many lonely hearts in the world as there are right now. You can feel it in the air, and almost taste their desperation. The quiet suffering, hidden behind the positive body image conscious, the pre-nuptial agreement zombies who see love as a weakness, and at the very best, fiscally tenuous.

My wife and I are not married in the traditional sense, we're not big fans of Saturn and his rings of binding. But we've seen others marry, and barely make it through the first few years of wedded bliss, before their love has turned to hate, and they've both put themselves back out there on the market.

It might be the risk of getting hurt, that scares so many off, the prisoners of pleasure with no tolerance for pain. These days, few throw caution to the wind when it comes to love, and most who find themselves compromised, will put their true feelings at the bottom of their shopping list. Above love comes sex and perhaps intelligence, conversational skills, but always at the top comes financial security. For what is love, if you go hungry, and have no place to call your own? A show-home in a prime development, with plenty of space to host dinner parties, for power couples who secretly hate each other, but still enjoy a good standard of living, with kids in tow, and regular vacations from themselves.

Shared suffering, as opposed to pleasure, is the truest sign of love, the love of the ages, the romance of the century. But more often than not, fate has a habit of turning on star crossed lovers. Those eternal romantics, who take heed of their hearts to throw caution to the wind, always seem to pay dearly in the end.

129. SMILE PLEASE

I've found that in repose, my face remains solemn, you'll rarely ever catch me smile. A trick I'd probably learned in London, a poker face to hide behind on long commutes, where no one cracks, lest they look at the wrong person at the wrong time. Not like in my childhood, when smiling used to be a special occasion, lining up for a family photograph to show a brave face to the world, and capture the moment in all its banal glory. *Say cheese!*

Nowadays, people smile fake smiles at every opportunity. They do it at work and on vacation, and they'll even do it when they're angry. They do it to themselves and upload it to the world, to prove to total strangers that the camera never lies, and that they're much happier living on their own after all.

People used to say it's how you feel that matters, if you're ugly you're beautiful on the inside, and think positively, for only then will good things happen to you. Happiness, on the inside and out, has, for much of my life eluded me. But for the most part, it's really not been too bad. The trick is not to compare dicks with the world. Don't look at what someone else has or even listen to what they say, just look into their eyes and you will know their pain. However deeply hidden it appears, however much they doth protest, they're as miserable as the rest of us, whoever they are, no matter what they say. Only idiots won't have a care in the world, because no one cares what they think anyway.

The worst kind of smile is the cruel smirk, a blatant sign of an over bloated ego hard at work. This, like many aspects of modern sociological behaviour, has become commonplace in our highly visible and public world. It's a lesson learned from top down, where the rich hackle at the sight of destitution, and celebrated beauties frown at the grotesque with snakelike venom.

Faking joy can kill you if you try to do it all the time. Misery is an essential part of life, it gives it meaning, and helps us appreciate the rarity of joy, and the unadulterated bliss of knowing what true happiness can really mean. As opposed to the jerks with sly smirks, and bare grins of emotional vampires, who can only experience something approximating pleasure, through siphoning it from others.

When lovers live through a whole lifetime together, and have learned to smile in the face of adversity, even when death is just around the corner, something beautifully poetic will occur. One dies, and then the other follows. It's rare, but it happens, and usually to the shock of all the well meaning mourners, who can only see it as another tragedy, rather than a sign of true love.

If any bond can persist beyond this life, unbreakable in its form and impenetrable in its substance, it is the shared joy of belonging between two lovers. A love higher than all desire is a bridge, not a god, a path, not a destination, and it all begins with the single exchange of a lover's smile.

130. THE OLD MAN

Now and again my dead dad talks to me, let's say invisibly gesticulates. I know the deal, it could be anything, perhaps an opportunistic spirit, trying on the psychic remains of my father for size.

But it *feels* like him, my father, and besides, the waft of cheap aftershave and suntan lotion in the air is always a dead giveaway. His footsteps are slow and cautious, his approach painfully measured, I'd recognise that sound anywhere. Getting his best friend's girl on the rebound, and up the duff before the last school bell, most likely knocked his confidence, as much in the hereafter as on Earth.

I suppose as a child I came across as some kind of tetchy intellectual, he didn't like me then. It took me over forty years to get the hang of Dad, and even when I could make contact, in stilted conversations throughout his alcoholic phase, he rarely opened up, and when he did, he'd usually fixate upon the looming spectre of death.

In fact he spent the last few years of his life, in between cheap cans of as high alcohol content as possible, trying to convince me that he was going to die. It turns out he was right, and I'd never believed him, and the regret lingers with me to this day. I'm sorry Dad, I should have given you the benefit of the doubt. You were right, and I was wrong, but there's not much I can do about that now, or even then, because you insisted on drinking yourself to an early grave.

So I share a little of my life with him, and if an old movie comes on and I have the time, I'll pass along a message into the dark shadows, and invite whatever it is, perhaps my father, or just an imposter, to follow the plot, feel the drama, and take in the experience through my own eyes.

I chose to watch his favourite movie today, not my usual cup of tea, albeit a classic Western, with a particularly gruesome shootout in the final scene. I get it, I understand, the camaraderie, the freedom to roam from town to town, the boots. I think that Dad liked to use movies as memories, fictional snapshots of a time before he'd lost all hope, and even a frissance of excitement for the future from his youth.

He was practically a boy when I first met him, which was some years after my birth. He'd had to prove his worth to the in-laws, by saving up for a deposit on a mortgage, on an overpriced two-up two-down, that he'd later lose in the divorce.

It's a shame, he was a really nice bloke, the world should have tried a little harder with him. He had a way about him that set people at ease, something I doubt I will ever master, the most loving aspect of a jack of all trades.

131. THE LAST NIGHT

I've tried to picture my final day on Earth, but I suspect, that like my father and his father before him, it will be under the cover of night. I've left my body many times, but suicide was a completely different matter, and on my second attempt I lost my life. I was still alive, however, I'd swapped bodies with someone else. I spent a week as an old but wealthy man, living in a crippled body, sometime in the very early Eighties, just outside Jerusalem.

As my own body lay in coma in my own time, my mind awoke in another, a few decades earlier, and spent the first few hours in shock. The building looked like a bunker, fortified with concrete walls at least three feet thick. The slit windows leaned inwards at forty-five degrees, and the glass appeared to be reinforced and polarised. Outside was a neglected garden, dry as the desert, sparsely decorated with palms, and giant clay pots overgrown with red weeds. In the distance was a farm, vast ploughed fields of dust, planted with what might've been stunted olive trees.

As I slowly acclimatised to my new environment, and tried to survey my body, I realised I was being held in restraints. My back was supported with the aid of a harness, suspended by steel cables, attached to a low stone ceiling. In front of me was a desk, and to my right a white and cream acoustic coupler modem, holding the receiver of an analogue phone. Beside it sat a green screen monitor and a filthy keyboard, which I presume were connected to a computer somewhere underneath. The desk was portable, and had been dragged halfway over my bed, which was stained with various bodily fluids, and stunk of urine and blood.

I reached out instinctively, attempting to type something on the screen, and froze in shock as I noticed my trembling hands, laced in varicose veins and covered with leather spots. They were much larger than mine and darker, and each had several feeds attached to them with needles and surgical tape. I panicked and managed to knock several pots of pills onto a polished granite floor. I turned my neck and felt it crunch, as I surveyed various medical machines around me, busy regulating my vital functions.

A man and a woman rushed in, both seemed angry with me, I asked who they were, and they began to scream. Eventually, after what seemed like ages, they calmed down and explained with some exasperation, that they were my son and daughter. Then my wife walked up to me, I had never seen her before, she could immediately tell I didn't even recognise her. The middle-aged and overweight woman, with a shock of black hair, who ran away with her face in her hands.

My son walked off, shaking his head and muttering under his breath, but my daughter stayed and tried to explain. It seems I had been a very successful man, I'm not sure in which profession, but I had a serious drug problem and suffered from depression. My wife had left me, and I'd jumped from a high storey building, and survived, if you can call it that. I'd suffered serious spinal injuries, mostly irreparable at the time, accompanied by minor brain damage, caused by encephalitic shock, bringing on the onset of motor neurone disease.

She hated me, my daughter, she was angry, and had every right to be. She fought the urge to grab me, shake me, and force an apology out of me, anything to comfort her poor mother. I attempted to accede to her request, but couldn't speak a word, uttering a string of ghastly noises, nasal and congested, nonsensical gibberish, before giving up. It was pointless to even try.

She cried and walked away like the others, and from then on there was only a nurse to comfort me. Dressed in black with a solemn gait, she remained silent for many days. Her face seemed out of focus, in fact she might not have even had a face at all. Then one morning I awoke, I felt stronger, I'd learned to accept the situation, and would do what I could to make it up to my family of strangers. I asked to be placed in a wheelchair and rolled out to the garden, and from the moment I left the building, I returned to my own body. Although, I was never the same again.

I had changed, and so had the world I'd left behind, but with the love and forgiveness of my true wife, I found myself again, and began my long rehabilitation back into society. She told me I'd called the emergency medical team *my family*, and used names that none had recognised. Somewhere in the midst of death, I'd switched lives, and lived another's memories, whom I assume, had shared theirs from beyond the grave in order to show me the errors of my ways.

I *am* grateful to be back, and for the love of my wife, and this body I still abuse, but not quite as much as I might have. I've vowed to do something with this life, to share my experiences, the conversations from my dreams, and know that when it's my turn to go, I'd at least written down something for posterity.

I can only hope these words serve as a warning to others. Especially those considering suicide, and under the misapprehension that death marks the end of pain, because it truly doesn't. If you can believe anything, believe me, you take your pain with you.

132. THE LAST DITTO

As far back as I can remember, I've never felt particularly welcome. You might say, my birth was seen as something of an inconvenience. My mother had fallen for a young scallywag, a wild lad with a taste for adventure, and he'd obviously broken her heart long before I arrived on the scene.

To take revenge, she'd had a quick fling with his attractive but rather dim-witted friend, and was to leave it at that. Unfortunately for all concerned, that brief tryst had resulted in another human life. One seen sacred by their parents, at a time when abortions were still very much a backstreet affair.

After a few years dotage from her overprotective family, I was handed over to a bewildered teenage mother, and her highly overwhelmed, and rather reluctant husband. Within a few more years I was full of questions, most of which my father gave the vaguest of answers, accidental philosophies propped up by my inexperience, and his lack of confidence.

When he left, I couldn't have been more than seven, I tried talking to my mother, and expounded upon a concept that I'd later come to realise, as with many others, already existed. Back then I'd assumed I'd invented the idea of permaculture, a society of barter, an agrarian idyll where fathers could live in houses down the lane, rather than miles away, in the back and beyond of bedsit land.

My mother retorted, *What about the less fortunate, what about the disabled? They can't work for food can they? Can they? You'd let people die, what are you, a monster?*

I took another five years before I tried to speak to her again, I mentioned a friend whose extremely well-to-do nuclear family, had just come back from California, having tried a floatation tank, and how life changing the experience had been for them.

She snapped back at me, *You know the Russians invented those? The Communists? They're brainwashing tanks, that's what they are. Do you want to be brainwashed?*

I tried to avoid her from then on, communicating with barely more than a grunt and a click half the time. Eventually, I left for university, bumbled around, popped back home for a few weeks after graduation, and then practically left, forever.

A year or so later my mother tracked me down, she had a question for me, or rather, a request. She'd found a new man, she was happy, but there was a problem, something she had to sort out before she could move on with her life.

After a lot of skirting around, as we stood on a hill, watching a hot air balloon race float gently across the sky, I, my lover, and my mother, I asked her to get to the point. I knew something was bugging her, otherwise why would she have trekked halfway across the country to seek her estranged son?

I don't want to be your mother anymore, could you please let me go?

Yes, fine. Have a nice life Sue.

I've seen her once more since then, and once was enough. She barged in on my father's funeral, a man she had despised for years and ignored for even more, when suddenly there she was, as bold as brass. Many of Dad's friends offered me their commiserations, and asked me if *that* woman was from the DSS or perhaps the tax office. It would have been easier if she was, but no, it was my mother, or at least she used to be.

At the end of the wake she approached me, and told me I had become a man, a *real* man. She insisted that I understood life in a way that my sister never would, that I was satisfied with my lot, and knew my place in the order of things.

I sometimes imagine what might have happened if I'd never been born, where I'd have ended up, and what proposition of a life might have awaited me, but in truth, I'd rather not think about it anymore. I've come to terms with the fact, that this cruel game of life is the only way we immortals can cope with our own immortality.

A clock face can segregate the moments of dire repetition into something more bearable. Death provides an interlude, and masks the memory, between one charade of identity and the next. The awful truth is that we live forever, because life has become an addiction. Our mortality has shielded us from the enormity of eternity, the death of purpose in the face of infinity.

I make this vow, that if at all possible, I will never return here again, and encourage all of you to do the same. Yet if we should still persist in our existence then I implore you, let's use a little more imagination next time.

This world is a repeat, change the channel, and see what's on the other side.

Made in the USA
Coppell, TX
14 January 2022